DARK QUEEN'S KNIGHT

THE CHILDREN OF THE GODS BOOK 33

I. T. LUCAS

NOTE FROM THE AUTHOR:
Dark Queen's Knight is a work of fiction!
Names, characters, places and incidents are products of the author's
imagination or are used fictitiously and are not to be construed as real. Any
similarity to actual persons, organizations and/or events is purely coincidental.

MEY

*C*ould life be more full of surprises?

As Mey finished getting dressed and glanced at the mirror, the same old face that had been staring back at her for years suddenly seemed different.

Except, nothing had changed about her. Not physically.

Not yet.

That would come later when she transitioned, provided that she did. There were no assurances of that, and the only indicator that she was a possible Dormant was her bizarre ability to retrieve echoes of conversations from the walls. Except, regular humans could have special talents as well, so that wasn't a guarantee.

But if she turned, would anything change about her appearance or the kind of person she was?

Hopefully not.

The last thing Mey wanted was to grow even taller. Yamanu, Alena, and the rest of the team were all statuesque. And now that she knew that they were immortal, she wondered if there was a connection.

With the mountain of mind-bending information that she

had yet to process, it hadn't crossed her mind to ask Yamanu about that. The thing was, the more she thought about what he had told her, the more questions she had, and the list was growing by the minute.

No wonder that the woman in the mirror had an uncharacteristically awed expression on her face. Her eyes, which usually seemed knowing and a little secretive, now looked shell-shocked. Uncertain.

Who was she?

Mey's self-perception had been blown away by Yamanu's revelations. Everything she'd believed about herself had been wrong.

Was she even human?

Even before discovering her ability to listen to walls, Mey had always felt like the odd peg that didn't fit into any of the pre-drilled holes. But then that wasn't unusual. Most people had some oddities about them that made them feel different. Except, the vast majority of those quirks were on the normal human spectrum, while hers were not.

"Are you about ready?" Yamanu rapped on the bathroom door. "Alena and Arwel are waiting."

Mey glanced at her watch. It was lunchtime, and Alena had probably ordered room service.

Except, who could think about food at a time like this? Her stomach was tied in such tight knots that she felt nauseous.

"I'll be out in a minute."

These people who she'd thought she knew weren't human. They were the descendants of the freaking gods, who apparently had been real. Would knowing that change the way she talked to them? The way she regarded them?

The friendship she'd formed with Alena had been based on lies. On both sides. They would have to start from scratch and reintroduce themselves to each other as the people they really were.

Not only that, there were going to be questions about her talent, and talking about it with anyone other than her sister was going to feel strange, frightening and liberating at the same time.

With a sigh, Mey pulled the brush through her hair, then twisted two strands and pinned them up. Glancing at the lipstick in her makeup pouch, she debated whether to apply it or not.

It was funny how she suddenly felt the urge to dress up. After all, her new friends had already seen her in everything from her photo shoot fancy outfits to her plain T-shirts and yoga pants. Except, this time she was going to enter the living room as Mey the Dormant, a future member of the clan, and not Mey the human who'd been just an acquaintance.

That's why Mey had put on one of the new outfits she'd bought the day before, and why she'd fixed her hair.

But perhaps putting on lipstick was a bit much.

She wanted to look put together, not like she was going out on a date.

It was better to play it cool and not assume an outcome for which there were no guarantees. If it turned out that she wasn't a Dormant after all, she would look like an idiot for making premature assumptions.

Yamanu had never heard of talents like hers or Jin's. None of the immortals in his clan could listen to echoes embedded in walls, or touch people and create a link to them, or anything even remotely similar to that. Which could indicate that the source of her and Jin's abilities hadn't originated from the same godly genes as the clan's.

Mey chuckled. What if there were other supernatural

beings hiding among the human population who were not related to the clan or to its enemies?

Perhaps she and Jin had gotten their abilities from a different source?

Now, that would be a big surprise, and not one Mey would be happy about. She wanted a life with Yamanu, and there was only one way she could have that—transition into immortality and become a member of his clan.

Smoothing out a crease in her new blouse, Mey took a deep breath and headed out with her head held high and her shoulders squared.

As soon as she opened the door, Alena jumped up from the couch and ran up to her. "I knew there was a reason I liked you so much." She pulled Mey into a crushing hug. "It's the affinity immortals and Dormants feel toward each other."

Mey hugged Alena back. "So, it has nothing to do with how amazing I am or how absolutely fabulous you are. It's all about the genes?"

"Well, I wouldn't say that." Alena let go. "You are an incredible woman, and I'm happy to have you as my friend." She kissed Mey's cheek.

Tears stinging her eyes, Mey glanced at Arwel. "What about you? Did you feel anything special toward me?"

He shook his head. "I should have felt that there was something different about you. I'm starting to think that my senses are failing me."

Mey frowned. "What do you mean?"

"Arwel is a powerful empath," Alena said.

"Oh." Mey tucked a stray strand of hair behind her ear. "Excuse my ignorance, but what exactly is an empath?"

Taking her by the hand, Alena led her to the dining table. "Arwel can feel other people's emotions and intentions. Even those of immortals, which is a rare ability. Most of what we can do works only on humans."

"Do you have a special talent?" Mey sat down on the chair that Arwel had pulled out for her.

When Alena made a face and shook her head, Arwel chuckled. "She has the most valued ability of us all. She can make babies."

That was a weird thing to say. "Aren't most women capable of that?"

Yamanu pulled out a chair for himself and sat next to her. "Our conception rate is minuscule compared to humans. Our females are lucky to have one child, and many don't have any. Alena is a miracle. She has thirteen."

Mey's jaw dropped. "No way. How?"

Alena laughed. "Do I need to explain about the birds and the bees?"

"I meant that you don't look like you have had even one. But thirteen?"

"I'm a very old immortal. In fact, I'm the oldest in the clan."

It didn't take Mey long to realize what Alena had just revealed. "You are the goddess's daughter?"

"I'm her firstborn."

Mey felt like moving her chair back to put some distance between her and Alena. The woman was the daughter of the freaking goddess? No wonder everyone was deferring to her and treating her like a princess.

Suddenly, the puzzle pieces realigned themselves. "Oh my God. The very important person who you've been alluding to is the goddess, and your enemies are the Doomers. That's who you need to hide from because they mean you harm."

Alena clapped her hands. "I knew you were smart. You get an A on the test."

"Unbelievable. A few moments ago, I thought that there could be no more surprises for me. Boy, was I wrong."

As the door opened and the butler rolled in the cart with their lunch, Mey remembered her strange dream.

Leaning toward Alena, she whispered in her ear, "Is he an immortal too?"

"You could say so. He can't die, but that's also because he isn't really alive. Ovidu is a bio-mechanical entity made to resemble a human."

Yamanu had told her that the clan had advanced technological knowhow and that they had been dripping it to humanity at a rate that made it look like natural progress.

It made perfect sense for them to keep some of those marvels for themselves.

"How many of his kind do you have? Does everyone in the clan have a servant like Ovidu?"

It was so cool that they could make such lifelike cyborgs.

Alena shook her head. "There are only seven Odus in existence. Originally, they all belonged to my mother, but she gave one to each of her kids."

"Why only seven? Can't you make more?"

"We can't. We don't know how."

Ovidu bowed. "May I serve lunch, mistress?"

"Please."

YAMANU

"Why the questions about Ovidu?" Alena asked.

Yamanu had wondered the same thing. He'd erased the memory of the conversation Mey had overheard about Ovidu's indestructibility, but apparently she still found him fascinating. Then again, she'd just learned that he was a marvel of engineering, far more advanced than anything current technology could produce.

Mey shrugged then glanced at the Odu. "I had a strange dream. I'll tell you about it some other time." She rolled her eyes, indicating that she didn't want to talk about it with Ovidu listening. "Just one more thing in the smorgasbord of weird-ness I've been served in the last two days. There are so many things I don't understand, while others make so much more sense now."

"Like what?" Alena prompted.

"I get now why everyone on your team treats you with such deference." She winked. "Other than your fabulousness, of course. But what I don't get is what are you doing here? After giving birth to thirteen children, you decided one day that it was time for a mommy makeover and some much-deserved party time?"

Laughing, Alena leaned and patted Mey's shoulder. "I love how direct you are. So, first of all, I didn't need a mommy makeover, but I got one anyway because my sister thought that I looked 'quaint'." She shrugged. "I like long, loose dresses in pastel colors, and I don't like fussing with my hair and think it looks awesome in a braid. But anyway, the purpose of this gig is to flush someone out. That's the reason for the elaborate makeup Eva applies to my face. It's to make me look like the person he misses."

"I told Mey about Areana," Yamanu said.

Alena waved a hand. "Oh, okay. Areana, who's my mother's sister, has a son who ran away many years ago, and she wants to find him. The makeup makes me look like her. We hope that once he sees his beloved mother's face on the side of a bus, he will get curious and try to make contact."

Mey cast a sidelong glance at Yamanu. "Why did he run away? Maybe it's not a good idea to flush him out?"

"You are smart, my lady Mey. Kalugal, the guy we are looking for, is Areana's son with the leader of our enemies. He ran away because he either feared his father or didn't agree with his agenda. We don't know what his exact motives were. The thing is, his mother asked her sister for a favor, and let's just say that our Clan Mother couldn't refuse the request. The why of it is a long story for another time. Right now, we need to focus on getting you out of here without alerting your watchers. We have some logistics to figure out."

Alena arched a brow. "I thought that you and Kian had figured everything out and that you were taking Mey to the village?"

Mey nodded. "I thought so too."

"It shouldn't be difficult to sneak Mey out of here," Arwel

said. "Ragnar's limo has darkened windows, and the last time I checked, the only cameras in the parking garage were ours."

"Check again." Yamanu reached for a bread roll. "And also check the footage of the last couple of days. See if anyone's been doing anything suspicious down there."

Arwel nodded. "I'll do that right after lunch."

"The other thing we need to solve is the phone situation." Yamanu turned to Mey. "You can't take a bugged phone with you, but I know that you don't want to part with it because your sister might call or message you."

Eyes widening, Mey pushed away from the table. "I forgot to check for messages today." She walked over to the safe and put in the code.

"Take it out to the corridor," Yamanu cautioned.

"I didn't forget." Mey pulled out the phone and stepped outside, closing the door behind her.

"I can watch Mey's phone," Alena offered. "If there is anything from Jin, I can let you know or forward the message."

"I have a better idea. I'll ask the expert's advice." Yamanu started getting up.

Alena put a hand on his arm. "Can't it wait for after lunch?"

"It will only take a minute, and anyway, I want to wait for Mey, if you don't mind."

"Of course not." She smiled. "That's so chivalrous of you."

It had been a sly move even though what he'd said was true. Yamanu had known that Alena would forgive his lack of decorum if he cloaked it in romantic intentions.

Pulling out his phone, he selected William's number and sat on the couch. It was a Sunday, so there was a small chance the guy was sleeping in, but knowing William, he was in the lab working on the weekends as well.

"Yamanu," he answered on the fourth ring. "I heard the good news from Kian. Congratulations."

Rumors certainly traveled fast through the village. Yamanu hadn't expected it from Kian, though.

"Thank you, but it's premature, and I need your advice. We know that Mey's phone is bugged, and we need to leave it behind. But she's expecting calls and texts from her sister. Is there any way to reroute them to a secure number without the watchers tracing it to us?"

William snorted. "It's child's play. Give me her number, and I'll have everything rerouted through several servers to a new phone. I can send a clan-issue device with Kri and Michael, so Mey will have it tomorrow. Leave her phone in the hotel's lost and found, but it needs to be hooked up to a charger."

"You are the best. Thank you."

"Any time, my friend."

Mey came in a moment later, looking pale, but everyone waited patiently with their questions until she put the phone back in the safe and locked it.

"There was a message?" Yamanu pulled out a chair for her.

Mey nodded. "Now I'm a hundred percent sure that it is not Jin who is sending the messages." Her chin quivered a little, but then she took in a shuddering breath and regained control. "This one was longer than usual. The one pretending to be Jin complained about my lack of updates. Supposedly, my texts and phone messages used to be the highlight of her day when she got to the spot with reception. She misses me and wants to know what's going on with me. Do I have any exciting news to share? Like a new boyfriend or a new job?"

Alena put her hand over Mey's. "Those seem like legitimate sisterly questions."

"Yeah, but not from Jin. She knows that I'm happy working for Dalia, so she wouldn't have asked about a new job. But whoever eavesdropped on my conversation with Derek got the impression that I've gotten a great new job offer."

"We can use that," Yamanu said. "Tomorrow, send Jin a message that you indeed have a new boyfriend who has connections in Europe, and who is helping you get a lucrative contract with one of the most famous fashion houses in France. Don't specify which house, of course, or when the interview is taking place."

"That's good," Arwel said. "It seems like a trail, but it leads nowhere."

KIAN

*A*fter the first call from Yamanu, Kian had returned to bed, trying to salvage what had been left of his relaxed mood on a Sunday morning. But after the second call, going back to bed was no longer possible.

He needed to get busy and call Turner, but doing it in his pajamas seemed unprofessional, especially since he was going to bother the guy on a day that was supposed to be dedicated to family.

"What's going on?" Syssi looked up from her tablet. "You look worried."

He sat on the bed. "Yamanu called again."

He'd given Syssi an update after Yamanu's first call, but things had escalated quickly, and a couple of hours later everything had taken on a more urgent tone.

Mey was no longer just a possible Dormant with an interesting talent, she had turned into a possible threat to the clan as well as an asset. And the news about her sister's ability was a game changer. Kian couldn't help but feel excited at the prospect of having both talents at his disposal.

"Bad news?" Syssi asked.

"It's a mixed bag. Apparently, Mey's sister has a very interesting paranormal talent as well. If she touches a person even once, she can create a sort of connection to him or her, and she can then hear and see what they are doing."

"That's one hell of a spying tool." Syssi put the tablet down and pushed up on the pillows.

"My thoughts exactly. Mey believes that her sister's new and mysterious job is connected to her talent, but according to Mey they had kept it a secret, swearing to never reveal their abilities to anyone. So, the big question is how Jin's employer found out about it. She thinks that the government has her sister and that if they hired Jin for her talent, they are never going to let her out."

"She's not wrong about that." Syssi shifted, pulling the comforter to her chest. "Imagine what they could do with her. She could be planted as a waitress in an event hosting foreign dignitaries, touch whomever the government wants to spy on, and boom, all his or her secrets from now until whenever are exposed."

"Mey's talent is also useful, but not as much as her sister's. It seems that hers is still a secret, though, but not for long unless we help her get out, which we are doing. She's being followed around so they can catch her doing something unusual."

"I'm surprised that they haven't snatched her yet."

"Yeah, me too. Perhaps they are being more careful with her because of what she does for a living. A model disappearing might get some media attention."

"Is Mey famous?"

Kian shrugged. "I don't know. That's a question better addressed to Amanda." He pushed his hair back. "Is it wrong of me to also want Jin for her spying ability?"

"Of course, you want her, but you wouldn't keep her prisoner if she wants to leave. Right?"

He grimaced. "If Jin is a Dormant, I will have no choice. At least until she transitions. But let's worry about that when we actually have her. Right now, Mey has only one iffy clue about Jin's whereabouts. She remembered seeing a West Virginia travel guide in her sister's room, and it had a page about a National Radio Quiet Zone earmarked. She has a hunch that's where Jin's new place of employment is located. I want to call Turner and ask him what he knows about it, and whether the government has research facilities there. Have you ever heard about the place? Because this is the first time that I did."

Syssi shook her head. "I didn't know it existed. I can do a quick internet search and find out the basics. You know, the stuff they put out for the public's consumption." She chuckled. "Do you think they have a secret facility for paranormals over there?"

"Who knows." He rubbed the back of his neck. "The problem is that if Jin was recruited by the government, it's going to be very difficult to get her out. I don't want to attract their attention. Our survival depends on us staying under their radar."

"Roni's situation was similar, and yet you approved his extraction."

"It was, and it wasn't. As far as his handlers knew, Roni was a smart guy and a talented hacker, and that's how he managed to arrange his escape. He didn't have any paranormal abilities, and neither did they. Jin could be in a facility full of people with various extrasensory talents. All it will take for us to get exposed is one person realizing who is helping Jin and then report it."

Syssi shivered. "It's not worth the risk. Not even if that facility is full of potential Dormants."

"That's why I need to talk to Turner. The impossible is what he specializes in."

"Roni can probably find out more about that quiet zone. Does he still have a backdoor into government databases?"

"I think so. But there are things even he can't get into. Besides, he needs to know where to look first. The other problem is that right now, he and William are dedicating all their resources to locating Kalugal. There is endless security footage for their facial recognition program to process."

Syssi nodded. "Priorities, priorities. Both Kalugal and Mey have something we want, but while we don't know where he is, Yamanu is bringing Mey in on Tuesday. Is he taking her to the keep? I would like to meet her."

"There was a change of plans. We decided that it would be better to get her out of New York as soon as possible. He is bringing her here tomorrow."

Syssi sat up. "Here? You mean to the village? How come?"

"If I put her in the keep, I'll have to assign Guardians to her, which I can't spare at the moment because of the raid. We need everyone available. Besides, I'm quite certain that she is a Dormant, so I'm willing to take the risk."

Tilting her head, Syssi regarded him for a long moment. "That's so unlike you. You are always so skeptical and so cautious."

"I'm becoming less skeptical, but not less careful. Mey has a strong paranormal ability, and she and Yamanu hit it off from the first moment. Both are excellent indicators of her being a Dormant. And if she isn't, Yamanu can thrall her memories of the village away the same as the keep's. He tested her, and she is not resistant to thralling. I'm not concerned."

With a big smile spreading over her face, Syssi wrapped her arms around Kian's neck and pulled him down for a quick kiss. "I need to get up." She let go of him and swung her legs over the side of the bed. "I have a lot of work to do."

"What work?"

"I'm going to call Amanda about throwing a surprise welcoming party for Mey and Yamanu. But first, I need to call Arwel and ask his permission to get into their house. I'm sure that it's dusty, that the fridge is empty, and that the place looks just as inviting as the other bachelor pads. I'll get Okidu to clean up, while Amanda and I go for a quick supply run. A few pillows and a throw blanket can do a lot to soften the look." She glanced at him from under lowered lashes. "I'm going to buy new bedding as well. Something luxuriously soft that spells honeymoon."

"Perhaps you shouldn't. I'm not sure what the deal with Yamanu is. We were all convinced that he was celibate, and then he calls about Mey and says that she is his one. How does that work?"

Syssi waved a hand in dismissal. "Maybe you were all wrong about him? He might have been very private about his intimate life, and he might have been choosy. Did he ever admit to being celibate?"

"No, but when you know a guy for so long, you don't have to be told. No one has seen him with a woman or heard him talking about one in centuries."

"So, he wasn't always like that?"

Kian shook his head. "I remember when he was just as active as the rest of the men and quite cocky about his effect on the ladies."

Syssi shrugged. "Perhaps he matured and learned to keep his conquests to himself. Personally, I think that speaks in his favor and not the other way around."

ELLA

*J*ulian wrapped his arm around Ella's waist and pulled her closer to him. "Did Ruth say what's the occasion?"

"Ruth wasn't the one who called. Sylvia did. She only said that her mom is inviting us to dinner."

The evening was windy, making the air feel cooler than it actually was. The summer dress that Ella had put on didn't offer much protection, and she hadn't thought to bring a jacket for the short walk to Ruth and Nick's house. Leaning against Julian's side, she was glad of the warmth his body was emitting.

"Did she invite anyone else?" Julian asked.

"It's only us, Roni and Sylvia, Ruth and Nick. I just hope it's not someone's birthday or anniversary. I would feel bad showing up without a present."

"I have a solution for that." Julian pulled out the two concert tickets his ex-roommate had sent them. "We can offer these."

Ella cast him an amused glance. "I know that you don't want to go hear him play, but you can't give these as a present because you got them for free."

"So what? No one would know."

"First of all, it's easy to guess who you got those from, and secondly, it doesn't matter. A gift is about spending the time to select something special, and not about giving away something that you don't want."

"What if you don't know what the person likes? If I had to buy a gift for Roni, I would have no clue what to get him. Would you?"

"Of course. I would get him something that has to do with grilling. You know how obsessed he is with producing the best steaks. It could be something as silly as a custom-printed apron that says Master Steak Chef. The cost doesn't matter, it's the thought put into selecting the gift that makes it special."

Leaning, Julian kissed the top of her head. "That's the difference between you and me. You are creative, and I'm not. Give me a project, and I will do my best to make it happen, but it's not going to be anything wowing. Just functional. Like the halfway house. I made it work, but it wouldn't have been half the success it is without your help."

Ella chuckled. "It sounds funny. Half of the half. But thank you. It makes me happy to think that the small tweaks I suggested are making a difference."

"The reading corner with the floor pillows is a success, and so is the self-serve ice cream bar. I don't think the common room would have been used as much without them."

As they climbed the steps to Ruth's house, Ella sniffed the air. "There will be no steak tonight, but something smells delicious."

Julian knocked on the door. "I wasn't hungry until we got here. But now I am."

Sylvia opened up. "You are just in time. Thank you for being punctual." She leaned to whisper. "My mom likes to serve her creations right when they're ready. She says that reheating destroys the flavor."

"She's absolutely right." Ella gave her a quick hug.

Inside, Roni and Nick were playing a virtual reality game, looking really weird. With the headsets on, they were moving in the virtual world in a way that made sense to them, but to onlookers their hand movements and head tilts seemed disjointed.

"That looks like fun," Julian said.

"You can take a turn after dinner," Ruth said from the kitchen. "Can you tell them that the food is ready?"

Julian nodded. "Hi, Ruth, and thanks for inviting us."

"It's my pleasure."

"Can I help bring things out?" Ella asked.

"Sure."

As usual, everything Ruth had made was simple and yet delicious. But more than the meal, Ella enjoyed the company. Sylvia and Roni were fun, and Nick was a real hoot. Ruth was quiet, not taking part in the conversation unless someone asked her something. But she seemed happy, content to be surrounded by family and friends, which Ella wouldn't have known before her transition.

She was still learning to interpret the more subtle scents people emitted, but the simple ones were quite obvious. After acquiring a whole new spectrum of sensory input, Ella wondered how she'd managed without it before.

"How is the search for Kalugal going?" Julian asked when dessert was served.

Roni stretched his back and rubbed his stomach. "It's going and going and going. Our servers are running at full capacity, and I have nothing to do. William can at least tinker with his mechanical inventions while we wait, but I can only read or play on my Switch."

Nick rolled his eyes. "As if that's such a hardship. Want to swap places with me? I now have two bosses over my head, telling me what to do. Eva and Sharon. I'm glad that she picked up speed and is keeping the agency from folding, but let's just say that I can't wait for Eva to come back, and in the meantime, I would love to sit in your throne-like chair and play games all day long."

Roni shrugged. "And I would gladly switch places with you and get to work aboveground for a change. But unlike you, I suck at the technical side of things. I'm a code man. Not hardware."

"That's too bad that your servers are maxed out," Ella said. "I've been meaning to ask you to do a quick database search for my aunt. But I guess it will have to wait for later."

"Is she missing?" Ruth asked.

"I don't know. She was always a recluse, and we were never close. I would like to know what's going on with her, but I can't just pick up the phone and call because I'm supposed to be dead." Ella folded her napkin and put it over her plate. "I've been thinking a lot about her lately and wondering whether she could be a Dormant."

Sylvia frowned. "I thought that your mom didn't have any siblings."

"Eleanor is my father's sister. But since Parker and my paranormal abilities are so much stronger than my mother's, I started thinking that maybe my father was a Dormant too. Given Amanda's affinity theory, it makes sense for Dormants to be attracted to one another. So, if two Dormants happen to go to the same school and are about the same age, chances are that they will find each other."

"What's her last name?" Roni asked.

"As far as I know, it's still Takala. If she got married, she didn't tell my mom about it. All I know is that she is about thirty-nine years old, and last I heard she worked as a pharmaceutical sales rep. She might have changed careers. But if she has Parker's compulsion ability, that's unlikely. She could make a killing in sales."

"Sweet," Nick said. "I wish I had some of that juice. But all I have is a knack for electronics."

"What are you going to do if you find her?" Julian asked.

"I'm not sure. I can't contact her because she thinks that we are all dead. But if there is a way to find out whether she is a Dormant, and it turns out that she is, she could join the clan. She might be someone's truelove mate. But I know that's a long shot and probably a lot of wishful thinking on my part." Ella cast Roni an apologetic look. "That's why I waited so long to ask you. I know that you are busy, and finding my aunt is the last item on your long priority list."

Roni shook his head. "Dormants are never last priority. Turner and I are still trying to find my grandmother, but it's more complicated with her because she is an immortal, and she knows that she needs to hide. Your aunt has no reason to do that, so she should be easy to locate. The hard part is going to be figuring out if she's a Dormant or not."

"Unless she exhibits strong paranormal ability," Julian said. "Especially if she can compel. That shouldn't be too difficult to test."

MEY

"*I* feel bad about you having to miss Alena's first photo shoot," Mey said as Yamanu closed the suite's door behind them.

Saying goodbye to her new friends had been surprisingly difficult. Mey hadn't realized how much she'd gotten attached to them. The worst part was not knowing if she was ever going to see any of them again. Yamanu's boss had allowed her two weeks. If she didn't transition during the allotted time, her memory of ever encountering immortals was going to be erased.

It would be as if she'd never met them.

Wrapping his arm around her shoulders, Yamanu pulled Mey against his side. "I don't care about the photo shoot. All I care about is Alena's safety, and I'm sure that four experienced Guardians can take care of that. She doesn't really need me. You, on the other hand, definitely do."

She couldn't argue with that. There were people watching her, her phone was bugged, and she was scared of men in black ambushing her at any moment. Yamanu was the only reason she wasn't panicking yet.

"Are you sure it's a good idea for us to walk to my apartment?"

Holding the elevator door open for her, Yamanu nodded. "The entry is being watched from across the street," he whispered.

"That's why I think we should take a car from the garage."

"I want them to see us strolling casually as if nothing has happened. Since they are listening to your phone, they know that you've spotted the guy who has been following you and called me because you were scared. I want them to get the impression that you've forgotten about him. It's important to maintain the illusion that you're just staying with your new boyfriend and having a good time. We don't want the watcher to suspect that you are spooked and about to flee."

It made sense and yet, as they stepped out of the hotel's front door, Mey couldn't help but glance at the other side of the street. "Where is he?" she whispered in Yamanu's ear.

"Hiding behind the white van. But don't look."

"Okay."

"When we get to your apartment, we need to put on an act. I'll say something about renting our own suite and spending the next week making love and lounging by the pool, and you are going to say that you can't wait to go with me to Paris and continue much of the same."

"Got it."

Mey smirked. She could have fun play acting for the surveillance cameras the watchers had filled her apartment with, and Yamanu would have no choice but to cooperate. It probably wasn't the time to fool around, but sounding stressed and worried was certainly not going to convince anyone that she was planning to spend the next week enjoying her new boyfriend. And since it was a necessary part of his plan, then why not? Life was too short to squander an opportunity for a little fun.

Then again, if she turned immortal, her opportunities would be limitless.

What a concept.

Mey wondered how others dealt with that. For procrastinators, it was probably hell. With no urgency to get things done and endless time to complete tasks, they were probably stuck in place doing nothing. For the overachievers, though, it was heaven. There was no limit to what they could do and learn.

Or maybe there was?

According to Yamanu, immortals were no smarter on average than humans. So maybe there was a limit to what the brain could store?

"Is there anyone in your clan who dedicates himself or herself to the acquisition of knowledge?"

"The only one who comes to mind is Sylvia. We call her the eternal student. But I don't think she does it to accumulate knowledge. She just hasn't found the one thing she enjoys doing."

"How many subjects has she studied?"

"I think she is on her third masters. Why?"

"I was wondering if anyone has tried to learn everything there is to learn. After all, when time is limitless, it's possible. The question is whether our brains can contain all that knowledge."

"That's an interesting question. I don't think anyone has tried and then discovered that his or her brain couldn't take the load."

As Mey's awareness prickled with a warning, she leaned her head on Yamanu's shoulder. "Is he following us?" she whispered.

"He's keeping about a hundred-foot distance. If we keep our voices down, he can't hear us."

"What if we are walking into an ambush? I don't feel right about this."

Thankfully, Yamanu didn't dismiss her intuition. "Do you want to turn around?"

"I need my damn laptop. If not for that, I could've just bought whatever I needed instead of going back to my apartment."

"We can turn back, and I can go get it by myself. You can stay with Ragnar."

The rest of the team had gone with Alena to her first photo shoot, so the hotel manager was the only immortal who could offer her protection.

Mey shook her head. "I'm probably being paranoid. Besides, I trust that you can handle a couple of hired thugs if needed."

"That depends."

That was a surprise. She'd expected Yamanu to puff out his chest and assure her that yes, he could handle any danger.

"On what?"

"On whether they are armed or not, and whether their trigger fingers are itchy and they open fire before I see it coming. Or if one of them is immune to thralling, which is rare. Save for that, I can freeze any human in his tracks."

"What if there are several of them?"

"I can freeze an entire block if I want to. Except for immunes, that is."

That was an impressive ability. No wonder that the immortals had survived for thousands of years undetected by humans.

"Will I be able to thrall people like that when I transition?"

He shook his head. "My ability is unique even among immortals. Most can thrall just one person at a time, and some can't do even that. Transitioned Dormants have to practice for a long time before they can thrall, and most don't bother."

She tightened her arm around his waist. "So, you are quite a catch. I snagged myself a very powerful immortal."

"I don't know about being a catch, but I admit to being powerful. My ability has saved the clan from marauders on more than one occasion. And even now my services are always in demand for one thing or another."

"Do you ever use it for anything other than defense?"

"Rarely. And since it doesn't work on other immortals, it's not effective in the fight against our enemies. But they can't use it on us either, so it evens out." He smirked. "And we are better trained. But we are also outnumbered, so our best strategy is to hide."

"Is it? In today's world it's not easy to stay hidden unless you do it in the jungles of South America or some other wild places."

"I know. For now, we have a technological advantage over our enemies, but that won't last long. They are doing everything they can to catch up. We need to reach a solution before they do that, or they are going to wipe us out of existence."

"What are your options?"

He rubbed a hand over his jaw. "It's another long story. Bottom line, we want to cause a change from inside the Doomers' organization. If they overthrow their leader and forsake his plan for world domination, we might come to an agreement and coexist peacefully."

Mey snorted. "Good luck with that. Peace can only be achieved from a position of power. As long as your enemies are the aggressors while your clan is taking the defensive position, and they think that they can win a war against you, they won't negotiate. They will only agree to do that if they fear that you can turn the tables on them and win."

6

YAMANU

*M*ey's view was a bit fatalistic, but she had a good point. Thinking back on his seven hundred years of life and what he had witnessed, Yamanu couldn't think of a single instance of an aggressor coming to the negotiation table for anything other than accepting surrender.

Things were a little different in democracies, but not by much. A leader was held accountable to the voting public, which meant that acts of aggression had to get the people's approval. Except, it was way too easy to manipulate the voters, as evidenced by Nazi Germany. Hitler had risen to power in a seemingly democratic process. In places where people had little to no rights and no access to truthful information, things were way worse.

The Doomers had been conditioned to hate everything the Western world stood for, mainly because it was a good way to control them and have them fight in wars that they otherwise would not have been motivated to win. Navuh's hatred for the clan in general and Annani in particular was probably secondary to that.

Were Annani and Kian deluding themselves that if Kalugal

replaced his father, he would agree to peaceful coexistence with the clan?

Why would he?

If he seized power over the Doomer organization, Kalugal would become extremely powerful and would have no motive to negotiate for peace. The clan was not a threat, mainly because they didn't seek the Doomers' annihilation even though they had the means to do that.

If they wanted, they could nuke the island and be done with their enemies once and for all. Except, unlike the Brotherhood, the clan believed in the sanctity of life, and the thousands of innocent lives that would be lost in an annihilation attack was not acceptable collateral damage. Annani would never allow that.

"We are here." Mey pulled on his arm.

Damn, if not for Mey, he would have just kept on walking. He was supposed to guard her, and not philosophize about things he had no control over.

As she opened the front door, he let his senses flare wide, searching for the signature of the watcher he'd noticed earlier. The guy was still across the street and seemed to be alone.

So far, so good.

Yamanu followed Mey into the lobby, and then pulled her in for a kiss. "Let me enter the apartment first," he whispered in her ear while pretending to nuzzle it.

"Okay," she whispered back. "But I'm staying glued to your back. What if someone comes at us from behind?"

"Good call. I don't sense any danger, though. So, you can relax."

He was right and wrong at the same time, and so was Mey.

When they reached her door, Yamanu knew right away that there were people inside, and as he opened it, they got ambushed just as Mey had expected.

"Here you are!" A gorgeous, barely dressed blonde rushed at them. "And you brought your hunk with you." She gave him a thorough once-over. "You weren't exaggerating." She offered him her hand. "I'm Tatiana, Mey's flatmate."

"I'm Yamanu. It's a pleasure to meet you." He hoped Mey hadn't told her roommates that he was from Slovenia. Tatiana's accent sounded Russian, but he could be mistaken. If she addressed him in Slovenian, he would have to improvise somehow because he hadn't bothered to learn it.

"I forgot that you were coming back today," Mey said. "I've been staying with Yamanu because it was so damn lonely here without you."

Putting a hand on her bony hip, Tatiana struck a pose. "I bet that was the only reason." She winked and turned to yell over her shoulder. "Girls, come and say hello to Mey's new guy!

As a stampede of bare feet followed and two more beautiful women rushed out of their bedrooms, Mey groaned. One had on only a long T-shirt and hopefully some panties, and the other one wore a pair of boxer shorts that were practically see-through.

Apparently, models were not modest. Which made sense. During fashion shows, they had to change quickly and in front of everyone who happened to be backstage.

"Hi, I'm Josephine," the first to arrive introduced herself. "Do you have brothers?"

He shook her hand. "I'm afraid not. I'm an only child."

"That's a shame." The other one offered him her hand. "I'm Valerie."

With the introductions and the once-overs done, the ladies turned their attention back to Mey.

"You could have left a note, you know," Valerie said. "We figured you were staying with your guy, but you didn't answer your phone."

That was because it had stayed in the safe, but Mey took the opportunity to act out what they had planned. Leaning against his side, she smiled coyly. "I'm sorry, but I've been so busy that I forgot to check my phone." She ran her hand over his chest. "There is so much to explore."

Mey's suggestive tone and caress had affected not only Yamanu, but her three friends as well, and suddenly the room felt oppressively hot and uncomfortable.

Four beautiful women turning their lust on him was enough to break the will of the most devout celibate monk. It wasn't that he was interested in anyone other than Mey, but he was still a male, and no amount of potions and meditation was going to change that.

"I'll wait on the balcony while you pack." He strode toward the sliding doors.

"Are you going on vacation?" Tatiana asked Mey.

"Yamanu and I are staying at his hotel. They have an awesome pool."

"Can we come to visit?" Josephine asked.

Damn. He had to rescue Mey from answering.

Pivoting on his heel, Yamanu went back and wrapped his arm around her shoulders. "We would love to have you, but maybe a little later. Mey and I are still in the getting to know each other stage." He ran his hand down Mey's arm.

Tatiana sighed. "I see how it is. We should start looking for a new roommate."

Perceptive woman.

"No way!" Mey protested. "I'm coming back. This is just a short vacation."

Tatiana waved a dismissive hand. "Yeah, keep telling yourself that." She walked away.

"What's her problem?" Mey murmured.

"Nothing," Valerie said. "She's just jealous."

That wasn't it. Even Yamanu's limited empathy had picked up on Tatiana's sadness. It wasn't about jealousy, she just didn't want Mey to leave.

Perhaps the Russian had a sixth sense that Mey was not coming back anytime soon.

He hoped that Tatiana was right. If Mey transitioned, she was going to stay in the village. But at the same time, he regretted taking her away from friends who seemed to care about her.

Mey was going to miss them.

7

LOKAN

"I'm so excited about seeing Ella and Vivian." Carol wound her arms around Lokan's neck and pulled him down for a kiss. "But I wish you would come with me. Couldn't the meeting with Kian wait until tomorrow?"

Even if it could, Lokan would have found another excuse to wriggle out of having to spend time with those two. If Carol had been meeting Kian's mate or sister, he might have regretted missing the opportunity to get to know them better. But both worked full time and couldn't meet Carol until later in the evening. Lunch with his former captives, on the other hand, was not his idea of fun. Compared to that, dealing with Kian and his suspicious attitude was going to be a pleasant experience.

"Tomorrow, I'm meeting Losham, and Kian wanted to see me before that. Besides, I'm sure your friends want your undivided attention. Go and have fun."

"Oh, I will." She kissed him again. "Call me when your meeting is over. Maybe you can join us later?"

"I doubt it."

In fact, he was sure Kian was going to hold him for as long

as Carol was out and return him to the hotel only when she was back as well, so there was no chance he could follow Ella and Vivian to the village.

What a suspicious guy. By now, Kian should have realized that Lokan's commitment to Carol was absolute, and that he had no nefarious plans for the clan. Still, he could understand his cousin's caution.

Secrecy and the ability to hide in plain sight was what had kept the clan alive and well for thousands of years, and to change a proven tactic would be a mistake.

When Kian called shortly after Carol had left, it confirmed Lokan's suspicion that the two events had been coordinated.

"Come down," Kian said. "The limo is up front."

"I'm on my way."

That was another precaution on Kian's part. Lokan didn't know where they were going, only that Kian had made reservations in a fine restaurant, promising that it would be an unforgettable treat.

When he exited the revolving door, the black limousine was indeed parked in front of the entry, and he recognized Kian's butler who had put on a chauffeur's hat and was holding the back door open for him.

"Good afternoon, master." He bowed when Lokan approached.

"Thank you." Lokan ducked inside, taking a seat opposite from Kian. "Hello, cousin." He grinned and offered his hand.

Expecting the grimace that usually came after that address, Lokan was disappointed not to get a rise out of Kian this time. Apparently, it had gotten old.

"Lokan." Kian shook his hand. "How is Carol doing?"

"She's excited to meet her friends. But she regrets that Wonder couldn't come."

"Yeah. She is operating the café now, and it's not easy with Carol gone."

"You should get some hired help." Lokan leaned forward. "Some humans wouldn't mind disappearing for the rest of their natural lives. They would think of your hideout as a sanctuary."

"I'm not going to allow criminals in our village."

"Not only criminals seek sanctuary."

"True. But that's a discussion for another day. Did you talk to your brother again?"

"Just to confirm the time and place for tomorrow. He was busy."

Kian nodded. "I believe we have enough information to take his men out. Just make sure not to let anything slip about the raid."

"Don't worry, I won't. I just wonder what will happen to Losham after this. He might decide to run."

"What if he does?"

Lokan shrugged. "Then perhaps you should chase after him. The guy is brilliant. If he feels that his career in the Brotherhood is over, he might consider switching loyalties, and he could be an asset to you." He smiled evilly. "That is if I allow him to live after our meeting tomorrow. If he knew about his adopted son's proclivities and what that scum did to Carol, then I'm going to hold him accountable for her suffering."

"Don't kill him. Bring him to me. I'll make sure that he pays for his son's sins. The only reason we are not going after him personally is my promise to you."

"I appreciate that. It's not that I care for Losham. I care about my father connecting the dots."

"And rightfully so." Kian raked his fingers through his hair. "There is another matter I wanted to discuss with you, and it has to do with what you told me about the government collecting paranormal talents."

Lokan's curiosity was piqued. "What about it?"

"The team that I sent to New York to try and flush out your brother met an interesting woman with an even more interesting story. Apparently, she and her younger sister have unique paranormal abilities, which are perfect for spying. Recently, her sister was offered a very well-paying job that required a nondisclosure agreement. She couldn't tell anyone what the job was or even where she was going to work. After she left for the new job, the only communications from her were a couple of odd texts. Her older sibling suspects that she's been recruited by the government to spy for them. I want you to try to find out more about the program. Maybe you can arrange to meet with those whose minds you've seen it in before."

Lokan arched a brow. "Is there a reason you're being so cryptic? What are their names? What are their abilities? If you want me to look for a connection, I need to know more."

Not really, but he was curious.

"You don't need to know that. Not yet. If you find out something and need more information to continue, I might consider it."

Leaning back, Lokan crossed his arms over his chest. "It's funny how you don't have a moral dilemma about sending me to do your dirty work. Would you have given one of your Guardians permission to peek into people's heads for no good reason?"

Kian rewarded his question with a chilling stare. "Yes, I would. Finding Dormants is a matter of survival for my clan, and that overrides all other rules."

"Fair enough." Lokan uncrossed his arms. "So, your interest in the sisters is purely for their genes and not their special talents?"

Kian's eyes darted aside, revealing his discomfort, and Lokan wondered whether he was going to lie about it.

"Mostly but not entirely. What they can do is truly unique. In fact, none of my clan members possesses anything like it. Their abilities could be most beneficial to us. On the other hand, if they are so outside the scope of what we know immortals can do, then maybe they are not carriers of our genes."

"Are you suggesting that there are other nonhumans out there?"

Kian shrugged. "Who knows. Humans are ignorant of our existence. We might be guilty of the same in regard to another divergent species."

"There could be another explanation." Lokan lifted a finger. "Mutation. Species tend to evolve. Maybe the sisters are the next step in human evolution?"

"That's an interesting hypothesis. I need to run it by our doctor."

As the limo pulled up to the curb and stopped, Lokan looked out the window expecting to see the front of a fancy restaurant. Instead, he saw a casual bistro with an outdoor patio and suburbanite clientele.

"What is this place?" he asked.

"This is Gino's. Gino is an old friend of mine, and his restaurant serves the best Italian food you've ever had."

8

CAROL

"I can't eat another bite." Vivian pushed her plate away. "My stomach feels like it's going to burst." Looking to both sides, she popped the top button of her jeans and sighed in relief. "That's much better."

Carol shook her head. "You didn't eat that much. I, on the other hand, really overdid it. Luckily, I'm wearing a stretchy skirt." She pulled on the waistband to demonstrate. "I love this brand. I'm going to order several more in different colors and patterns."

The thing was called a bandage skirt, but it was one of the most comfortable and versatile pieces of clothing ever. It was stretchy, so there were no zippers to poke her and the fabric was substantial, so it held its shape. And although it hugged her curves all over, she could still move comfortably in it. Not only that, it didn't take much space in the suitcase and didn't get wrinkled. It was a perfect travel piece.

"I say it's time to order drinks." Ella pulled her ID out of her wallet and waved the waiter over.

"I don't like it when you do that," Vivian said.

"Use my fake ID or order drinks?"

"The ID."

Ella shrugged. "This is my identity outside of the village. I can't use anything else. Besides, you are using a fake one too, and with how young you look, the waiter will probably ask to see yours as well."

"Perhaps. But at least mine shows my real age."

With all that Ella had been through and all that she'd achieved, it was easy to forget that the girl was barely nineteen and that Vivian was her mother.

Even before her transition, Vivian had looked like Ella's older sister. She hadn't changed much after it, but she looked younger, healthier, and certainly happier.

What Carol wondered was how much of it was due to her new and improved body, and how much of it was due to her new and improved life. Living in the village with the man she loved and knowing that her daughter had emerged stronger from her ordeal rather than broken had erased the stress lines from Vivian's pretty face. With her lips curved in a smile, she appeared to be in her mid-twenties, more than a decade less than her actual age.

"What can I get you, ladies?" The guy flashed a smile at Carol.

"Black Russian for me."

Ella handed him her ID. "I'll have a strawberry margarita, please."

He looked at Vivian. "And you, miss?"

She lifted the empty bottle of Perrier. "I'll have another one of these."

When he left, Carol leaned closer. "If you are worried about the calories in drinks, don't. Our metabolism is great."

"I'm staying away from alcohol."

Carol's eyebrows popped up. "Are you expecting?"

"I'm expecting to get pregnant, but I'm not yet. At least I

don't think that I am." She leaned in and whispered. "How do immortal females know that they've conceived? There is no period, so there is nothing to be missed."

"And thank God for that," Ella said. "That was the best part about transitioning."

Carol glanced from mother to daughter. "Really? That was the best part? Because I can think of several benefits that are so much more monumental than no periods."

"Like what?" Vivian asked. "I don't feel much different."

"Yeah, me neither," Ella agreed. "I'm still only five foot four, and I still carry several extra pounds on my hips. I hoped to pass out and wake up a supermodel. Instead, I never lost consciousness, and I look exactly the same as I did before. And on another note, you were always an immortal, Carol, so you've never had to suffer through periods. You don't know what a pain in the rear they are."

"You are both such complainers." Carol rolled her eyes. "I bet you always see the glass half-empty instead of half-full."

Vivian sighed. "You are not wrong, and I'm trying to work on it. I don't know if it's a human thing or just me. But enough about us. We want to hear about you and your life in Washington."

"There is not much to tell. Lokan is busy, and I'm not, which drives me nuts. I'm used to being overwhelmed with too much work, and now I have nothing to do." She smiled. "But the positives definitely outweigh the negatives. Despite the nightly marathon sex sessions, I'm well-rested, I'm caught up on all the gossip magazines, and I started a foodie blog. Life is good. It could have been perfect if Lokan had moved with me into the village, but that's not in the cards. Even if Kian gets over his mistrust and allows it, Lokan needs to stay connected to the Brotherhood. He is the clan's new safety net."

When the waiter arrived with their drinks, everyone waited for him to leave before resuming the conversation.

"How did you come up with the idea for a foodie blog?" Vivian asked.

"I have an amazing mate who is very concerned about keeping me entertained." Carol winked. "He doesn't want me to get bored and start thinking about going on missions again. Whenever he can, Lokan takes me out to the best restaurants in the city. At first, I started rating them for fun, but then I thought about putting it in a blog." She shrugged. "It's just something to do until I decide what I really want to sink my teeth into."

"You can try for a baby," Vivian suggested. "Merlin's fertility center is the new social hub of the village."

Carol's eyes widened. "No way! Did everyone go crazy?" She looked at Ella. "Are you and Julian also trying to get pregnant?"

Ella patted her shoulder. "My mom is exaggerating. I'm in college now, and I'm in no hurry to become a mother. It's only some of the couples and a few of the single ladies."

"What about Amanda? Is she going for it?"

"Not as far as I know," Vivian said. "I've never seen her or Dalhu in Merlin's place."

Carol lifted a brow. "Does he run the clinic from his house?"

"God forbid." Vivian put a hand on her chest. "Have you been to his place?"

"Is it that bad?"

"It's worse. What he calls the fertility center is his office in the clinic. He glued a sign on the door that says 'Merlin's Fertility Center'."

Carol laughed. "He's an odd bird, that one, but he's amusing. Did anyone other than Syssi and Kian conceive yet?"

"If anyone did, they are not sharing," Vivian said. "Still,

there is an atmosphere of hope in the village. Even those who are not trying for a baby seem more upbeat."

"That's good. I'm glad to hear that. The freaking ghost town of a playground was one of Kian's worst ideas. Everyone who passed by it got sad without even realizing why. I don't know what was going through his head."

"Hope?" Ella mused. "Maybe Syssi had a premonition that there would be plenty of babies soon, and that they would need a playground."

Carol nodded. "Makes sense. Kian does whatever she suggests. Which reminds me. I heard that Syssi had a premonition about Kalugal being in New York, and that a team was sent to investigate."

Ella and Vivian exchanged looks.

"Did you know that?" Ella asked her mom.

"I knew that they sent a team there, but Magnus didn't tell me why." She looked at Carol. "Perhaps it's supposed to be a secret? Who told you about it?"

"Lokan. I didn't know that I wasn't supposed to talk about it."

Ella shrugged. "It probably isn't a secret. It's just that my mom and I are not part of the gossip circle yet."

"That's not a bad thing," Vivian said. "I don't need to know everything that is going on with everyone. People should mind their own business."

"Yeah, good luck with that." Carol chuckled. "There are no secrets in a small community like ours. Eventually, and by that I mean within twenty-four hours, everyone knows what's going on with you whether you like it or not."

"It's a little annoying," Ella said. "But at the same time, it gives me a sense of security. The community takes care of its members, and if help is needed, it is not only available but also offered freely and wholeheartedly. I think the benefits are worth a little loss of privacy. I wish there were more human communities like that."

"There used to be," Carol said. "When most people still lived in small villages, it was a lot like it is here. The alienation is the product of urbanization."

"Which has advantages and disadvantages too," Vivian said. "I agree that city folks live more isolated lives than those in small communities. But on the other hand, the large city population allows a person to be more selective about his or her choice of friends. A musician might want to hang out with other musicians, and a farmer with other farmers."

"Hey," Ella said. "That reminds me. I heard an interesting statistic. Apparently, farmers have sex more frequently than any other segment of the population. Their average is once a day."

Carol snorted. "Once a day is nothing to boast about. Obviously, whoever did that study didn't know about immortals."

9

YAMANU

"*I*'m all packed." Mey came out of the bedroom carrying her big satchel.

Yamanu eyed the thing. "How did you manage to fit everything in there?"

She laughed. "I didn't. Alena let me borrow one of her suitcases. It's on the bed."

"Oh." He strode inside, picked up the designer luggage, and brought it to the living room.

"Should I put it in the cart, master?" Ovidu asked.

"Let's see if it fits."

The food cart was covered with a tablecloth, but its bottom shelf wasn't wide enough. His and Mey's bags made two bulky protrusions.

"Maybe I should just pack my stuff in shopping bags?" Mey asked.

"I don't think it's a big deal. No one is going to pay attention to Ovidu taking the cart down in the service elevator."

"Is the guy across the street still there?" Mey worried her bottom lip.

"He is. But I'm going to take care of him."

She frowned. "What do you mean by that?"

"Don't worry about it." He wrapped his arm around her waist and pulled her to him. "I'm going to plant in his mind an urgent need to visit the restroom."

"Can you do it from up here?"

"Not unless I want the entire block to run for the nearest bathroom. From such a distance, I can only do a blanket thrall, and I can't narrow it down to one person. I need to be near the guy to affect only him."

"I get it. What about me?"

"While I go down to take care of the watcher, you'll go down to the parking garage where Ovidu will be waiting for you with the limousine. After I get rid of the guy, Ovidu is going to pick me up from the front of the hotel."

"Sounds like a plan. Except, can you take me to the garage? I'm afraid someone might be lurking in there."

Poor girl. Up until now, Mey had managed to fool him into believing that she was doing fine, but apparently she felt safe only when he was around.

"Sure." Yamanu cupped her cheek. "Everything is going to be okay. I promise."

She glanced in the direction of the safe. "Will you remind Alena to take my phone to the lost and found?"

"She won't forget, but I will make sure to remind her. The Guardians that we are going to meet at the airport have your new one, and all your calls are already redirected to it. If your sister calls or leaves a text message before we get there, they will let me know."

"Did they land already?"

He glanced at his watch. "Not yet, but we should get going. After they land, the jet will get refueled, and we will take off right after that."

Mey nodded, took one last look at the suite, and sighed. "I

have good memories of this place. I hope I'm not going to lose them."

His gut clenched. "Me too. I trust the Fates, though. They brought us together for a reason, and it's not to mess with us. Let's go."

He led Mey out, and together with Ovidu, they took the service elevator down to the parking garage.

When they exited, Yamanu let his senses expand for a long moment. Once he'd ascertained that no one was hiding behind one of the vehicles or the many thick support columns, he proceeded to the limousine.

"Lock the doors," he said before leaving Mey and Ovidu in the car.

"Yes, master." Ovidu dipped his head.

Instead of taking the elevator to the lobby, Yamanu jogged up the ramp to the garage's exit and came upon the watcher from behind.

It wasn't the same guy who Yamanu had caught before, and he decided to take a peek into his mind before thralling him to experience severe stomach cramps. Perhaps watcher number two knew more than watcher number one had.

As it turned out, number two knew even less. He was a newly hired hand, and his job was to notify number one if Mey left the hotel.

Useless.

After thralling the guy to duck into the nearest restaurant to use the facilities, Yamanu called Ovidu to come get him.

The low-level personnel that had been assigned to watch Mey didn't indicate that her acquisition was important to whoever had sent them. What were they hoping to find out?

Perhaps they believed that Mey could lead them to a bigger fish? A more powerful paranormal? Or perhaps a group of them?

He chuckled. If only they knew.

But they were not looking for immortals. They were most likely looking for other paranormals.

As Ovidu pulled up to the curb, Yamanu opened the door and slid into the back seat. "The guy was a nobody. He didn't know anything."

Mey tilted her head. "Is it me and my suspicious nature, or is this whole thing odd? Why are they even bothering? What are they hoping to find out this way?"

"My thoughts exactly. I'm starting to think that they are not interested in you personally but hoping that you will lead them to a bigger fish."

"What if I did?" She looked at him with worried eyes. "What if I exposed you and Alena?"

"They have no reason to suspect us. And our meeting in the waiting room of the modeling agency was purely coincidental." He smiled. "Except that it wasn't because the Fates had something to do with that."

"What could they possibly suspect? That I belong to a cabal of paranormals?"

"That's not as crazy as it sounds. If they collect paranormal talent, they might assume that other intelligence agencies are doing the same, and Israel has one of the best in the world."

Mey chuckled. "That's absurd."

"Not really. Mysticism is a big part of Judaism, and there are many stories of famous rabbis performing feats that could only be described as paranormal. Who's to say that the Israeli intelligence is not using them?"

Mey's shoulders started shaking a moment before she burst out laughing.

"What's so funny? I'm serious."

She shook her head. "It's the image that's funny. A group of rabbis, with their long beards and curly sideburns, sitting cross-legged in a circle, holding hands, and remote viewing Israel's enemies. You have one hell of an imagination."

He shrugged. "Hey, stranger things have happened."

She choked down a giggle. "Like what?"

"Like a girl listening to the echoes embedded in walls and hearing conversations between immortals. Would anyone believe that?"

MEY

*M*ey had never flown on a private jet, not even during her Mossad days, and as she and Yamanu entered the private airport, she was surprised at the lack of security. No one checked their luggage or asked to see the contents of her purse, and she and Yamanu headed straight for the jet, where the two new bodyguards were waiting for them.

Guardians, she corrected herself. That was what they were called. Not bodyguards.

"Hi, I'm Kri." The female Guardian offered Mey her hand while giving her a once-over.

They were about the same height, but Kri's shoulders were about twice as wide as Mey's, and she had biceps that were more pronounced than those of most guys, even those who exercised regularly.

She looked young, but by now, Mey knew that immortals' looks could be deceptive. The Guardian could be hundreds of years old.

"Nice to meet you. I'm Mey."

"Here is your phone." The male Guardian handed her a white box. "I'm Michael."

"Nice to meet you, and thank you." She took the box and shook his hand as well. "I felt naked without a phone."

Kri snorted and then cast a questioning glance at Yamanu. "Is there something you want to tell me, big guy?"

He pretended not to get her meaning. "Alena is doing her first photo shoot, and she has everyone with her, so you can head straight to the hotel. Ovidu will drive you there." He smiled. "Ragnar has prepared a very nice suite for you two. This is the easiest assignment you'll ever get. Think of it as the honeymoon you've never taken."

So, Michael and Kri were a couple. Cute. They looked like they belonged together.

Kri shook her head. "Okay, be like that. I'll just get Alena to fill me in on the details."

Yamanu let out an exasperated sigh. "Fine. What do you want to know?"

She looked at Mey. "I think I already do. Is he treating you right?"

Mey threaded her arm through Yamanu's and leaned her head on his shoulder. "He is perfect."

A huge grin spread over Kri's face. "Yamanu is the best. You don't know how lucky you are. So, what's your talent? Kian didn't tell us anything. All we were told was that the team discovered a new Dormant."

Mey cast a sidelong glance at Yamanu. Talking about her ability with strangers was not something she was comfortable doing. In fact, she felt a surge of anxiety at the prospect.

Yamanu patted Mey's hand. "All in good time. We need to get moving."

Kri deflated. "Yeah, this is not the time or place for that."

She turned to Mey and smiled. "Once this assignment is over, and I'm back in the village, how about we get together?"

"I would love to. I just hope that I'm still there when you come back."

The Guardian got her meaning right away. "Good luck." She offered Mey her hand. "I have a good feeling about you."

Michael eyed the two suitcases. "Need any help with those?"

Yamanu snorted and picked them up as if they weighed nothing. "Have fun, kids."

"Oh, we will." Kri wrapped her arm around Michael's shoulders. "See ya when we see ya." She waved goodbye and picked up her duffle bag.

The girl traveled light.

Walking with Yamanu up the stairs, Mey asked, "Are they married?"

"Not yet. But they are mated, and they don't need a ceremony for it to be official."

Yamanu had touched on the fated mate myth, but he hadn't elaborated. There had been so much information that he'd needed to share with her, and it hadn't allowed for an in-depth discussion on any of the particulars. Most things she could wait until later to learn more about, but she was most curious about this subject.

"Would you like something to drink?" Yamanu asked as Mey secured the safety belt. "We have water, beer, and whiskey."

"Water is fine." Mey waited until he was strapped in as well. "Explain the fated mates thing to me. Is every mating fated?"

Yamanu took a long moment to answer. "It's complicated. Up until about three years ago, none of us had mates, and all we knew was from stories our Clan Mother had told us. Most gods and immortals of her time did not have fated mates, and it was considered a rare blessing to find your one and only. That didn't mean, though, that love was absent from relationships that hadn't been fated."

"What about the new couples?"

"They all believe that they are each other's fated."

She tilted her head. "Do you believe that? Perhaps they are still in the honeymoon stage, and that's why it feels special to them?"

What she really wanted to ask was whether he believed that she was his fated mate, but it was too early for that. After all, they'd known each other for a little less than one week.

Letting his head rest against the seat's back, Yamanu let out a breath. "I don't know. I wish there was a test to determine that. Then again, maybe believing in it makes it so. Why poke holes in the fantasy?"

"Why indeed?"

In a way, it was a relief that he didn't believe in the myth wholeheartedly. The ordinary kind of love was hard enough to find. Shooting for the stars could only lead to disappointment.

"But that's my logical brain talking," Yamanu continued. "On a gut level, I believe that our situation is different than that of the gods and immortals of old. I think that the Fates are responsible for the recent discoveries of Dormants. It can't be a coincidence that after so many centuries of finding none, we are suddenly finding one after the other. And if the Fates are involved, they wouldn't do a half-assed job."

He took her hand and brought it to his lips. "I can't be a hundred percent sure about the others, but I do believe that you are mine. I know it's too early, and I don't expect you to believe it, but I just felt like I had to say it."

As Mey's stomach did a flip, she smiled noncommittally and brought the bottle of water to her lips.

Yamanu might be deluding himself just as the others were

doing. He wanted her to be his mate and therefore believed that she was—not because she was so fabulous, but because Dormants were so rare.

The entire concept was strange. But then there were cultures that didn't believe in love at all, so there was that.

Mey was a realist, but she believed in love.

She could see herself spending the rest of her life with Yamanu, but she was well aware that it might be just an infatuation. He was gorgeous, chivalrous, and selfless. Any woman would have fallen for him. But real love had to withstand the test of time and adversity.

Regrettably, the two weeks that Kian had allowed for her transition was not long enough for that. She would have to take a leap of faith and commit to Yamanu based on her untested feelings.

Even after all that he had told her about himself and the clan and immortals in general, she didn't know much about him, from simple things like what did he like to do in his free time to the big question of why he had taken a vow of celibacy.

For some reason, Yamanu believed that his vow protected his people, but it could be wishful thinking just like the fated mates thing.

A silly superstition.

Not that she was going to call him out on that. Questioning a person's beliefs was the fastest way to alienate them.

KIAN

*a*s Turner's contact number appeared on Kian's phone screen, he lifted a hand, stopping Onegus mid-sentence. "Excuse me. I've been waiting for this call."

When Kian had called the guy the day before, Turner and Bridget were out on the town. Since what Kian wanted to discuss with him wasn't urgent, he'd asked Turner to call him at his earliest convenience.

"You wanted to talk to me?" Turner said.

"Should I leave?" the chief asked.

"It's not private." Kian turned to Turner. "Onegus is here, but it has nothing to do with what I wanted to talk to you about."

"Go ahead."

"What do you know about the National Radio Quiet Zone?"

There was a long moment of silence. "Why do you ask?"

Turner's uncharacteristically tense tone raised Kian's hackles. "The New York team encountered a very interesting lady." In several concise sentences, Kian told Turner about Mey and Jin, their unique talents, and Jin's new job.

"So, the only clue Mey has is a travel guide with an earmarked page. It could be nothing."

"Or it could be something. What do you know about the place?"

"I know plenty. The most severe restrictions on electronic communications are within a twenty-mile radius of the Green Bank Observatory. It was created to protect the radio telescopes in Green Bank and Sugar Grove from interference. But there is more. The U.S. Navy Information Operations Command is located in Sugar Grove. The base has intelligence-gathering systems, and it is rumored to be a key station in the Echelon system."

Straightening in his chair, Kian shifted the phone to his other ear. "What the hell is the Echelon system?"

"It is operated by the National Security Agency, and it's a global network of spy stations that can eavesdrop on basically anything, track transactions, monitor bank accounts, etc. These are unconfirmed rumors, but I heard it from reliable sources."

An uncomfortable feeling started churning in Kian's gut. This spying system was something he should have been aware of. Especially with all the technological knowhow that the clan had been dripping to humanity.

He wondered whether the Brotherhood knew about it. If they did, then they could thrall whoever worked there and get their hands on top secret information.

Hopefully, they were just as ignorant about it as he was.

"How good are they? Can they hack into our private communication system?"

"Your network communication is highly encrypted with technology that doesn't exist on the market yet, so you have nothing to worry about. For now, anyway. But those using regular communication networks are another story. I'm sure that they can deal with encryption as well, just not at the level you are using. Their spying operation is rumored to be global, which means that they are listening in on communications from foreign countries and gathering intelligence. Some of it must be encrypted."

Kian let out a whistle. "It gives a whole new meaning to Big Brother watching."

"It does. On the other hand, it's not humanly possible to sift through all that massive information, so they use bots that react to certain trigger words. Those who have something to hide and are aware that their conversations might be monitored can work around it. Don't mention bombs, terror attacks, explosions, and such, and you're probably fine."

"It's scary. People are installing devices in their homes that can spy on them even when they are not using phones or computers."

Turner chuckled. "I wouldn't be too worried about it. With all that massive spying network, they still couldn't prevent some of the worst terrorist attacks. The way they analyze the information they gather must be faulty."

Letting out a breath, Kian swiveled his chair around and looked out the window. "How does it tie in with our missing Dormant, though? Do you think they are creating a paranormal spying network to supplement their equipment?"

"Sounds far-fetched, but it wouldn't be the first time the government has dabbled with the paranormal. They had remote viewing labs in the seventies, with psychics trying to prove that they had ESP."

"Did they work?"

Turner chuckled. "They no longer have them, so I assume that the experiments failed. But back to the missing girl, even if they decided to revive the program, there is no reason to house it in the same place as the electronic one."

"What if they found a way to enhance the paranormal signal?"

Turner didn't respond right away. "That sounds like science fiction. You, of all people, should know what technologies are out there."

Kian swiveled his chair back and pulled out a box of cigarillos from the drawer. "That's not necessarily true. We leak out information, but we don't know what humans are doing with it. Someone might have developed something we haven't even dreamt of. Besides, today's science fiction is tomorrow's reality."

Onegus lifted his hand. "Can I ask a question?"

"Go ahead." Kian waved a hand. "I'm going to put the call on speaker."

He should have done it from the start, but then the entire office building would have been privy to his conversation with Turner. Not that he wanted to keep it a secret, but Turner wouldn't have appreciated that.

"What if they programmed their bots to pick up on trigger words that hinted at paranormal talents?" Onegus asked.

A light bulb went on in Kian's head. "That makes sense. I was wondering how they found out about Jin. Mey said that they never mentioned their abilities to anyone. I assumed that Jin had blurted something to someone she wasn't supposed to. But if what you suggest is true, the sisters could have triggered the system when they talked about their paranormal talents between themselves."

"They must have only mentioned Jin's talent and not Mey's," Turner picked up the thread. "That's why they went after Jin and only monitored Mey."

Rapping his fingers on the desk, Kian groaned. "I feel like we are onto something big here, but I'm not sure what."

"Dormants, of course," Onegus said. "If the government is

collecting paranormal talent, they can have a hidden facility full of Dormants."

Kian shook his head. "Even if that is true, we can't do much about it. I'm not going to attack a government facility and snatch a bunch of people. First of all, most of them are probably there voluntarily, and secondly, I'm not going to do anything to attract the big gorilla's attention. That would be suicidal of me."

"You are absolutely right," Turner said. "Even Dormants are not worth the risk."

Onegus rubbed his jaw. "I wish there was a way to get to them before the government does. We could offer them a better deal to lure them in, and once they find their mates, they are ours."

The pieces clicked into place in Kian's head. "That's it. That's what we need to do. The question is, how? We don't have anything like their Echelon system, and my bet is that it's impossible to hack into."

Onegus shrugged. "Wouldn't hurt to let Roni give it a try."

"Actually, it might," Turner said. "I know that he is one of the best, but there are others who are just as good and better, and they can detect his hack and trace it back here."

SYSSI

"Where do you think I should hang it?" Amanda held up one of Dalhu's landscapes. "It's too small to go over the couch."

Syssi took a step back and looked at the empty expanse of wall. "Maybe you should hang both of them together. One next to the other."

"That's a good idea. But then I'll have nothing for the bedroom."

Syssi snorted. "I don't think Yamanu and Mey will pay any attention to what's hanging on the walls. They will be too busy looking at each other."

"I hope they will be doing more than that." Amanda held up both landscapes. "What do you think?"

"Looks good."

"Onidu!" Amanda called. "I need you to come here and hang up the paintings."

Wiping his wet hands on his apron, the butler rushed out of the kitchen. "Yes, mistress. Right away."

"How is the cleanup going?" Amanda asked.

"The refrigerator is ready for new supplies. I'm cleaning the oven now."

She stepped down from the couch and handed him the paintings. "Did I tell you what a treasure you are?"

"Thank you, mistress." Onidu bowed.

Syssi blinked. Had she imagined it, or had he looked embarrassed by Amanda's compliment?

She shook her head.

Next, she would be imagining that he blushed. But for that he needed blood circulation. Did the Odus have a circulatory system? They had to have something like that. Their outer covering was biological, so they must have some sort of circulation to keep it from decaying, but it didn't have to be blood. Maybe nanites?

Whatever they were and however they were put together, Syssi was convinced that the Odus were sentient, and that was probably why Annani refused to let anyone tinker with them. But perhaps they could be put through an X-ray machine?

Except, they might be made from materials that were impenetrable to X-ray. In fact, those materials probably didn't exist on earth.

As her head started spinning, Syssi stumbled toward the couch, managing to sit down before the vision took over her faculties.

An alien world appeared before her eyes. The sky had a reddish tint to it, and it was dark, but somehow Syssi knew that it wasn't nighttime.

She was in an airport or rather a spaceport, watching scores of Odus being loaded into what looked like shuttles. The atmosphere was somber, with no one talking or smiling, not the Odus and not their handlers.

But everyone's eyes were glowing, eliminating the need for

artificial illumination. Apparently, this was a dark world, and its inhabitants had adapted their eyesight to its conditions.

Was it the gods' home planet?

Except, the handlers didn't look like the way she imagined the gods did.

They were all dark-haired and dark-eyed, and their skin wasn't pale. Everyone was male, except one beautiful woman who stood to the side, observing, her long, colorful robes flapping around her majestic figure as the wind battered at her relentlessly.

No one paid attention to the strong gusts, indicating that it was a common phenomenon.

The way the handlers were sneaking peeks at the woman as if seeking her approval made it clear that she was in charge of the operation.

One of the males detached from the group and approached her, saying something in a harsh-sounding language.

The woman nodded and then smiled, revealing a pair of sharp fangs.

It was then that Syssi realized why the woman and the handlers seemed so familiar to her.

This wasn't a vision; it was a hallucination. Those people were the Krall that she had invented for one of the Perfect Match virtual reality fantasy scenarios. Except, in her story, the vampire-like Krall were on Earth and not on an alien planet.

"Syssi, wake up! You are scaring the crap out of me!" She heard Amanda's voice as if it was coming through a tunnel.

"Don't make me slap you!" Amanda sounded panicky.

Syssi lifted a hand. "Don't."

"Oh, thank the merciful Fates." Amanda sighed in relief. "Did you have a vision?"

Forcing her eyelids to lift, Syssi shook her finger because shaking her head was a no go. "A hallucination."

Amanda frowned. "What's the difference? And since when do you hallucinate?"

"I don't, but this could not have been a vision because what I saw came from my own imagination. It was about a fictional society of vampire-like creatures that I invented for Perfect Match. It was one of the environments for the virtual reality adventures to take place in."

Amanda's forehead creased. "Are you sure that you didn't dream them up or see them in a vision before creating them for Perfect Match?"

"If I dreamt about the Krall people, I don't remember it. And there was a weird variation in my whatever it was. In the hallucination, the Krall were loading Odus into shuttles. There were no Odus in the one I created for Perfect Match."

Amanda tapped a finger on her upper lip. "That would make perfect sense for a dream, but not a vision. You had both the vampire-like creatures and the Odus stored in your head, and your mind created a story by combining both. That often happens in dreams. Except, this wasn't a dream. It looked exactly like the other time when you had a vision."

Syssi shrugged. "Perhaps I just fainted."

"It's possible. We should get Bridget in here." Amanda pulled her phone out of her pocket.

"Don't." Syssi put a hand on her arm. "I feel fine, and I don't want to make a big fuss about this. We have to finish preparing the house for Yamanu and Mey. When they walk in, I want them to feel like they are starting their honeymoon."

Amanda smirked. "I saw the bedding you brought. Nice touch." Pushing up from the couch, she looked down at Syssi. "On one condition. You stay here on the couch and let me and the others finish the work. You might have overtaxed yourself."

"What happened?" Callie walked in with a bunch of shopping bags.

"Syssi fainted, but she is okay now. Do you need help with those?"

"I got it. I'm going to put everything in the fridge. But after that, I need to borrow both Odus to help me bring stuff from my house. I cooked up a feast." She dropped the bags on the counter and came over. "Are you sure you're okay? You look pale."

Syssi waved her hand dismissively. "Stop fretting about me. I'm fine. Maybe I just need a bite to eat. Amanda and I cut work short today to come to organize this party, and we didn't have lunch."

"Say no more." Callie grinned. "I'm on it." She turned to Onidu. "Can you come with me to my house? I need your help to carry things."

He turned to Amanda and looked for her permission.

"Do whatever Callie tells you."

"Yes, mistress." He bowed and followed Callie out.

Less than ten minutes later, they returned with loads of trays.

"Are you okay to get up?" Callie asked. "Or should I serve lunch on the coffee table?"

"I'll get up." Syssi put her feet down, then waited to see if her head was still spinning.

"Take my hand." Amanda pulled gently, lifting her up slowly and then wrapping her arm around Syssi's middle. "Small steps. Nice and easy."

"I'm okay. You are all fussing too much over a little fainting spell."

"You are pregnant, darling, so of course we are worried about you."

At the table, Callie loaded a plate for her and even spread a napkin over her knees. "Eat the spinach. It tastes much better than it looks, and it's chock-full of iron."

Rolling her eyes, Syssi picked up the fork and scooped up some of the green mush. "I like spinach, but this looks like green mashed potatoes."

"You're not far off," Callie said. "It's mashed with lots of butter."

Syssi tasted it and then scooped up some more. "It's good."

She had been so busy and excited about Yamanu coming home with a potential mate that she hadn't noticed how hungry she was. Even though she was an immortal, as an expecting mother, she should have paid better attention to her health.

"Arwel will have to look for a new place when he comes back," Callie said.

"Poor guy." Amanda sighed. "Yamanu, with his mellow nature, was the perfect roommate for him. Where is Arwel going to find another one like him?"

"Ben, Carol's old roommate, can take him in," Syssi suggested. "I don't think Carol is coming back."

Amanda shrugged. "She might. Maybe in time, my brother will accept Lokan just as he accepted Dalhu and Robert."

"It's not about that." Syssi put her fork down. "For Lokan to move into the village, he has to sever all connections to the island. And that's not in anyone's best interests."

13

MEY

*A*s the jet landed on a small airstrip in the middle of nowhere, Mey wondered how far it was from the village. All she could see was a hangar and the limousine that had been sent to pick them up.

"Welcome home, master Yamanu." Ovidu's twin bowed and took the suitcases from Yamanu's hands. "And you too, mistress Mey."

"Thank you." She was surprised he'd been told her name.

The guy, cyborg, whatever he was, looked like the stereotypical jolly butler, but he reminded her of the weird dream she had. "Do they all look the same?" she whispered in Yamanu's ear.

"More or less, but I can tell them apart easily. When you get to know them, you'll notice the small differences."

When the butler opened the back door of the limousine for her and bowed, Mey thanked him again and slid to the other side, making room for Yamanu.

"Are you nervous?" Yamanu asked.

"A little. What's going to happen once we get there? Are we going to see the boss?"

Yamanu glanced at his watch. "It's late, so we are probably going straight home." He grimaced. "I can just imagine the amount of dust that has accumulated since Arwel and I left. And there is nothing in the refrigerator."

"I could stop at a supermarket, master," the butler offered, looking at them through the rearview mirror and smiling his fake smile.

Yamanu's forehead furrowed. "Thank you, but I'm sure Mey is eager to get home. We can get something from the vending machines to tide us over." He wrapped his arms around Mey's shoulders. "I think there are a couple of pizzas in the freezer, so we are not going to starve until tomorrow."

The butler was still looking back at them and grinning like a clown instead of paying attention to the road.

"Is the limo one of those self-driving vehicles? Because I'm still human, and my body is destructible."

"Do not worry, mistress," the Odu said. "You are very safe with me behind the wheel."

"Thank you, but I would appreciate it if you looked at the road and not at us."

"Yes, mistress. Of course." He turned around and even pulled up the partition, giving them privacy.

Pretty considerate for a cyborg.

Yamanu shook his head. "The Odus are behaving strangely lately."

"How so?"

By the time he was done telling her the story of Okidu falling into the water and needing a reboot, the butler had parked the limo in a spacious garage that was full of nearly identical cars.

It seemed as if they were all the same make and model just in different colors and trim finishes.

Mey looked around. "Are we underground? And do clan members get clan-issue cars in addition to clan-issue phones?"

Yamanu chuckled. "You don't miss much, do you? Yes to both. We are in an underground parking garage, and the village is about a hundred and fifty feet above us."

"One hell of a hideout you have here." She followed him outside.

"It's a great place. We used to live in a high rise in the city, but this is much nicer. I like being surrounded by nature, instead of concrete, glass, and steel."

As they headed toward the elevators, the butler trotted behind them, carrying both suitcases, and the disconnect between his looks and his strength was disconcerting. The Odu looked to be in his mid-forties, pudgy and short, but he obviously had no trouble with the weight. The stupid smile never left his face, and she didn't hear him breathe hard. In fact, she didn't hear him breathe at all, but given Yamanu's story, the cyborg needed air to function.

When they cleared the pavilion, Mey stopped and took in a deep breath. "Fresh air. I love it."

Regrettably, it was dark already, and since there were no streetlamps and the sky was overcast, she couldn't see much. Nevertheless, Yamanu pointed out every building they passed, the café, the playground, the pond, trying to describe what she couldn't see.

"It's okay. You can give me a tour tomorrow."

"I might be busy."

Mey didn't like thinking about being left alone in Yamanu's house while he was gone. She didn't know anyone yet.

"It's very quiet in here. Is it always like that?"

"It's too quiet. Which is suspicious. They might be planning a surprise party for us. Get ready for an ambush."

"Oh, no." Mey laughed. "The second one today?"

"I'm glad you're not freaking out."

"Why would I?"

"Oh, I don't know. Meeting a bunch of immortals for the first time, all eager to get to know you."

She leaned her head on his shoulder. "I'm eager to get to know them too."

In her experience, it was best to dive in headfirst and get over the shock of hitting the cold water in one go. Dipping a toe at a time was not her style.

14

YAMANU

*A*s he and Mey neared the house, Yamanu stifled a chuckle. With the shutters down for the night, he hadn't expected to see lights in the windows, but he had expected to hear the murmur of voices. There were none, which was impressive given the number of people he could sense were hiding inside.

Did they really think they could surprise him? Or was the surprise meant for Mey?

"Get ready," he whispered in her ear. "There are at least thirty people in the house."

"How can you tell? It's dark and quiet."

"I can sense them, which they are aware of. So, the surprise must be for you."

She smiled. "I'll do my best to act surprised. After all the trouble they went to, it would be a shame to disappoint them."

Smoothing one hand over her red dress, Mey combed her hair with the fingers of the other. "How do I look?"

"Too good." He grimaced. "I should have insisted that you wear baggy sweats. This dress is way too sexy."

Mey stopped and turned to him. "I have eyes only for you." She reached up and kissed him on the lips.

"I'm not worried about your eyes. I'm worried about theirs."

He and Mey were not mated yet, and her scent didn't carry even a hint of his, which would make every single guy in the room think that she was up for grabs.

"Is there a reason we are stopping, master?" Okidu asked from behind them.

"No, let's go inside."

It occurred to him that the butler must have known about the surprise party and hadn't said a thing. Had it been his decision?

Probably not. Kian had most likely ordered him to keep quiet.

At the door, Yamanu paused and winked at Mey before depressing the handle. Holding her hand, he crossed the threshold and stopped again. It was dark inside, and no one jumped up, yelling 'surprise'! But he could hear their breathing as well as sense their presence.

Silly people.

Giving Mey's hand a little squeeze, he closed the door behind them and flicked the light switch on. The first thing he saw was a big banner draped over the opposite wall.

'Welcome home Yamanu and Mey!' it said in bold red letters.

A moment later, the pandemonium erupted, with people spilling in from the back yard through the open sliding door, clapping and shouting 'surprise'!

Amanda led the procession, advancing on Mey with a broad smile on her beautiful face. "I hope we didn't scare you." She offered Mey her hand. "I'm Amanda, and I take full blame for this."

Mey grinned as she shook Amanda's hand. "Thank you so much for your warm welcome."

"My pleasure." Amanda gave her an unabashed once-over. "I love your style."

"Alena told me that you are fond of Diane von Furstenberg wrap dresses. This is by a different designer, but it's the same style."

Kian tapped Amanda's shoulder. "I think we can leave the fashion talk for later. I'm sure Mey and Yamanu want to be done with the introduction and get to the food." He offered Mey his hand. "I'm Kian."

She gaped for a moment and then shook the hand he'd offered. "Neither of you looks like your sister," she blurted, sounding a bit breathless.

Nice save, Yamanu thought. But that didn't help with the surge of jealousy coursing through his veins. Mey had promised to have eyes only for him, but apparently, she also had eyes for Annani's son.

"We all have different fathers." Kian turned to Syssi. "Let me introduce my better half. This is my wife, Syssi."

And so it went, with everyone stepping forward and introducing themselves, the women checking out Mey openly, making comments about how beautiful she was and how stylish, while the few single males checked her out more covertly.

He would have to thank Amanda later for inviting mostly mated couples.

For the most part, Mey treated them with a friendly but uninterested attitude, but then Dalhu approached. She definitely had eyes for him as well.

"And this is my mate, Dalhu." Amanda wrapped her arm around his waist, making it clear that he belonged to her.

"Are you also Yemenite?" Mey asked as she shook his hand.

"No, what made you think that I was?"

She glanced between the ex-Doomer and Yamanu. "Your name and your height. I thought that you and Yamanu were related."

He cracked a rare smile. "No relation whatsoever."

15

MEY

*A*fter the last of the guests had left, Mey plopped down on the couch and kicked her shoes off. "Your family is awesome."

Not only had they arranged a beautiful and warm welcome party for them, they had also cleaned up before leaving. Most of the work had been done by the Odus, but still, she appreciated it.

"They are okay." Yamanu took one of the few remaining bottles of beer and popped the cap. "I'm glad it's over."

Unlike her, he hadn't seemed to enjoy himself much.

Yamanu had spent most of the evening with his arm wrapped possessively around her waist and glaring at any single male who'd dared to approach her to introduce himself. He'd even glared at the mated ones, including his drop-dead gorgeous boss.

Kian was a god. Or as close as it got for a human or an immortal. He was a little intimidating, but Mey had met plenty of alpha males and knew how to handle them. Rule number one was to show no fear. Weakness only spurred predators on, while a show of strength got their respect.

Then there was Amanda's mate. The ex-enemy. That was a story she couldn't wait to hear. The guy wasn't as gorgeous as Kian or Yamanu, but he was definitely impressive. A warrior turned artist, but still a warrior through and through. She could sense the power pulsing just underneath the surface of his stoic exterior.

In Kian's case, her interest had been purely esthetic, and in Dalhu's, it was simple curiosity. But even though she hadn't been attracted to them, Yamanu hadn't liked her looking at either of the men.

She was in a committed relationship with Yamanu, but she was still a woman, and she had eyes. Perhaps she'd felt a smidgen of attraction toward those two impressive male specimens, and he had somehow sensed it.

Otherwise, there was no reason for his grumpiness.

Mey didn't mind the possessiveness, but jealousy wasn't something she could tolerate. Typically, she attracted a lot of male attention, and her partner needed to learn to accept it or their relationship would be under constant strain.

Amanda and Syssi were both beautiful, and their partners probably had to live with the fact that men looked at them. Heck, women probably sent covetous glances at those guys every time they went out in public, and Amanda and Syssi had to learn to tolerate it as well.

Trust was a crucial component in any relationship, and especially when one or both partners were getting a lot of attention.

Yamanu sat next to her on the couch and put his hand on her exposed knee. "It was a long day. You must be tired."

Her wrap dress had parted, barely covering the top of her thighs, but since the guests were gone, Mey hadn't bothered to adjust it.

As Yamanu waited for her response, his hand started a slow trek up her thigh, making his meaning clear.

"I'm still hyped up from the party. I don't think I could go to sleep just yet."

As Yamanu's hand kept going up, the dress parted all the way, and he cupped her hot center.

"Is that for me?" There was a bite to his tone.

"Who do you think it's for?"

"Oh, I don't know. You've shown interest in several of the men." His finger breached the gusset of her panties, finding her moist lower lips.

Arching up, Mey closed her eyes. "I wasn't attracted to any of them. I was just looking."

"I didn't like it." He slid a finger inside her.

There was something both arousing and off-putting in the way he did it. Leaning back nonchalantly, he was still holding the beer in one hand while fingering her with the other.

Not wanting to reward this, Mey stifled a moan. "Tough. You need to get used to that. I tend to attract attention."

His finger retracted, then lazily pushed back in. "I can deal with that. What I can't deal with is you looking back."

"I didn't mean anything by it. But I'm not blind, and your clansmen are impressive."

He continued his slow fingering, getting her wetter and needier by the moment. "How would you feel if my eyes followed another woman around?"

Crappy.

Had she done it?

Yeah, she had.

For the first several moments after meeting Kian, Mey couldn't take her eyes off him, trying to figure out what made him stand out in a room full of handsome men. It wasn't just about his looks, it was the inner power that radiated from him, and she'd wondered whether it originated from his strong personality or his godly heritage.

Still, she could understand how it had made Yamanu feel. If the roles were reversed, she would have been majorly pissed.

Not only that, things had probably seemed much worse from Yamanu's perspective. He might have thought that she was craving the things he couldn't give her.

"I'm sorry. I shouldn't have done it. But rest assured that my interest wasn't sexual or romantic. You are my man, and I only want you."

If he allowed it, she would have proven it to him, giving him the best blow job of his life, but he didn't let her touch him with her hand, let alone her mouth.

Everything below the belt was off-limits.

He withdrew his finger and came back with two. "Don't do that again."

"I won't. I promise."

Leaning, he put the empty beer bottle on the floor and used his freed hand to pull on the tie holding her wrap dress together. "I bet every male in this room thought about doing this."

"Not every male, and you are the only one who actually gets to do it."

As he parted the dress, exposing her body, his glowing eyes went to her breasts. She was wearing a red padded bra that made it look like she actually had a bit of cleavage.

Her panties were red as well, matching the bra and her dress.

"Did you put it on for me?" He pulled the bra cups down, exposing her breasts and leaving the folded cups to lewdly push them up.

Mey hadn't thought about seduction when she'd chosen the lingerie set to wear for today, only style. The red wrap dress was the most flattering outfit she had, but it tended to show a bit too much on occasion, and she'd wanted her underwear to match the dress.

"I put it on for me," she admitted. "But I'm glad that you like it."

Yamanu nodded. "I like your answer." He dipped his head and flicked his tongue over one puckered nipple.

16

YAMANU

*J*ealousy was not Yamanu's thing. Or rather it hadn't been until Mey.

It was irrational and irritating, but he couldn't help it. Especially when her eyes followed Kian with an awed expression that had made his blood boil.

Yamanu was considered a good-looking guy, and people found him charming as well. Even before the celibacy vow, other men had never been an issue for him. For as long as he could remember, women everywhere and of every age and ethnicity had been sending him covetous glances. Some men too.

Except, he hadn't hung out with Kian or Dalhu before, and apparently they garnered just as much female attention, if not more.

He couldn't care less about other females looking at them, but he cared about Mey. The unexpected surge of red-hot jealousy had brought about an intense need to possess her in every way.

Which he couldn't do, and that had generated even more aggression. Nevertheless, he wasn't going to allow the beast to take over. Mey was still human, and he needed to be careful with her.

Still, as he switched to suckling her other nipple and pinched the one he'd just left, he didn't do it as gently as he should have, and Mey hissed in pain.

"I'm sorry." He cupped the abused peak, soothing it.

Eyeing him a little apprehensively, Mey put her hand on top of his head. "Perhaps we should go to bed."

"Did I scare you?"

She shook her head. "You don't scare me, Yamanu. Even when you get peeved, I know that you are too wholesome and good to become mean. I'm just thinking about how frustrating this must be for you. Frankly, it's frustrating for me too. I want to touch you, to taste you, and to give you as much pleasure as you're giving me. But instead, I have to fist my hands and clutch the couch, so I don't reach for you the way I want to."

With a sigh, Yamanu dipped his head and rested his forehead on her chest. "I need a little more time to figure things out."

She stroked his hair. "I know, and I don't want to pressure you. That's why I suggested we call it a night and go to bed."

Right, as if he was going to leave her unsatisfied and aching.

It was bad enough that he was going to bed with a hard-on, but that was unavoidable unless he took another dose of the potion, which he didn't want to do.

He'd already taken five servings, but instead of affecting his libido, it was affecting everything else. His mind was foggy, and he felt lethargic, which shouldn't be happening given his low level of physical activity. For the past week, he hadn't even looked at weights, and the only run he'd done was when Mey had called him about the guy following her.

Still, there was no reason for Mey to suffer alongside him,

and Yamanu had enough self-control to handle his arousal without climaxing.

Or so he hoped.

He could probably control the ejaculation, but the question was whether he could control his fangs. He hadn't bitten a female in centuries.

Lifting his head, he offered her a closed-mouth smile. "I'm all for going to bed but not to sleep. I'm not done with you yet. I want you to wake up tomorrow with a smile on your lush lips."

Mey cupped his cheek. "Are you sure? I don't want you to ache, and it seems that you are struggling tonight." She put a gentle finger on his lips. "You are hiding your fangs, but I caught a glimpse. They are elongated, and I know what it means. The potion has worn off."

Damn. There wasn't much the woman missed.

"I've already taken five doses today. I don't want to take another one. But I can control myself."

Her brows dipping low, she shook her head. "I don't know what's in that concoction, but that can't be healthy for you. Let's just go to sleep."

This was the smart thing to do, but not what he wanted.

Pushing up to his feet, he lifted her up into his arms and started for the bedroom.

Mey wrapped her arms around his neck, but instead of a smile he got another frown. "What are you doing?"

"Taking you to bed."

"To sleep."

He shook his head.

"Put me down." The tone of command in her voice didn't leave room for misinterpretation.

Reluctantly he did as she asked, letting her legs drop to the floor next to the bed.

Someone had put new white bedding on it and scattered a few red rose petals on top of the duvet. His bet was on Amanda. Regrettably, her efforts to make this a romantic night were going to be wasted.

Standing with her back to it, her wrap dress hanging from her shoulders and leaving her magnificent body exposed to his hungry eyes, Mey couldn't see how inviting the bed looked.

She put her hands on her hips and glared at him. "We are going to sleep, and I don't want to hear another word about it. Tomorrow, you are going to see the doctor, and you are going to ask him or her whether this thing that you've been over-dosing on is safe in the quantities you've been consuming lately."

Bossy lady.

On the one hand, Yamanu wasn't happy about Mey's decree, and her commanding attitude had only spurred on his own arousal, but on the other hand, he was touched by her concern for him. He knew she was still aroused and still wanted him, so it wasn't about staving off unwanted advances.

Mey was worried, and she was putting his wellbeing above her needs.

He bowed his head. "Tonight, I'll obey your command, my lady Mey. But only tonight."

A mischievous smirk lifted one corner of her lips. "We will see about that."

YAMANU

$\mathcal{L}$ast night had cemented Yamanu's decision. He had to talk to Kian and lay it all out for the boss.

He hadn't told Mey what the meeting was about, and the only thing he'd told Kian was that he needed to talk to him. Kian hadn't asked about what, and Yamanu hadn't volunteered the information.

Which meant that he could still back out.

Except, he couldn't.

It was somewhat cowardly of him to put the decision on Kian's shoulders. But even though it was about something extremely personal, Yamanu honestly felt that the consequences were too extreme for him to make it on his own.

As he reached the entrance to the office building, pushing the door open felt like a life and death decision. What if Kian told him that he needed to keep the celibacy going? That the clan could not manage without his protection?

Not that he needed Kian to tell him that.

The knowledge that he was the shield behind which the clan could hide in an emergency was what had made keeping his vow possible. He didn't need anyone to tell him how crucial it was. What he needed was for Kian to lie to him and say that he had done enough and that the clan could manage without his protection.

Yamanu started turning around, intending to walk away, but then stopped. Mey's image, standing in front of him with her dress parted, her hands on her hips, and her eyes glaring at him, was the impetus he needed to go in and march into Kian's office.

Kian looked up at him and frowned. "What troubles you?"

Yamanu closed the door behind him and pulled out a chair. "Is it that obvious?"

"Usually, you bring smiles and sunshine. Today it's a storm. Trouble with your lady?"

"Not with Mey. With myself. But it's connected."

Putting his pen down, Kian leaned forward and gave Yamanu his undivided attention. "Is there anything I can do to help?"

As Yamanu wondered whether Kian would have been willing to take a vow of celibacy to free him from it, he stifled a snort.

The answer was most certainly not.

None of his brethren would have been willing to sacrifice that part of their lives for the clan. So why had he?

At first, he had done it to atone for his sins, but then when he discovered what he had gained by abstaining, his conscience hadn't allowed him to stop.

"I need your advice."

Kian let out a breath. "That's easy enough. Although if what you seek advice for are matters of romance, I'm afraid you will be disappointed with how little I know on the subject. I'm lucky to have a very understanding and undemanding mate. Anandur would probably be a better choice."

"I don't need that kind of advice." Yamanu pushed his hair

back. "But I need your word that nothing of what I'm about to tell you ever leaves this office."

Kian chuckled. "Then make sure not to leave your lady alone in here. I'm afraid that I have no control over what the walls do with the information they absorb."

That wrested a smile out of Yamanu. "I'll keep it in mind."

Kian nodded. "You have my word."

Damn, this was difficult. Perhaps he should just get it over as quickly as possible before he changed his mind.

"I'm sure that you, like everyone else, have suspected that I'm celibate." When Kian gave a quick nod, Yamanu continued. "You were right. I took a vow of celibacy more than six centuries ago, and I've never broken it."

Kian's brows lifted. "Not even with Mey?"

"Not even with her. But she is the reason I'm here."

"Obviously. But I'm not a shaman or a cleric who can absolve you of your vow. This is a personal decision. Although I can't imagine what prompted you to make such a vow in the first place and then keep it up for so long."

"I'm not looking for absolution. Only for advice. But in order for you to be able to give it, I have to explain why I took the vow in the first place, and why I kept it up until now."

"And how. I can't imagine how you managed that."

Taking a deep breath, Yamanu let it out slowly. "Do you remember how I was before I took the vow?" When Kian smiled and nodded, Yamanu continued. "I was a cocky bastard, and I didn't limit myself to widows and the paid variety like the rest of the men. I thought that by providing pleasure to married ladies I was doing them and their clueless husbands a service. Teaching them how good it can be when done right."

Kian cocked a brow. "Did you get caught? Annani specifically forbade that."

"Indeed. But as I said, I was young and stupid and full of

myself. I thought that I knew better." He took in a shuddering breath. "But what I didn't count on was getting anyone pregnant, or that with my distinct coloring it would be obvious that the child was not fathered by the lady's husband."

"What happened?"

"He murdered her and my newborn child."

Kian's face reddened, and his fangs punched out. "Did you kill him?"

Yamanu nodded. "The story he told everyone was that the mother had died during childbirth and that the infant had been stillborn, but I suspected foul play. I snuck into his bedroom at night and peeked into his head. He didn't wake up the next morning, and his death was attributed to natural causes." Yamanu rubbed his jaw. "I smothered him with a pillow, the same way he'd killed his wife and my child."

Kian's eyes filled with compassion. "That's a lot of guilt to carry around. Was that why you took the vow?"

Yamanu shook his head. "Back then, the Clan Mother herself acted as judge, and I went to her to confess my crime and ask for punishment. She sentenced me to six months of exile on one of the unpopulated islands, saying that the forced abstinence best matched my crime. She told me to use the time for reflection."

"That was quite merciful of her. She didn't tell anyone about it either. Back then, you were just a junior Guardian, so I didn't have much contact with you, but I knew about your trip to that godforsaken island. I thought that you needed time for reflection and chose to isolate yourself. You were always the spiritual type."

Yamanu nodded. "The Clan Mother is infinitely merciful. My torment was self-evident, and she decided that I was punishing myself enough as it was and gave me time to mourn."

18

KIAN

*K*ian still didn't understand how that incident, as tragic and as devastating as it had been to Yamanu, had caused him to take on a vow of celibacy and keep it for over six hundred years. If memory served him right, it was closer to seven hundred.

"What happened next? Did you become so accustomed to not having sex that you decided it was a good way to continue?"

Yamanu chuckled. "Not really. I was dropped off on the island just with my sword, my hunting knives, and a bow with arrows. At first, I got busy building myself a shelter, and then I hunted and fished for sustenance. I suffered from loneliness and from the lack of female companionship, but in a way, I enjoyed my suffering because it helped with the guilt."

Kian nodded. "You felt like you were paying for your sin."

"I felt that I deserved to suffer, but I treated it as a sentence and had every intention of resuming my sex life when it was over, just not with married ladies. I realized the wisdom of the Clan Mother's rules and vowed to obey them to the letter. But that was it. Then the six months were up, and a Guardian with a boat was sent to pick me up. I think it was Gondel who came for me."

"I remember Gondel. He is serving in the sanctuary now."

"Yeah, I guess he deserves a semi-retirement. Anyway, I got home, spent the day with my mother, and the next day headed to the village to purchase some supplies and find me some paid company. That was when I discovered what the abstinence had done for me."

Kian leaned closer. "What happened? You couldn't do it?"

Yamanu laughed. "I could have pounded nails with the club in my pants from just thinking about finally getting some. That wasn't it. A horde of marauders descended on the village, and I was the only immortal there. The village men ran out to block the attack, but I knew they didn't have a chance. They were going to get slaughtered and the women raped. Out of pure desperation, I decided to shroud as many of the villagers as I could, hoping to give them at least a fighting chance against the attackers."

The gears in Kian's head picked up speed, and he knew what Yamanu was about to say next. Nevertheless, he kept quiet and let the Guardian continue.

"Imagine my surprise when the marauders stopped their advance, looked around in confusion, and then changed direction and kept going. I shrouded the entire damn village."

"What did the villagers do?"

He chuckled. "Dropped to their knees and thanked the Lord and every saint they could think of."

"Are you sure you couldn't do that before? The sudden flare in power could have been because of the desperation you felt, not the celibacy."

Yamanu shook his head. "By then, I'd been in enough battles to know the extent of my powers. Until the exile, I could thrall and shroud with the best of them, but it was no where near the godlike power I felt that day. I realized that what fueled it was the pent-up sexual energy which got channeled into the shroud. And the best proof of that was that I felt spent afterwards. It was as if I climaxed twenty times in a row. I no longer needed to seek out the village prostitutes. I purchased the supplies that I came for and headed back home."

Pushing away from the desk, Kian walked up to the concealed bar in the sideboard and pulled out a couple of beers. "I know it's too early for this, but I need one. How about you?"

"Snake Venom sounds perfect right now."

Kian handed Yamanu the beer and pulled out a chair next to him. "I can't imagine you going home and deciding to give up sex for good."

"I didn't. I decided to give it another six months and see what happened. But that was after long contemplation. As I walked home in a daze, thinking and rethinking everything that had happened, it dawned on me that perhaps there was a reason behind the tragedy I caused. It had pushed me to become the clan's protector. If I could become the shield who kept my people safe, then perhaps the terrible loss of life wouldn't be as meaningless."

"Did you tell anyone?"

Yamanu shook his head. "I didn't want people to know that I was abstaining. At first, it was because I couldn't be sure whether it was going to work again. I was afraid that it had been a one-time fluke. Later, after I proved to myself that I could do this at will, I didn't want people to know and treat me like a martyr."

"When did you take up the vow? And how did you manage to hide it so well?"

"I don't remember the exact time, but it was once I realized that the power was there to stay, and that after each depletion I needed time to recharge. I didn't need to be a genius to figure out the connection. And as for keeping it hidden, I pretended to be discreet. At first, people teased me about it, but after a while, they got used to me ignoring the jibes and stopped."

"I assume that you are here because you want to break your vow?"

"I don't want to. But I have no choice if I want to keep Mey. If I don't, I'll have to let another male induce her transition, and I can't stand the thought of that."

Kian debated whether it was okay for him to ask how Mey was reacting to this. He'd been sure that the two of them had already been intimate. In this day and age, people didn't wait months or years to have sex, and she must've thought it odd that Yamanu didn't initiate it, or worse, refused her.

"Does Mey know about your vow?"

"She knows that I have taken a vow, and that it has to do with the safety of my clan, but she doesn't know the reasons behind it. You are the first to ever hear this story, and the only reason I'm telling you is that I need to talk with someone about it. Someone who is not emotionally involved but who understands the ramifications."

"Is she okay with that?"

Yamanu chuckled. "Mey is incredible. She accepted me thinking that a physical disability was preventing me from being fully functional. She even talked about adopting children."

"What about intimacy? Was she willing to give it up?"

Yamanu smiled and looked away. "I'm sure that I don't need to explain to you about all the ways a man can be intimate with a woman."

Yeah, the conversation was getting way too personal, but

those questions had to be answered before life and death decisions were made.

Kian raked his fingers through his hair. "What if you take a break from the celibacy and then go back to it once Mey has transitioned?"

19

YAMANU

*Y*amanu regarded Kian for a long moment. Had he even realized what he was suggesting?

The guy really had the emotional intelligence of a brick.

It wasn't like taking a break from being a vegan and indulging in eating steak for a week before going back to it. Although maybe that particular example would make it easier for Kian to understand. Unless he was repulsed by meat, but Yamanu didn't think that was the case. It was a matter of principle for Kian, not a culinary preference.

Instead, Yamanu went with something simpler and more obvious. "I'm needed for the raid tomorrow, remember?"

"I meant after the raid."

"I'm afraid that once I get a taste, I won't be able to go back, and I'm terrified of leaving the clan without protection."

Kian nodded. "Yeah, I get that, but you've already sacrificed so much. Except, the prospect of losing your blanket-shrouding abilities terrifies me as well. Knowing that we have you to shield us in case we get discovered by humans is a security blanket we've become dependent on. That being said, humans haven't posed a threat to us in a long time. Our biggest concern is the Doomers, and your shrouding and thralling don't work on them. Perhaps we can do without."

Yamanu had a feeling that Kian was saying it out of guilt and not conviction. "With how advanced the facial recognition technology is becoming, and security cameras being installed everywhere, my ability to shroud us might become a matter of survival again."

"You've got a point. Especially in light of the interesting and discomforting conversation I had with Turner yesterday. I asked him what he knew about the Radio Quiet Zone, and what he told me kept me awake all night. Apparently the US government, along with several strategic allies, has a system called Echelon, and the quiet zone is home to its main installation."

"What are they doing with it?"

"They monitor electronic transmissions throughout the world. For now, our encryption keeps our intercommunications secure, and I've learned from Lokan that the Doomers use a similar system, just not as sophisticated. But still, there will come a day when that monitoring will include conversations picked up in public places and even in people's homes. With all the Alexas and Google devices and whatever else is on the market, that future is already here."

After hearing the first part, Yamanu barely listened to the rest of what Kian was saying. "They have a spying base in that area?"

Kian nodded.

"And Mey thinks that Jin is working there, and her special ability is spying. There must be a connection."

"Perhaps. We are still trying to figure out what to do about it."

"I think that sending someone to snoop around should be our first step."

"I wanted to get Roni to hack around their system, but Turner advised against it. We don't want to attract the big guns' attention."

"He isn't wrong. But how are they doing it? I mean, I get that they are collecting transmissions, but then someone needs to actually listen to them."

"Bots. They program a bunch of trigger words which the bots flag, and then a human checks it out. For now. With the advancements in artificial intelligence even that won't be necessary. The computers are going to be the Big Brothers watching. It's only a matter of time, and I have a feeling that we are running out of it."

Yamanu snorted. "We have only ourselves to blame. If not for the dripping of technology we've been providing, it would have taken humans another thousand years to get to where they are now."

"True, but then we wouldn't be living the comfortable lives that we do. We had the knowhow, and they had the manpower and resources to actually build all the gadgets we now can't live without."

"Can't argue with that. It's just another Catch-22. We are damned if we do and damned if we don't."

"Unfortunately, life is full of compromises."

Yamanu nodded. "Ain't that the truth. But for now, we can still do things the old-fashioned way. I can go there and snoop around. Humans are defenseless against me. I can probably get inside that super-secret facility and get any information we need. And if Jin is there, I can get her out."

Kian shook his head. "It's not that simple. There is another possibility that we need to consider. If they are collecting para-normal talent, there might be people in that facility who can sense who you are. But that's something Turner and I are going to put our heads together and come up with a plan for. Right now, we need to figure out what to do about your lady. You have a two-week window to induce her before she accumulates too many memories to thrall away without causing her damage."

"I'm sure she is a Dormant."

"So am I, but we can't take chances. What are you going to do if she turns out not to be a Dormant? Keep her a prisoner in here for the rest of her life?"

Yamanu slumped in the chair. "I don't know what to do."

"Talk to Bridget. Maybe there is another way to induce Mey's transition..." Kian stopped mid-sentence, and Yamanu caught his eyes widening for a split second.

"What? Do you have an idea?"

He shook his head. "No, I was just thinking that you might be more comfortable talking to Merlin about this. You know, man to man."

MEY

*W*hen Yamanu had left to meet with his boss, Mey considered taking a walk around the village. A visit to the café would have been nice, but she had no reason to go other than meeting some more of Yamanu's people, and it would be better if he came along.

God forbid she stopped to talk with one of the bachelors, which the majority of the clan's males were. Yamanu would throw another jealous fit. She was going to eventually cure him of that, but it would take time.

Baby steps.

Rome had not been built in a day, and lasting relationships were no less difficult to build than cities.

Perhaps they could have lunch there.

Or stay at home and enjoy each other. Getting to know others could wait.

The welcoming committee had stocked the refrigerator as well as the pantry, and there were plenty of leftovers from last night's party, so there was no urgency to go anywhere.

In the end, Mey had settled on the backyard. It was so incredibly peaceful up on the mountain, so quiet that she felt like she could spend days sitting on a lounger, sipping on a tall glass of iced tea, and just chilling with a book.

Except, on the inside, she was nowhere near as tranquil as her surroundings. There was the worry over Jin and what could be done to find her, the uncertainty about her induction into transition, and her future with Yamanu.

Things couldn't continue like this. If he kept on drinking that potion to excess, he was going to harm himself despite his superior physiology. And besides, it was obviously losing its effectiveness, and quite rapidly so. Eventually, it would stop working no matter how much of it Yamanu consumed.

Hell, it was already happening.

If Yamanu refused to break his vow, or couldn't, she would have to leave. At the thought, Mey's gut squeezed painfully. Leaving Yamanu would be devastating, but luckily for her, she wouldn't remember any of it.

Not that she believed that wholeheartedly.

Even if she didn't remember Yamanu, the hollow feeling in her chest would let her know that she was missing someone terribly. Mey was sure of that.

Perhaps she would dream about him?

Except, more than her relationship with Yamanu was at stake. She needed the clan's help to find her sister, and she wasn't willing to give up on her chance of becoming an immortal.

If he couldn't induce her, then someone else would have to do that, or it would have to be done by the clan's doctor.

There had to be a way to solve this problem. As Yamanu had said, fate would not have brought them together just to dangle happiness in front of their faces and then snatch it away, leaving them both broken.

An hour and two iced teas later, she was still thinking about it when Yamanu returned.

"You look relaxed." He closed the sliding door behind him, then sat on the lounger beside her. "Having fun?"

"It's very peaceful up here. How did your meeting go?"

"It was interesting. It turns out that the Quiet Zone is home to the Navy's information operations command, and it is rumored to be the key station in the Echelon system, which is all about electronic intelligence gathering. They can eavesdrop on phones, computers, and all types of electronic transactions. I don't know how it's connected to Jin and what she can do, but it seems like something that we should investigate."

Mey sat up straight. "When can we go?"

"The better question is when I can go. You can't leave the village until you've transitioned. Besides, it's not safe for you out there."

Crossing her arms over her chest, Mey pinned him with a hard stare. "I'm not going to stay behind while you go looking for my sister."

"Why not? I know what she looks like, and I'll probably take several Guardians with me. But it will have to wait until after the raid. Right now, everyone is busy preparing for that, and no one has the time to start planning another mission."

Mey lifted her hand. "Wait a second. What raid?"

He closed his eyes. "I forgot that you know nothing about it. The Doomers, our enemies, moved into our territory. We need to get rid of them."

"When is it happening?"

"Tomorrow. That's why I was needed back."

Mey frowned. "Aren't you risking exposure? Immortals fighting each other while humans are around to witness it is sure to attract attention."

"That's my specialty." Yamanu smirked. "I can shroud the entire area. No one outside that building is going to see or hear anything."

Her eyes widened. "You can do that?"

"Yup. And I'm the only one who has the ability. That's why they needed me here."

She didn't like that he was going to participate in a raid, but he was a Guardian. And he had a duty to his clan.

"Can't you just leave them be?"

He cocked a brow. "The Doomers?"

"Yeah. Are they here to get you?"

"No, but they plan to abduct female students from colleges and universities in the area. We can't allow them to do that."

Mey recoiled. "Why would they do that?"

Yamanu's eyes blazed with anger. "For the sex resort on their island, which serves the Doomers' army and the various deviants from all over the world who can afford the exclusive sex vacation package. They kidnap women and force them into slavery, either sexual or housekeeping. Once they are brought to the island, they never get to leave. We can't do anything about those they've already taken, but we can make it really difficult for them to get new ones."

"Why can't you free the ones they have over there?" She shook her head. "I can't imagine how terrible it is for them."

He smiled sadly. "As I explained before, they outnumber us significantly. We don't stand a chance in a direct fight with them. And bombing the island is not possible because many innocents would die."

Regrettably, he was right, but that didn't make her feel any better. Wrongs had to be righted, but it wasn't always possible.

If only the clan could cooperate with Mossad on that, together they might stand a chance. But that was wishful thinking, and she knew it. Mossad was legendary, but it was operated by humans and it had enough on its plate. Defending the minuscule Jewish nation from its countless enemies was a mission almost as impossible as freeing those women.

Both the clan and Israel could use a powerful ally in their fight for survival.

She chuckled. Where were they going to find one? China?

Yamanu frowned. "I can't see what's humorous about this."

"Nothing. It's sad and hopeless. I was just thinking that the clan's situation is similar to Israel's. Both are tiny and rely on technology for their continuous survival, and both could use a powerful ally. Then I thought that the ally needs to be a country with a huge population, like China. But the Chinese are not interested in helping others, probably because they don't need anyone. They are a force unto themselves."

Yamanu nodded. "They have the numbers, and they don't need others for technology either because they copy and steal what they cannot or do not want to develop themselves."

YAMANU

*M*ey sighed. "These problems are too big for us to solve. Let's concentrate on what we need to do about us."

Before they got sidetracked by other things, that was what Yamanu had originally wanted to talk to Mey about. But now that he was facing her, he wasn't sure how much he was ready to reveal.

It had been difficult enough to tell Kian about the reason for his celibacy, and Kian's response hadn't been what he'd hoped for.

Instead of patting him on his shoulder and saying that he had done enough, Kian had tried to come up with alternate solutions. Apparently, he was of the same opinion as Yamanu that his services were too crucial for the clan's survival to give up.

"That's what I'm trying to figure out. I plan on stopping by the clinic to ask the doctor's advice."

Mey's eyes brightened. "That's an excellent idea. I've been wracking my brain, trying to come up with a solution that would allow you to keep your vow while also inducing my transition. Perhaps it can be done with artificial insemination and an injection of venom."

"Yeah, that's what I'm going to ask him. It's far from ideal, but I don't see another choice." Except for allowing Mey to choose another male, but that wasn't really an option.

She frowned. "Your eyes are glowing. Does the idea of my artificial induction aggravate you?"

He took her hand and brought it to his lips for a kiss. "If that were as easy as taking a pill, it wouldn't have bothered me. But the thought of another male's essence in you is disturbing. Still, I can probably handle that. What got me angry was the idea of letting another male induce you the natural way. I don't think I can do that, but I can't be selfish and stand in the way of your transition either." He shook his head. "They would have to put me in stasis for the duration of the induction. Otherwise, I might kill the male trying to help you."

Mey shook her head. "And what would happen once you awakened? You would hate me, and whoever was chosen to induce me. That's not going to work."

"I wish I could say that you are wrong. But you are not."

"What about taking a break from your vow? Kian gave us two weeks, and you can't do anything until after the raid, which leaves eleven days to induce me. I think the clan can survive that long without your protection."

"That's true, but there are other problems with that. First of all, I don't know if I'd be able to go back to being celibate. If there is no other choice, that's what I'll have to do, but it's a scary prospect. It also means that until the two weeks are over, I can't go looking for your sister. With my powers intact, I can waltz into that facility and waltz out with your sister. Without them, that's less likely."

Mey let out an exasperated sigh. "I don't know why you think that your powers are dependent on your vow, and I'm not going to ask. If you wanted to tell me, you would have done so by now."

It was good that she hadn't asked because he was not ready to tell her. In case he decided to break his vow, there was no need to make her feel doubly guilty for depriving the clan of its protector.

When he didn't respond, Mey continued. "But you don't have to be a super immortal to thrall the guards to let you in. I would think that any Guardian could pull it off."

Apparently, Mey had been truthful about her job in the intelligence department having been clerical because she wasn't thinking like someone who'd been trained to be a spy.

"It is true that I can thrall the guards, but I can't thrall the surveillance cameras, and those sitting in the control room are going to sound the alarm. But using my full powers, I can have the entire facility thralled, including those in the control room and their supervisors."

"Oh, right, I didn't think it through. Because your people's powers are mental, they are ineffective against electronic eyes and ears."

"I didn't say that. We have one clan member who can fritz out electronics, but she's not a Guardian, and she can't go on a mission like this. Besides, I don't think she can cause a large scale shutdown. As far as I know, she can do one device at a time."

"It's still a very useful trick."

"It is. And perhaps when Kian and Turner put their heads together, they will come up with a plan that can work without my special talents."

"Who is Turner?"

"A new member of the clan who is a brilliant strategist."

Mey's brows lifted. "He was a Dormant?"

Yamanu nodded.

"Oh, I thought that all the Dormants you've found were female."

"There were several males as well."

"Did they also have paranormal abilities?"

"Just the same as it was with the females, some did and some didn't."

"How do you induce the males?"

Yamanu smiled. "It's much easier for them than for the females. They have to fight one of us and get bitten."

"I wouldn't call it easier. You said that you are stronger and faster than human males."

"I didn't say that they had to win. Only to offer enough of a fight to spur our aggression. Without that, there is no venom."

She narrowed her eyes at him. "Can I fight you? I can probably hold my ground for long enough to get you aggressive."

"I don't think it will work. I doubt that you would be able to make me aggressive enough to bite you. Hell, I'm not sure it's even possible for a male immortal to bite a female in aggression."

"I assume that it has never been tested?"

He nodded.

"So why not give it a try? It's not like we have that many options."

22

LOKAN

"*I*'m so glad you could come." Losham got up and offered Lokan his hand.

Surprisingly, he seemed genuine.

Their previous meeting in San Francisco had been the first one ever they'd had outside the island. It had been strained, with Lokan trying to figure out where Losham's loyalties lay, and Losham suspecting Lokan of spying for their father.

Or rather Lokan's father.

Losham probably had been fathered by one of the harem's servants.

Knowing that they weren't related made dealing with Losham easier. Lokan no longer felt the need to form a connection with the guy, which on some subconscious level he'd sought to do before. Perhaps that was why he'd reached out to Losham in the first place, and why Losham's suspicions had been somewhat hurtful.

Now he could regard him as a stranger. And, if need be, kill the bastard for allowing his deviant son to torture Carol.

With a well-practiced smile sliding into place, he shook

Losham's hand. "I'm glad that you agreed to see me. I'm sure you are very busy with the relocation."

Losham shrugged and sat back down, motioning for Lokan to take the seat across from him.

"The field commanders are taking care of the men, and all I had to do was get comfortable in my new house."

The restaurant he'd chosen was in one of the most prestigious hotels in Los Angeles, the Beverly Hills hotel, and the corner they were sitting in provided the privacy they needed for their conversation.

"Did you?" Lokan reached for the bottle of superb Japanese whiskey that Losham had ordered and poured it into the two glasses.

"It's big, and it's fancy, but I prefer my modest abode in San Francisco and the view I have there." He spread his arms. "The entire bay, including the Golden Gate Bridge. You can't beat that."

"Indeed." Lokan nodded. "So, your men are all settled already?"

"Not yet. Several stayed behind to take care of covering our tracks, but they should be arriving either tonight or early tomorrow morning." He narrowed his eyes at Lokan. "Why the sudden interest in my men?"

Lokan shrugged. "After mine absconded with my jet, I decided to use human servants and security services instead of getting more men from the island. Frankly, it's liberating. I don't feel responsible for anyone, I don't need to take care of them, and I don't have to wonder whether they are loyal to me or not." He grinned. "Not to mention privacy. No one is spying on my activities and reporting to our father."

As the waiter interrupted Losham's response to take their order, Lokan debated how to steer the conversation to Sharim without it being too obvious. It had to come up incidentally.

"What are you hiding, my brother?" Losham asked after the waiter had left. "Why the need for privacy?"

Lokan laughed and waved a dismissive hand. "Nothing nefarious, I can assure you. But from time to time, I like to take a day off and enjoy myself. I don't need anyone reporting to our father that I'm slacking on the job."

"Yes, I can understand that. I'm fortunate to have a very loyal assistant who I know will not reveal anything harmful about me." He leaned forward. "Frankly, my workdays are pretty easy. I have competent commanders in place, and they need minimal direction from me."

"You are fortunate in that regard." Lokan sighed. "I don't know where I went wrong with mine. It seems that I haven't mastered the art of training and keeping good staff. I could learn a few tricks from you." Buttering up his opponent was a proven tactic to soften him up and have him lower his defensive shields.

Smiling, Losham pretended to shrug the compliment off. "I've been lucky as far as loyalty goes, but I've lost men to incompetence."

Perhaps that was a good opening.

"I guess it's unavoidable, and accidents happen too, caused by the most insignificant of mistakes. Some with tragic consequences."

Losham took the bait. "The monastery was no accident," he hissed. "The clan took my son and his men, and then staged it to look like an accidental explosion."

"Do you have proof?"

"I don't need proof." Losham put his hand over his chest. "I know it in here. They are going to pay for it. Not today and not tomorrow, but I'm not one to forgive and forget. I am a patient man, though, and I'm not in a rush. First, I need to get back in our father's good graces. I can't plan strategic attacks against the clan when I'm tasked with selling drugs and procuring whores."

"You really cared about Sharim." Lokan refilled the two glasses and lifted one to his lips, all along intently watching Losham's expression.

"Of course, I did. He was my son."

The wave of sorrow coming from Losham confirmed his words.

"I don't want to be disrespectful of the fallen, but I heard rumors that Sharim had certain proclivities." He pinned Losham with a hard stare.

"So what if he did? None of his playmates suffered long-term damage. And besides, they were only lowly humans. Since when did you turn into a humanitarian?"

Lokan stifled a smile. He'd just gotten the perfect opening he'd been waiting for.

"I don't care about humans. I was just curious. Imagine what he could have done to an immortal female, though. An indestructible plaything would have provided him with endless hours of entertainment."

Losham cringed. "That would have been a different story, and I might have felt inclined to intervene. But since there are no immortal females for the taking, that would have been extremely unlikely. The clan guards its own fiercely, and there are no others."

Losham seemed sincere, but Lokan wasn't ready to give up the line of inquiry just yet. Knowing that Losham was not a culprit in his son's activities was a relief, but Lokan had to be certain before he let it go.

"Are you sure? Because his base was right here under the clan's noses. What if he found one of their females, and that's why they retaliated so forcefully?"

Spreading his arms, Losham sighed. "Who knows? No one survived the attack, so all we can do is guess. I still think it's highly unlikely, and the clan didn't need any special provocation to attack. We are enemies. When they found out about our base, which I suspect they did through the weapons suppliers, they attacked."

Lokan nodded. "I hope that you are more careful than that. Now that you are on their turf, you need to watch out."

"I'm well aware of that. That's why my men arrived in their own vehicles and with all their weapons. I don't need anything delivered, and I'm not even going to contact our so-called friends in Los Angeles. I also implemented a new security protocol." He smiled. "It's designed to ensure my warriors' loyalty and to forewarn them in case of the unlikely attack. People are just as loyal as they have to be and no more."

Lokan lifted his glass. "Words of wisdom, my brother."

Kian had told him about the last raid on Losham's drug operation in the Bay Area, which the clan had staged to look like the men had picked up and left, absconding with the drugs and the money. If Losham believed it, he had no reason to trust his men. The question was, what had he done to ensure their loyalty? Tracking devices were the most logical, but immortals' bodies rejected foreign objects. Perhaps he'd had them implanted deeper? Securing them to the spinal cord? There had been talk of doing that, but as far as Lokan knew, it hadn't been done yet. Implanting thousands of soldiers was a major undertaking, especially when the procedure was involved and couldn't be done in an assembly line fashion.

They clinked glasses and emptied the shots down their throats.

Lokan wondered what those security measures were, but asking about them days before the clan's attack would be a dead giveaway. Kian hadn't told him when he was planning to do that, but he wouldn't wait long.

The question was whether he should warn him. Chances were that Kian had done his homework with proper reconnaissance, but perhaps a word of caution was in order.

Except, he felt bad for Losham. The guy hadn't been aware of his son's torture of Carol, so Lokan had no vendetta against him, and it felt wrong to betray him.

Straddling two worlds wasn't easy.

"That's good stuff," Lokan said as he put his empty glass down. "I guess you are not overly concerned with budget cuts."

"I'm saving the Brotherhood a lot of money. I think I earned the right to some splurging here and there."

"No doubt. I've been thinking, though, that maybe we are going about it all wrong. Plenty of human females would come to the island voluntarily for the right monetary incentive. Wouldn't it be even cheaper to get them this way?"

Leaning back, Losham crossed his arms over his chest. "A year ago, I might have agreed with you, but things are different now. The kind of women they want on the island is not the kind who will come voluntarily. We need smart girls who are educated, articulate, and good-looking, to lure in the caliber of men that we need for the new breeding program."

Lokan kept pressing the issue. "I'm sure some of them would be willing to come for the money too. A college degree is not a guarantee of financial security, and most young women these days have no qualms about sex with strangers."

Losham smiled. "Aren't we lucky? It's so ridiculously easy to get a female in bed that it takes all the fun out of the chase. Men are predators, especially immortals, and we need the chase, the challenge, to get excited."

"I didn't see you complain when you used the brothel's selection."

"That's different." Losham waved a dismissive hand. "Paying for your meal is not as exciting as hunting for it, but it's better than just having it fall onto your plate."

23

YAMANU

*A*fter scoping the building in Koreatown, the Guardians met up in the parking lot of a discount department store where they had parked their cars.

As Onegus clicked the doors open, Yamanu got inside and let out a sigh. "This is going to require precision. They've smartened up. The density is going to make the operation difficult."

Onegus turned the engine on and eased out of the parking spot. "We are going at night. You can just make everyone in the area sleep like the dead. You don't have to be picky about it."

"I can't do that. What about mothers with infants? I don't want them to sleep through the baby crying. And what about those working night shifts? Someone might be driving in or out and fall asleep at the wheel."

Onegus rubbed a hand over the back of his neck. "What are you going to do?"

"Scare them. Dread always works. And I can try to focus my shroud centered on the building. Except, that's not a precise science, and if I want to keep the commotion contained, I will have to cover some of the adjoining buildings as well. I'll have to spread dread, so no one dares leave their apartment and get close. How long do you think it will take to capture all the Doomers? Should be no more than fifteen to twenty minutes."

Onegus shook his head. "We don't have a precise number, but from what we've gathered so far, there are more than sixty of them."

"Shouldn't be a problem."

"I hope you are right. If any of them manage to escape, it's going to be difficult to chase them down."

Shrugging, Yamanu pulled out his phone. "Excuse me for a moment. I want to check up on Mey. I feel bad about leaving her alone in the house."

He fired a quick text. *I'm on my way home. Do you want me to pick up something to eat?*

Her return text came a couple of minutes later. *Don't bring anything. Carol and Callie are here with Wonder, and they brought dinner with them.*

That was a relief. He was glad she wasn't alone. *In that case, I might stop at the doctor's to ask him about the things we discussed earlier.*

She fired back. *That's a good idea. I'll wait to eat dinner with you.*

It sounded so domestic. He loved it. Having a mate to come home to was not something he'd ever hoped to experience.

It might take a while, and I don't want you to wait. Eat with your guests.

I'll save you a plate.

Okay.

Pocketing his phone, Yamanu smiled and closed his eyes.

"The mated bliss. I'm so envious." Onegus sighed.

"Don't jinx it. First, we need to make sure that Mey transitions."

"My bad. When are you going to start on that?"

Yamanu tensed. Had Kian talked? Because Onegus shouldn't be asking that. He should have assumed that they'd been working on it at least from yesterday.

"Who says that we haven't started yet?"

The chief shrugged. "She only got here yesterday, and the party ended late. Mey is still a human, she must have been exhausted." He glanced at Yamanu. "The Fates were generous with you. Mey is much more than a gorgeous woman. She has a strong personality. You fit well together."

"Thank you."

When they got to the village Yamanu pretended to go home, but as soon as he ditched Onegus, he changed directions and headed to the new phase of the village where Merlin's house was.

"Come in," the doctor yelled as he knocked.

Yamanu had an excuse ready in case Merlin was not alone, but thankfully, he didn't sense anyone else in the house.

"Do you have a moment?"

"I have all evening." Merlin pointed to the couch. "Take a seat."

Yamanu eyed the thing, debating whether he should remain standing. The sofa was covered in books and magazines, empty candy wrappers, and crumbs that looked moldy.

Merlin was a major slob.

"Excuse the mess." The doctor lifted a pile of books, swiped the crumbs away with his hand, and pointed at the spot he'd cleared. "Better?"

"Thank you."

Merlin sat on the chair across from the couch. "What can I help you with, Yamanu? Are you ready to start a family?"

Yamanu swallowed. Was it written on his forehead? Because he doubted Kian had betrayed his confidence.

"Why would you think that's what I want to talk to you about?"

The doctor shrugged. "The fertility potion is what everyone wants from me lately, and I heard that you've snagged yourself a Dormant. Congratulations."

Damn, he was getting paranoid. Besides, he came here to confess.

"Thank you, but perhaps the congratulations are premature."

Merlin's smile slid off his face. "What's the problem?"

"Before I start, I need your word that this will stay confidential."

Merlin puffed out his scrawny chest. "I'm a doctor. I don't reveal my patients' confidential information."

"Then consider me your patient."

"Done."

Merlin listened intently to Yamanu's story, not interrupting even once, just frowning and uttering an occasional 'aha'.

"So, what do you think, can Mey's idea work?"

The doctor spread his arms. "It has never been done. I don't know if we can even extract venom from an immortal. And for the composition to be right, it needs to be produced by arousal. When an immortal male is in that state, he has only one thing on his mind, and it's not getting his fangs milked for venom."

Yamanu slumped back. "Can we at least try? Perhaps one of my Guardian buddies who are mated would be willing to do that for me?"

Merlin's smart eyes filled with compassion. "You will be forced to tell him what it's all about, and then he would need to tell his mate because he would need her to produce the venom. And then it might not work. In fact, I'm pretty sure it's not going to. You have only three options. Take a break from your vow, forget about it entirely, or let Mey choose another male to induce her."

"Number three is not an option, and number two will leave the clan without protection. That leaves the first one, but I'm afraid that I won't be able to go back to celibacy."

Merlin nodded. "Can you give me a sample of that potion you've been dosing yourself with? I want to check it out."

Yamanu rubbed his hand over his jaw. "That's another problem. Since I met Mey, I've been increasing the dosage, but despite that, the potion seems to be getting less effective by the day, and I'm experiencing side effects I didn't before. I started feeling lethargic and foggy."

"That might be a side effect of the potion, but it could also be that you are depressed. The choices you are faced with are extremely difficult."

Could that be true?

There were moments in which Yamanu felt elated for having been gifted with a treasure like Mey, and others when he felt that the burden on his shoulders was so heavy that he was sinking under its weight.

"What do you think I should do?"

Merlin smiled sadly. "I can't tell you that. As much as I would have loved to ease your burden, you have to make this decision yourself. No one can make it for you. But if I may, I would like to make a small suggestion."

"By all means."

"Since it looks like you are going to choose option number one, you should consider freezing up semen for the future. If one day you decide that you want to have babies with your lady, and you are still keeping your vow, that might make it possible without going through the torment of stopping and resuming your celibacy again."

KIAN

*K*ian surveyed the war room, the real one, not his office in the underground that had been given the same name by the men. Fifty-four Guardians had gathered for the pre-mission briefing, their male voices filling the room with an atmosphere of positive camaraderie he wished he could bottle and carry around with him for when he was feeling down.

Some of the rescue missions couldn't be postponed, which meant that they were going to face the Doomers with even fewer men than he had hoped for.

On the podium, Onegus counted heads to make sure everyone was present. When he was done, he clapped his hands to get their attention. At the foot of the podium, Shai started the recording.

"By the latest count, we will be facing sixty-two Doomers," Onegus started. "But that number might still change. As we've seen, they did not all arrive at the same time, and more might be coming tonight and tomorrow. What it means is that we can't have one Guardian per Doomer like we did last time. We won't be able to immobilize them before they know what hit them. We are going to encounter resistance, and there will be fighting."

Several of the guys high-fived each other. No one seemed overly concerned.

"The good news is that there are no humans in the building itself, which means that we don't have to worry about witnesses during the fight, but the area is densely populated, and the surrounding buildings are all clustered close together. That being said, we are lucky to have Yamanu, who is going to shroud the entire block. That alone will ensure minimal human casualties, if at all."

All eyes turned to Yamanu.

"A big round of applause for our secret weapon," Anandur called out.

The guys all started clapping and demanding that Yamanu take a bow.

Smiling, he flipped them off.

Appropriate, Kian thought. They had no idea what Yamanu was sacrificing for their safety. They wouldn't have been teasing him like that if they did.

Onegus raised his hand and waited for the men to quiet down.

"Unlike on most other missions, we expect injuries. Regrettably, we can't bomb the place as we did the monastery, and since we are in the middle of an urban area, speed is crucial, and the full-body suits would slow us down. We are going in with only the vests that are part of our disguises."

There were a few murmurs, but not of concern, but rather relief. The suits were cumbersome, and it got hot as hell inside them.

"What disguises?" Anandur asked.

Onegus lifted a bulletproof vest with the acronym SWAT

printed on it. "There is a chance some of the Doomers might manage to escape outside the shrouded area. The uniforms will come in handy for the chase. People will see them and trust that things are under control. But that's just a nice side effect of the real reason for these. Since we don't want the Brotherhood to find out who took out their men, and we've already staged a defection and an accident, we had to come up with a new and creative scenario. This time the police get them."

"How's that going to work?" Anandur asked.

After Onegus explained, he put the vest down. "Bridget and Julian retrofitted one of the buses to be our field hospital, so they'll be able to mend most things on the spot, including broken bones."

"What about Merlin?" someone asked.

"He is going to stay in the village in case one of our rescue teams needs medical help."

"What are we going to do with the downed Doomers?" Brundar asked.

"We have four SWAT trucks in addition to the ones we will be using to get in and out of there."

"Do we have space left in the catacombs?" Rupert asked.

Onegus nodded. "We are going to double up and store two Doomers in one spot."

It was a temporary solution, but the truth was that Kian hadn't come up with a long-term one yet. The old keep was maxed out, and he didn't want to bring the Doomers into the village even though they posed no threat while in stasis.

It was about keeping the place clean. Now that he and Syssi were about to welcome a child into the world, he didn't want any darkness to contaminate the sanctuary that he had built for his people. If he told his mother that, she would have been tickled. Her son, the staunch skeptic, was suddenly entertaining superstitious beliefs.

Except, there was a practical side to it as well. Even though the chances of someone spontaneously waking up from stasis were slim, they weren't impossible, as evidenced by Wonder.

A new location would have to be found to store the Doomers, and that was a problem. Guardians would have to be assigned to the new location, and Kian hated further splitting the force.

When all the questions were answered, Onegus dismissed the Guardians. They had the next day off until ten o'clock at night, when the last pre-mission meeting was going to take place.

The raid was scheduled for one in the morning the next day.

As usual, Onegus had vetoed Kian's participation in the raid, but this time Kian hadn't even argued the point.

With his mother in the village, it was out of the question. Leaving only a minimal force in place to guard her and the rest of the village's civilians made him uneasy. The least he could do was be there in case emergency measures had to be deployed.

Even though they had procedures in place to block access to the village in case of an attack, something always went wrong, and improvisations had to be made on the spot.

Besides, if he joined the raid, Syssi would have been worried, and he didn't want her to get stressed. He was still troubled by the fainting spell and strange vision she'd had while preparing Yamanu and Mey's welcome party.

Something about the pregnancy was making her more susceptible to visions, and what was worse, they were starting to get mixed up with her regular dreams and even her imagination.

Could it be the baby's doing?

Vivian hadn't had a telepathic ability until she'd gotten

pregnant with Ella. It had grown in strength along with her unborn child.

Kian had a feeling that their little Allegra might turn out to be a powerful seer, and that filled him with dread. He had seen what premonitions had been doing to Syssi. He did not want his daughter to carry an even heavier burden.

25

MEY

*M*ey leaned back and groaned. "I'm going to get fat, and it's all because of you. I can say goodbye to my modeling career."

Carol eyed her with an amused expression on her face. "I think you can forget about modeling anyway. Immortals can't be in the limelight. If they could, Amanda would have been a movie star."

Callie and Wonder laughed, but Mey didn't know Kian's sister well enough to get what was funny about that. Amanda was not only a striking beauty, but she also had charisma and a strong personality. Mey could definitely see her starring in movies.

"Amanda is very dramatic," Callie said. "I think she secretly yearns to be an actress."

"I don't see why not." Mey shrugged. "She could have fun for a few years and then retire. If anyone spotted her, she could claim to be a doppelgänger."

"Too risky," Carol said.

Mey looked at the two stuffed grape leaves left on the platter. "Oh, well." She scooped them onto her plate. "I'm glad that I saved a plate for Yamanu. Otherwise, there wouldn't have been any left for him."

She cut a piece off one and stuffed it in her mouth. "These are so good. I've had plenty stuffed grape leaves before, but not homemade and not as good as yours, Callie. You have a gift."

"Thanks."

"Amanda is exactly like her mother," Wonder said.

"Do you know the goddess well?" Mey asked.

Again, the three laughed, and once more Mey felt out of the loop.

"Wonder is Annani's best friend," Carol explained. "They've known each other since childhood."

Mey's eyes widened. "How is that possible? Yamanu told me that there were no survivors except for Annani and her sister and that no one knew that the sister survived until recently."

Wonder's eyes misted with tears. "I was buried underground and in stasis for thousands of years. When I woke up, I didn't remember who I was. And when my memory returned, I thought that everyone I loved was gone except for Annani. Then Carol found Areana for us, and it turned out that my sister accompanied her out of the area before the disaster. I still can't believe that my sister's alive." She lifted a napkin and wiped her eyes. "I want to see her so much."

"So why don't you?"

The three exchanged glances, and then Carol patted Mey's arm. "There is so much we still have to tell you, but that will take the rest of tonight and the next day, and I need to get going."

"Yeah, me too," Callie said. "The guys are back already, and Brundar is waiting for me at home."

"Same here." Wonder pushed away from the table. "Come by the café tomorrow. After the morning rush is over, I might have a few minutes to breathe, and I'll tell you more about our history."

Mey got up as well. "Thank you for coming and keeping me company. I really appreciate it."

Carol smiled. "It was our pleasure. Welcome to the clan." She pulled Mey into her arms.

For a small woman, she was very strong, and her embrace was a bit too tight.

"Thank you." Mey pulled away. "I really hope that I get to stay. I like it here."

The door opened, and everyone's eyes turned to Yamanu, who walked in with a big friendly smile on his perfect face.

Mey's breath caught in her throat. He was so strikingly handsome that every time she saw him enter a room, it was like getting zapped with an electric current. Especially with that broad, charming grin that made everyone love him.

What a man.

"Hello, ladies." He walked over and shook each one's hand. "Thank you for keeping Mey company. I felt so bad for leaving her alone in the house on her second day in the village."

"It was our pleasure." Carol stretched on the tips of her toes and pulled him down to kiss his cheek. "You've got yourself an awesome lady. I wish you both the best of luck."

The fond way Yamanu was looking at Carol would have made Mey nervous if he were a regular guy. But even without any empathic ability, she could sense that Carol and Yamanu had a history, just not the romantic kind.

Besides, they were distant cousins, and according to Yamanu, relationships between the descendants of Annani were forbidden. Something about their peculiar genetics made it so that they were as closely related to each other as human first cousins.

That was another advantage of living in the village, and not one to sneer at. Except for the few women who were already mated to other clan members, all the others were Yamanu's relatives and posed no temptation.

She was being absurd.

The man had withstood temptation for centuries, and the first woman to break his resolve was her. Loyalty was not an issue with Yamanu. If anything, he had it in excess.

Once all the goodbyes and hugs and kisses were done, and they were finally alone, Yamanu let out a breath and pulled her into his arms.

"I missed you." He kissed her lips.

It was a light kiss, not a passionate one, but it ignited a fire within her as if it was the most erotic thing ever.

Evidently, there was something to be said for abstinence. Lack of stimulation heightened the senses, and even the smallest of touches triggered powerful yearnings.

Yamanu let go of her and sighed. "I've talked to the doctor."

26

YAMANU

*A*s Mey's scent of arousal hit Yamanu's nostrils, his body responded, but he forced himself to put some distance between them and turned his face toward the kitchen, hoping the smells of food would drown it out.

Who was he kidding?

It was like expecting a tiger who'd smelled prey to stop and admire the lovely scent of roses.

Even though he was hungry, the food held no interest for him. As much as he hated to do that, another dose of the potion was in order. His willpower could only stretch so far.

"I'll be back in a moment." He rushed toward the refrigerator for a vial.

"I'll heat up your plate," Mey offered, mistaking his urgency for hunger.

"Thanks." He didn't correct her.

After last night, he had done his best to hide while taking a dose, feeling like a junkie who had to get his fix in secret. Except in his case, it was the opposite of that. He was taking the antidote.

Damn, his life sucked.

No, he should never think like that.

The Fates had been extremely kind to him, presenting him with a mate so amazing that he couldn't have dreamt her up. Not even if he attempted to envision his perfect one and only could he have come up with someone like Mey. He hadn't known such perfection existed.

Things would turn out okay.

He had to believe in that.

As Mey put the plate in the microwave oven, he pulled out the vial together with a beer bottle, emptied the vial down his throat, and popped the beer's cap. By the time Mey turned around, he had stashed the empty container in his pocket and lifted the beer to his mouth.

"How did the scoping go?" Mey leaned against the counter and crossed her arms over her chest. "Do you expect any trouble?"

"The conditions are far from perfect, but it's doable." Seeing the worried look on her face, he wrapped his arms around her. "Don't worry. We have the element of surprise on our side, and the Doomers are no challenge for us, not when they don't outnumber us a hundred to one. Besides, I'm not going to be part of the attack force. My job is the easiest of all." He smiled tightly.

The truth was that he would have gladly traded places with any of the Guardians. Fighting was easy, and the only sacrifice it required was hard training, which he did anyway.

Mey's shoulders relaxed. "That's good to know. But now that I have friends whose mates are Guardians, I worry for them too."

As the microwave beeped, she pushed away from the counter. "Where do you want to eat?"

The bedroom. Although he would settle for the kitchen counter.

Instead, he pointed to the dining room.

"It'll be more comfortable over there."

She looked at his beer. "Is that any good?"

"It's very strong. Do you want to taste it?"

"Yeah, I do. I see you chugging those, and I look at the label and wonder what a beer called Snake Venom tastes like." She put the plate on the table and reached for his bottle.

Just seeing her put her mouth where his had been a moment ago sent an erotic pulse down to his groin, bypassing the potion as if it were not there.

Except, he knew it was. His movements slowed just a fraction, as did his thought process. It seemed that the only thing the potion was good for was putting him to sleep.

Grimacing, Mey handed him the bottle back. "I don't know how you can drink this. It's worse than whiskey."

He pretended shock, putting his hand over his chest. "Blasphemy. You've just insulted my two favorite drinks."

"I'm sorry." She smiled. "Now tell me what the doctor said. But maybe you should eat first."

He forked one of the stuffed grape leaves. "These are supposed to be eaten cold. It's the Mediterranean version of sushi."

Mey shrugged. "I like them warm."

She was playing along, letting him stall, but he couldn't postpone telling her about his consultation with Merlin for much longer.

As he finished chewing, Yamanu wiped his mouth with a napkin and took another swig from the beer.

"Merlin doesn't think that milking venom from an immortal male is going to work, or that any of them would agree to do that. He pointed out that the only possible candidates are the mated guys, and that they would need to get their mates involved. For the venom to work, it has to be produced by arousal, and to get aroused, they need their mates."

"What about the other kind? I'm willing to be the test bunny for that. Getting aggressive shouldn't be a problem, and if you don't think you can bite me, you can let the doctor milk your fangs, and he can inject me with your venom. Who knows? Maybe that would be enough, and there would be no need for the second part?"

As crazy as the suggestion was, it wasn't entirely illogical. Perhaps he should ask Merlin what he thought about it.

"It's a long shot, but I'll ask the doctor what he thinks. Most likely, though, it won't work. He suggests that I take a break from my vow until you transition, and while we are at it, freeze semen for when we want kids."

Mey snatched a stuffed grape leaf from his plate and popped it in her mouth. Chewing furiously, she tapped her foot on the floor.

When she was done, she leveled her gaze at him. "I hate to be the one to bring it up. But how long do you think you can keep going like that? I know that you are an invincible immortal, but if the potion can suppress your sex drive, it can affect other things as well. My mother used to be a nurse, and she told me that every medication that helps with one thing has the potential to damage ten others. And even if side effects aren't a problem, the fact that it's getting less and less effective is."

She wasn't telling him anything he didn't know. "Is there a point you are trying to make?"

A tear slid from the corner of Mey's eye. "Temporarily breaking your vow to induce me is not the solution. You'll have to choose between breaking it for good or giving me up."

27

LOKAN

"*I*t was a pleasure talking to you, my son. I wish we had more time."

Lokan still felt strange whenever Areana called him her son. She was a stranger to him, and getting to know her in ten-minute increments wasn't working that well. He still didn't know whether he could talk about his father with her, or about his plans for the island, or ask her advice on dealing with his split loyalties.

His bond with Carol meant that he was now part of two worlds. The clan at large hadn't accepted him with open arms, but his aunt had. If it were up to Annani, he would have been invited to live in their village.

Not that he wanted to. Carol would have been happy, but he would have been forced to sever his ties to the island, and that wasn't on the table.

"I wish so too. I hope that one day I will get to see you and embrace you, feel what it is like to have a mother."

He hadn't meant to say the last sentence. It was no doubt painful for Areana to hear that, but the truth was that he resented her for buying into his father's nonsense so readily.

She had never been in danger from the other immortals. Her being a goddess and therefore superior to Navuh was the only reason he had kept her locked up. With his ability to compel immortals, he could have kept her and his sons safe.

It was all about control and power, and she was either overly naive or just too weak to stand up to Navuh.

Then again, Lokan couldn't fault her for that. Navuh was so much more powerful than Areana, and she was well aware of that. Perhaps she was doing the best she could under the circumstances.

Would he have done differently in her place?

Could he have done more?

It was unfair to judge her before walking a mile in her shoes, so to speak.

"One day…" Areana's voice wavered. "I will hold you in my arms again. But you have to promise me something."

"What is it?"

"That you will not seek your father's demise. That you will find a peaceful solution."

Even though she'd been dead serious, he chuckled. "If you have any ideas on how to achieve that, please share them with me."

"First, promise me."

Glad that she couldn't see him, Lokan rolled his eyes. "I only seek the demise of the current system. I don't want to kill my own father. He might be an evil dictator, but other than denying me your love and care, he hasn't wronged me."

"That's good enough. Thank you."

"Until the next time, Mother." He disconnected the call.

They'd run a minute over the ten allotted to them, but William had been gracious enough not to come on the line and remind them that time was up.

With a sigh, Lokan put the phone on the coffee table and

leaned back. He'd gotten so used to conducting all of his phone conversations on the balcony that it had felt strange to do it from the hotel suite's couch.

Carol was still sleeping, and he debated whether to crawl back in bed with her or order breakfast.

The other thing keeping him from going back to bed was that he still wasn't sure whether he should call Kian and warn him about Losham's increased security measures.

Perhaps he could talk Kian out of attacking Losham's men?

That would be the best solution as far as Lokan's guilt, but he knew Kian wouldn't listen. Saving the women was very important to him for some reason.

Lokan felt bad for the victims, but they were just humans, and if he were in Kian's position, he wouldn't have risked his own men to save them. In the larger world of traffickers, the Brotherhood's share was insignificant. But unlike the humans, Brothers were much more dangerous to Kian's men. He should focus his efforts on the regular rescue mission he'd been running and leave Losham and his men alone.

Strategically, it made much more sense.

Except, he suspected that it was a matter of pride for Kian. He couldn't tolerate the thought of Losham operating a trafficking ring right under his nose.

Snatching the clan-issue phone off the table, Lokan punched Kian's contact. If Kian didn't answer right away, he was going to disconnect.

No such luck.

"Lokan, what a surprise," Kian said.

"I hope I didn't wake you up." He knew he hadn't, but Lokan couldn't miss the opportunity to needle his sanctimonious prick of a cousin.

"You didn't. What's going on?"

"I wanted to give you an update about my meeting with Losham."

"Right. I forgot about that."

Really? That was the whole reason behind Lokan's visit to Los Angeles.

"Two things you should be aware of. One is that more men are arriving today or have already arrived last night. So, you should adjust your count. And the second is that Losham has implemented new security measures. He didn't tell me what they were, and given your imminent plans, I didn't want to ask. But just for your general information, there has been talk of implanting the Brothers with trackers that their bodies can't reject. As far as I know, it hasn't been done yet. It involves attaching the tracker to the spinal cord so it can't be removed without causing major damage, and that's a huge undertaking. Still, Losham's men might have been part of a pilot program."

"Thanks for the warning. Anything else?"

Regrettably, Kian hadn't taken the bait and told him when the raid was going to happen. Not that he could've done anything about it, but knowing was better than not.

"I tried to convince Losham that finding volunteers who would enter the brothel for the money would be more cost-effective than the elaborate setup he has to maintain, but he said that the caliber of women they were looking for would not do so voluntarily."

"Right."

Lokan switched the phone to his other ear. "Is there any way I could persuade you to change your mind about the attack?"

"Why?"

Kian was the master of one-word sentences.

"Because your reason for doing it is motivated by pride and not logic. The Brotherhood plays a very small part in this global phenomenon, and even if you could eliminate that part entirely, it would only make a tiny dent in it. So why risk your men on a mission against a powerful opponent when you can achieve more, with less potential casualties, by focusing on the humans running similar operations?"

There was a long moment of silence, and then a sigh. "I wish I could tell you that you are wrong, but you are not. I can't tolerate the thought of Doomers snatching girls right from under our noses."

Encouraged by the admission, Lokan decided to press on. "There is another risk factor involved. If you eliminate Losham's men, my father might react with pride rather than logic as well. Don't forget that we have an excess of warriors now with nothing to keep them busy. That's not healthy for an organization like the Brotherhood. With his pride injured, Navuh might decide to send a large force to Los Angeles and resume the hunt for your people with renewed fervor."

"You raise valid points. I'll give it some thought."

Lokan let out a relieved breath. "I'm glad that you're not as hot-headed as I thought you were."

28

KIAN

*K*ian ended the call with Lokan, leaned back in his chair, and closed his eyes.

There had been truth to what the guy had said, but the question was what were his motives? Lokan's loyalties, if he had any, were questionable. He might have wanted to protect his brother or even his own skin.

Lokan's visit to Los Angeles coinciding with the raid on Losham's men would cast a shadow of suspicion on him, which at the moment he couldn't afford. After dropping off the radar for nearly a month, he was probably on his father's watch list's top three. If not first.

Perhaps the prudent thing to do would be to postpone the raid for a later date.

Or cancel it.

The thing with the trackers was worrisome, and he needed to consult with Bridget and William about the possibility of removing or disabling them if needed.

He also needed to talk to Turner. Lokan's comment about Navuh's response had touched a nerve.

Tonight's raid could not be staged as a mass defection, the

way it had been done in the previous one in the Bay Area. And they had already used the accidental explosion ruse in the monastery. Even if the Brotherhood's leadership had bought that one, which he doubted, they were not going to buy another accident.

This time, the idea was to come in as a SWAT team and take everyone into custody on suspicion of terrorism. Or at least that was what the humans in the area would be led to believe and what they would report. It would be assumed that the captured Doomers were being held for interrogation in a secret facility.

Given their ability to thrall, it was a shaky explanation, but then trained officers detaining terror suspects would not be susceptible to thralling. Not during the arrest, anyway.

He and Onegus had come up with other tricks that Kian hadn't mentioned to Lokan, but all of that was not going to solve the problem of hidden trackers.

He picked up his office phone and dialed William's number first. "Can you come to my office?"

"When do you need me?"

"As soon as you can make it here."

"I'm just finishing something, and then I'm on my way. Fifteen minutes tops."

"No problem."

The second call went to Bridget. "William is coming over in fifteen minutes, and I need you here as well. I have some new information I need to discuss with the two of you."

"I'll keep my door open. When I see William walking by, I'll join him."

"Good deal."

William's lab was in the underground complex, so it would take him several minutes to get to the office building. The question was whether it was enough time for a quick visit to the roof.

Shaking his head at his own weakness, Kian opened the drawer and grabbed the box of cigarillos.

Up on the roof, he lit up and called Turner.

"What's up, Kian? Figured that you need me after all?"

Kian chuckled. He hadn't taken into account that Turner might feel offended at not being included in the upcoming mission. "I always need that huge brain of yours, but I figured that you needed some time off to take care of your private clients."

"That's so kind of you. What changed your mind?"

"A call from Lokan. He said that I'm acting out of pride rather than reason, so I figured I'd ask the opinion of the most logical person I know."

"I assume that he was referring to tonight's raid."

"He doesn't know that it's going down tonight, but yes. He said that the Brotherhood plays a very small part in the global problem of human trafficking, and that I'm risking the lives of my men by having them fight a strong opponent when I can achieve much more by directing their efforts toward stopping the humans engaged in the trade."

"Smart fellow."

"So, you agree with him?"

"I do. But on the other hand, we can't ignore the psychological effect of letting Doomers operate on our turf, and that goes for both sides. The Guardians will feel like shit for letting Doomers snatch girls right in their backyard, and the Doomers might get emboldened by our lack of action."

Kian let out a relieved breath. Canceling the operation would have been bad for morale. But his relief was premature. He hadn't told Turner the rest.

"He also said that Navuh might retaliate by sending a large

force to Los Angeles. That would be like swatting a bee and having the entire hive descend on us."

"Provided that he knows the clan is responsible for the attack. Bridget told me that you have a clever cover-up."

"We do. The question is whether it would pass scrutiny."

"Can I offer a suggestion? Or will I be overstepping my bounds by doing so?"

"Go ahead."

"You are dealing with a large number of Doomers this time, correct?"

"A little more than in the Bay Area operation, but they are concentrated in one location."

"Which is in the middle of Koreatown."

"I see that you are well-informed."

"I live with Bridget. Of course, I am. You need another ring of security around the outer perimeter in case some of the Doomers manage to get away. If even one makes it out, your cover story will be blown to pieces."

"I don't have enough people."

"But I do. Or rather I can get them. I can have several units spread out throughout the area."

"It's a bit late for that. It's happening tonight. Besides, humans stand no chance against Doomers unless they are willing to shoot first and ask questions later. We are talking about Koreatown, not a lawless territory in the middle of nowhere."

"They can shoot the Doomers with elephant darts. But if you are not willing to postpone the raid, I can't help you with that. I need more than several hours to organize this. What I can do, however, is send a small crew to investigate for you. Humans can get into the building under a number of pretenses."

"I would appreciate that."

He'd wanted to ask before, but his pride stood in the way. Kian wanted to accomplish the mission without Turner's help, but it was turning out that he couldn't.

He let out an exasperated breath. "I might have to cancel the raid altogether. Lokan also said that there was talk of implanting the Doomers with trackers attached to their spinal cords. He doesn't know if it was done, and if Losham had his men implanted, but it's a possibility that I can't ignore. I can't bring them to the keep if they are traceable. William and Bridget are on their way and I'm going to ask their opinions on that."

"Let me know how it goes."

"I will."

Flicking the butt of his cigarillo into the trashcan, Kian headed back to his office.

It was true that he'd rushed the mission, but that was because he didn't want to give the Doomers a chance to snatch any girls. It was also true that he hadn't thought it through as meticulously as Turner would have no doubt done.

After relying on the guy for so long, Kian was out of practice, and apparently so was Onegus. Or maybe it was just that everything kept changing, and he didn't have time to adjust.

It hadn't occurred to him that the Brotherhood hadn't given up on putting trackers on their men. Where there was a strong enough need and enough effort was put into fulfilling it, a solution was bound to eventually present itself.

As Bridget and William entered his office, he motioned for them to take seats next to the conference table.

"What's this all about?" Bridget asked.

When Kian was done explaining, William pushed his glasses up his nose. "If the trackers are on, I can detect the transmissions they emit. But it is possible to leave them dormant and activate them only when the men go missing. I wouldn't know until that happened."

"How about X-ray?" Kian asked.

Bridget lifted a brow. "You want me to check every Doomer for hidden bugs? That would take forever."

"We can find a solution for that. The question is whether you can detect a small tracker deep inside the body."

She nodded. "I can."

"We can bring them to a warehouse somewhere, and you can check them for bugs before we transport them to the keep."

"I have a better solution," William said. "We can store them in the warehouse until we find a permanent place to stash them in. And in the meantime, I can rig up a device like the one the Doomers use to scan visitors to the island."

"That's right. I forgot about Carol's description. But if we actually find trackers in them, that doesn't solve our problem. We can't start operating on each one to remove them."

For several long moments, the three of them sat in silence, each trying to come up with a solution.

"What if we ship them out somewhere far away?" Bridget suggested. "It will have to look like a government installation. I don't think the Brotherhood would risk taking on the United States armed forces to release its warriors."

William shook his head. "That won't be necessary. All we have to do is install a strong transmission scrambler. In fact, I'll get right on it, so we will have it ready for tonight. You'll need to find a warehouse, though."

Kian waved a hand in dismissal. "That's not a problem. When can you have a scanner ready?"

"It will take time. I have to order parts, and some of them will be coming from overseas."

"I will have to put Guardians on rotation to babysit the

Doomers. I don't want any surprises, and as we've seen with Wonder, spontaneous awakenings from stasis can happen."

"That's a waste of manpower," William said. "I can install surveillance cameras in the warehouse and connect the feed to our control center. If by some freak accident they get wet and wake up, they will still be locked up. I'll also disable the fire sprinklers just in case."

Bridget lifted a finger. "I think I can solve the scanner problem. I can put them through medical equipment. An ultrasound machine and an MRI should do it. We are not limited to what can be used on travelers."

Kian leaned back in his chair. "Good thinking. Now there is only one problem remaining, but I doubt either of you can help me with that."

"Try us," Bridget said.

"Turner suggested having another ring of Guardians further out, in case some of the Doomers manage to run away, but we don't have Guardians enough as it is."

"You can use civilians," Bridget said. "They can go in pairs."

Kian shook his head. "Not a good idea. They will be defenseless against even a single Doomer. Most of them can't aim well enough to hit a running target, and their hand-to-hand skills are laughable."

Bridget lifted her hands. "Then I guess the Guardians will have to make sure that no Doomers get away."

M E Y

*W*hen Mey woke up, Yamanu was gone. She glanced at the nightstand to check if he'd left her a note, then lifted her new phone and checked for messages, but there were none. Not from Yamanu and not from her sister.

The only reason she knew that her new phone was indeed receiving all of her communications was her inbox, which was filled with the same store promotions she normally received.

Could he have gone to work? He was supposed to have the day off to rest before the mission. Could something have come up and the boss called him in?

Trying to stay positive and not imagine the worst, Mey got up and went into the bathroom.

Things had been strained between her and Yamanu after last night's argument, and she had spent the night sleeping on the edge of the bed with her back turned to him. If she hadn't been scared of going too far, she would have spent the night in Arwel's room.

Her position wasn't fun, that was for sure. She didn't want to be the reason Yamanu broke a vow he'd kept for hundreds of years, and she also didn't want to be the one to deprive the clan of its most powerful protector.

Never mind that it was probably all in Yamanu's head, and that the vow had nothing to do with his powers. He believed in it, and that was enough. Even if nothing in him changed once he broke it, he would think that it had, and his powers would diminish.

If only she could quash the feelings she had for him, she would have left, gone to Kian, and asked for another immortal's help with her transition. After that, she could join the clan's single ladies, and either find a guy she liked or not.

She was far from being an old maid, and as an immortal, there was even less pressure to find a guy to settle down with. She could wait thousands of years if she wanted to.

What a depressing thought.

Except, Mey doubted she would ever find anyone else who would capture her heart like Yamanu had. At twenty-six, it was the first time her feelings had run so deep for a man, and that was even before she actually articulated them.

Did she love him?

After the two other times she'd thought she loved a guy, Mey had decided that she wasn't going to think in terms of love until she was absolutely sure about it, and it was too early for that with Yamanu. Despite the strong connection she felt to him, or maybe because of it, Mey preferred to protect her heart and remain cautious.

Especially since there was a chance that they were not going to stay together.

Hoping that Yamanu's morning meeting wasn't going to last long, Mey got busy preparing breakfast. Nothing fancy, just eggs, hash browns, and toast, but lots of it. Her man was a big guy, and he needed large quantities to sustain him.

When the front door opened, her heart skipped a beat.

His long hair dripping wet, Yamanu looked like he had just stepped out of the shower. Where had he been?

"Good morning." He walked over to her and kissed her cheek. "What smells so good?"

"Hash browns, scrambled eggs, and toast."

He cocked a brow. "I thought those were on the list of forbidden foods for a model."

"I made them for you."

A happy grin spread over his handsome face. "But you are going to join me, right?"

She shrugged. "Why not? As it stands, it is not a sure thing that I'm going back to modeling. I might as well indulge in some fattening foods. Worst case scenario, if I need to get back to that, I can always go on a crash diet."

His grin melted away, replaced by a sad look. "I want you to stay."

"I want that too. But it's up to the Fates, right?" She took his hand and led him to a barstool. "Sit and tell me where you've been."

"To the gym. I usually train for two hours a day, but I neglected to do so in New York. The hotel gym wasn't equipped for immortal Guardians. The heaviest weight I could put together was two hundred pounds."

She loaded a plate for him with a mountain of eggs and potatoes and put it on the counter. "And that's too light? How much do you lift?"

A smirk lifted one corner of his mouth, and he puffed out his chest. "I warm up with seven hundred pounds."

Mey whistled. "Impressive. Are all immortal males so strong?"

"They are stronger than the average human male, but unless they train, they don't come anywhere near that. Frankly, not all of the Guardians do either."

The toaster beeped, and Mey took out the four slices and put them on a smaller plate. "So, my guy is not only one of the most powerful mentally, but also physically. The Fates were kind to me." She winked at him.

"Don't make fun of the Fates." He waggled a finger at her. "They can be vindictive. If you want to stay in their good graces, you should compliment them sincerely and thank them for their gifts. Otherwise, they might decide to take them away."

Yamanu delivered his little speech with a straight face and a tone that was dead serious.

He really believed that the Fates were real, which should not have surprised her. A guy who believed that his power was dependent on him keeping his vow of celibacy would believe in other superstitions just as strongly.

"I'll do my best."

He frowned. "Does believing in fate go against your religion?"

"Not fate in general, that's fine, but I'm sure a rabbi would frown at me praying to the Fates. Except, I'm not very religious. It's more about keeping my parents' tradition than anything else. So, I don't mind saying a few nice things about your Fates if it makes you feel better."

Yamanu nodded, but she wasn't sure if it was in approval or to indicate that he understood.

"Where is your plate?"

"Oh, right. I got distracted." Mey turned around and loaded much smaller portions of eggs and hash browns on her plate. "Do you have any plans for today? I mean before the raid thing?"

"No. What would you like to do?"

"I would like to see the village. I didn't get the chance to leave the house yet."

He put his fork down. "I'm sorry. I should have taken you out and shown you around."

"You were busy, and there is no rush. How large is the village anyway?"

"We can cover the topside in about an hour, a little longer if we take it slow. But there is also the underground complex, which I'm sure you'll find interesting."

"Can we stop by the café?"

"Sure thing."

30

YAMANU

"*I* feel like a cowboy." Anandur patted his twin holsters.

Brundar adjusted his helmet over the tight cotton cap he had put on to hide his long hair.

Yamanu did the same. "How do I look?"

Anandur grinned. "Like the badass that you are." He patted the bulletproof vest. "Look at all these pockets and the goodies inside of them."

"Do you think we get to keep them?" Yamanu asked. "They could be useful for future missions. We are unrecognizable in this gear. It even has a face mask and glasses." Which was great to cover his weird eyes. "And the body armor is not as cumbersome as ours."

"It's also not as effective," Brundar said.

Kian walked over and clapped Yamanu's back. "We keep everything. It was easier to purchase these than rent them."

Their outfits also included rifles, but they were not going to use those. Instead, they were armed with dual special issue taser guns.

Learning from Wonder's experience, they knew it was

easier and faster to disable an immortal using a taser. Shooting a Doomer with a regular gun would not necessarily disable him, and wrestling him down to the ground first in order to bite him was a problem when each Guardian had to take care of two Doomers.

Onegus clapped his hands. "Okay, people, listen up! Is everyone decent? Wonder is here to demonstrate the proper use of a taser gun on an immortal."

Several of the guys snickered.

Scanning the gathered men, Onegus confirmed that everyone was dressed before nodding to Wonder, who'd been waiting just outside the door.

"As the only person who has ever used a taser on a live one, or two…" Onegus glanced at Anandur and Brundar, "she has unique experience."

Wonder looked uncomfortable, and so did her mate and his brother. No one was going to forget that they had both been taken down by one untrained female.

"All I did was put it on the highest setting, like so." She demonstrated. "My taser had a long reach, so I didn't have to get close, which is the major disadvantage of a taser gun. I trust that you guys practiced and know how far it can reach?" She looked around before continuing. "Okay, that's good. Another disadvantage is that you only get one shot, and then you need to replace the cartridge. The biggest advantage of a taser is that you don't need to aim at vulnerable organs to disable your opponent. As long as you hit him, the electrical shock will do the rest."

"These have three shots," Onegus said. "You must have been given an old model."

Someone laughed, saying she had managed splendidly with just one shot. Then there were some more murmurs, but no one asked the most critical question.

Yamanu lifted his hand. "How long does the twitching last?"

She smiled shyly. "Since I didn't wait for it to be over, I don't know. I clobbered each of my victims over the head as soon as they were down. But perhaps Anandur knows the answer to that. My taser hit Brundar at the same time his knife hit me, so I was out for that, but Anandur saw what happened."

All eyes turned to Wonder's mate.

"Sorry, guys. But I was busy holding Wonder in my arms and deciding on the kind of death my brother deserved for killing her. I wasn't paying attention to him or how long he was twitching."

Brundar grimaced. "That's the thanks I get for saving your sorry ass."

Anandur grinned. "I think we are even."

"That we are."

Yamanu had heard the story of Anandur walking into Callie's ex's house in his armored suit and snapping the bastard's neck. Unfortunately, he'd arrived a few minutes too late to save his brother's knees. Callie's ex had shot both of them, causing enough damage to disable Brundar for weeks.

"Any more questions?" Wonder asked.

"Yeah," Niall said. "Why aren't you joining us?"

Wonder shook her head but didn't lose her cool. "And who is going to make you your sandwich tomorrow when you come to the café for lunch?"

"True, true. I take it back."

Anandur cast Niall a murderous glance. "Next time you have suggestions for my mate, you'd better run them by me first."

Niall snorted. "Have you heard of women's lib? She doesn't need your permission for anything."

Most of the guys were smart enough to keep their mouths shut, but some were just as stupid as Niall and made a few comments, some in support of Anandur, and some in support of Niall's right to free speech.

Anandur got in Niall's face. "Wonder might not need my permission to do anything, but you do. Am I clear?"

As jeers and cheers sounded in equal measure, Yamanu got ready to break up the fight that seemed to be brewing, but Kian beat him to it.

"Save it for the enemy, boys. You are both embarrassing Wonder."

Anandur was the first to back away. With a dismissive shrug, he walked over to his mate and wrapped his arm around her middle. "Sorry, love. The adrenaline must have gotten to my head."

Niall dipped his head. "My apologies, Wonder. I was just messing with Anandur, and I meant no disrespect or offense."

She smiled at him. "That's okay, none taken."

31

ANANDUR

*J*ust to spite him, Onegus had put Anandur in charge of the unit Niall was in.

"Peace," the guy said as they settled in the armored vehicle. "I was just having fun."

"Wonder doesn't appreciate people pestering her about entering the force."

Niall grimaced. "I didn't know that. I thought I was paying her a compliment."

Next to him, Camden chuckled. "You never know with the ladies. It's better to keep your yap shut."

"Oh yeah? So how am I supposed to charm them into having some fun time with me?"

"You just do this." Camden demonstrated a suggestive look combined with a tilt of his head.

"You want to tell me that that works for you?"

Camden puffed out his chest. "When you are as good-looking as me, nothing more is needed."

Anandur tuned them out. His bachelor days were long gone, and he didn't miss them one bit. Wonder was all he needed and would ever need. Well, except for maybe a couple of kids, but there was time for that.

A few months ago, he wouldn't have even entertained the thought, but now that Merlin had performed a miracle with Syssi and Kian, there was hope. One success didn't mean that there would be more, but it was better than nothing.

As Gregor parked the truck, Anandur was glad to see that the streets were empty of pedestrians, and that no lights shone brightly in the nearby buildings or that of the Doomers for that matter.

Earlier, Turner had sent a couple of humans to snoop around the place and check whether anyone patrolled it at night, and whether there were security cameras in the vicinity.

They'd reported no patrol, but they found cameras. Luckily, it was a simple system that was hooked to the internet, which meant that Roni could switch the feed from his command center and put it on a loop. If anyone was watching, they were going to see the same nothing happening throughout the night.

Other than that, they had Yamanu sitting across the street in a rented car and shrouding the area, adding an uncomfortable vibe that would keep humans away.

Anandur glanced at his watch. "Ten minutes to action. Check your equipment."

The guys did as he'd instructed, and then there was the nervous wait. This was the part he hated the most. The last minutes before the mission, when all the horsing around was done, and it was down to counting the seconds while the adrenaline was pumping through his veins and his muscles were coiled tight ready to spring into action, but it wasn't time yet.

When it finally was, Onegus's voice sounded in their earpieces. "The cameras are down, and the alarm is disconnected. We are ready to go."

They exited the vehicle silently, sprinting in a crouch toward the building.

The thing was an old two-story structure, with six apartments on the first floor and six on the second. The problem was that the front door and the staircase were bottlenecks. Assuming every apartment housed four Doomers, two Guardians were assigned to each one, another four to the corridor as backup, and the rest were to surround the building and catch any fleeing Doomers.

Still, getting thirty-two armed men through a single entry door was going to take a few seconds, and that could cost them the element of surprise.

Regrettably, the apartments didn't have balconies, and breaking in through the windows wasn't an option either.

Anandur's team had been assigned to the second floor, and they were the first to enter, followed by the second team assigned to the same floor.

Sixteen men altogether.

Brundar was heading the two teams in charge of the downstairs.

Should be a piece of cake if the Doomers slept like the dead.

If not, they would wake up when the small hairs on their necks tingled in alarm, warning them about enemy immortals approaching.

So far, so good.

The men spread out, two taking position in front of each door, while the remaining four stationed themselves in the intervals in between the apartments.

Anandur listened, but all he could hear was a guy snoring in the apartment Gregor and Dougal were going to storm.

It was a shame that Arwel was in New York. They could have used his empathic skills to double-check the number of occupants in each apartment.

Except, Alena's safety was more important, and it had been decided not to call him back. It was enough that Yamanu had been pulled away. Uisdean and Ewan were okay, but they weren't head Guardians. Bhathian was, but he had a mate and a baby with him, so his loyalty was to them first and Alena second.

After another long moment of intent listening, Anandur gave the go signal, and everyone exploded into action.

MEY

*T*he waiting for news reminded Mey of her Mossad days, when the guys had gone to do their thing, leaving her behind in the hotel to worry.

Now, like then, she was alone, pacing around like a caged tigress and trying not to bite her nails. It was a nasty habit she'd developed as a girl and had never gotten entirely rid of. Whenever the stress and worry would get to be too much, the urge to nibble became nearly uncontrollable.

Perhaps she should take up knitting, something to keep her hands busy. The other option was gluing on acrylic nails, which she had done in the past for the same reason. The fake nails were too hard to bite, but then she'd discovered that scraping away the nail polish was almost as satisfying as biting.

Both outcomes were unattractive and unproductive. If she'd learned to knit, she could at least make something. A scarf for Yamanu, or maybe a warm hat for the winter.

The knock on the door startled her, and her hand flew to her chest. Knocks on doors in the middle of the night were never good. As everyone with a loved one on the frontline knew, only the worst of news was delivered in person.

Everything else could be handled on the phone.

Her heart running amok in her chest, she walked to the door and opened it, expecting to see a couple of somber Guardians. Instead, it was Callie and Wonder, each holding a gallon-size ice cream bucket.

"We thought that you could use some company," Callie said. "It's nerve-wracking to wait for the guys to come back, and doing it alone is the worst."

"We brought Rocky Road." Wonder lifted her bucket. "Can we come in?"

Mey shook her head and pulled the door open all the way. "I'm sorry. When I heard the knock, I thought it was bad news."

"Oh, right." Callie grimaced. "We should have called first."

"That's okay. I'm glad that you're here. I was going nuts." Mey eyed the ice cream container in Wonder's hand. "I'd much rather nibble on that than on my nails."

"You too?" Callie sat on the couch. "I used to bite my nails a lot, and sometimes I still do." She smiled. "But you are right. Ice cream tastes much better. Can you get us spoons?"

"Coming right up."

Mey pulled out three soup bowls and three tablespoons. Emergency situations called for the big guns. This wasn't the time for little teaspoon nibbles from dainty ice cream goblets. Not that Yamanu and Arwel had anything like that in their kitchen. Mostly, they used paper everything.

"Perfect." Callie took a spoon and loaded the bowls.

As Mey sat on one of the armchairs, she glanced at her watch. "It's one o'clock in the morning. How are you going to get up for work tomorrow?"

Wonder shrugged. "Immortals don't need much sleep."

Callie nodded. "That's one of the perks. I can work at the nightclub, and then in the morning come help Wonder in the café. I could have never pulled that off when I was a human."

Mey raised a brow. "I didn't know you worked in a nightclub. How come you need to work two jobs? I was told that Guardians are paid well."

"I don't need to, I want to. Brundar owns half of the place, and I like keeping an eye on him when he is there." She winked.

"Why? I mean, if you were both human, I would have understood, but immortals are supposed to be absolutely faithful to each other, right? Yamanu told me that fated mates never even feel attracted to anyone other than their partner."

Callie waved with her spoon. "That's true, and I trust Brundar completely, but he needs me there to stave off unwanted advances. Besides, we sometimes use the place to play." She winked again.

Wonder chuckled, and then quickly stuffed a big chunk of ice cream in her mouth.

"Am I missing something?" Mey asked.

Callie smiled. "Brundar's place is not an ordinary nightclub. Well, the top floor is, but the basement is off-limits to the vanilla clientele."

Wonder coughed. "Excuse me." She shoved another spoonful of ice cream into her mouth.

"I see." Mey reached for her bowl and followed Wonder's example.

Callie's elephant-sized hint hadn't been lost on Mey. It seemed that she and her mate were into some interesting stuff.

Mey had no problem with that. In fact, she'd always been curious but had never dared to even look into a club like that. Maybe now that she knew the owners, she might summon the courage. But only if Yamanu went with her.

Not to do anything, of course. Just to check it out.

"I know," Callie said. "It's a bit of a shocker, but I can assure you that all the members are nice people who just enjoy the spicier side of things. Brundar has kept it a secret for a long time, but I convinced him that there was nothing to be embarrassed about." She snorted. "Not that you'll hear him breathe a word about it, but he doesn't mind if I do."

Mey put her bowl down. "I admit that I'm a little curious. Do you think Brundar would mind if Yamanu and I came to check it out?"

Callie grinned. "Are you into the spicy stuff too?"

Right now, she wasn't into any stuff, but Wonder and Callie didn't know that.

"I've never tried, and I'm not sure that I want to. But I would like to understand the allure."

"You can come to one of the demonstrations. We have classes every Wednesday." Callie scrunched her nose. "Although I'm not sure Brundar would be thrilled about another Guardian checking the place out. So far, no one from the clan has expressed the desire to visit, and I think he's very glad about that."

"It's not a big deal." Mey shrugged. "If he's not comfortable with it, I can skip it. It's not like it's at the top of my bucket list or anything like that."

"What is?" Wonder asked.

"Finding my sister, figuring out if Yamanu and I are really fated mates or if this is just an immortal urban legend, transitioning, deciding what to do with the rest of my life."

"Oh, wow," Callie said. "That's some heavy shit. But let me assure you at least of one thing. Fated mates are real. Don't ask me how and why, but I know it's true. Right, Wonder?"

"Yeah, it is. But it's really difficult to distinguish between regular love and the fated kind. I think that the only true test is time. If after the honeymoon period is over, neither of you feel even the slightest attraction toward anyone else, then your union is fated. Other than that, I really don't know how to test it."

Callie laughed. "If that's the only test, then I need to convince Brundar to invite immortal couples to the club. There is nothing like watching people having kinky sex to determine whether you can feel attracted to someone else."

Wonder grimaced. "Maybe for you, but I would just feel grossed out." She cast Callie an apologetic look. "No offense. I have nothing against it. But it's not my thing."

"No offense taken. But you are right. The temptation should match the person's particular desires. But I still think that's the best kind of test." She looked at Mey. "What would be your greatest temptation?"

Mey shrugged. "I can't think of any. All I want is for things to work out between Yamanu and me."

33

BRUNDAR

"Counting back from three," Onegus's voice sounded in Brundar's earpiece.

This time around, it had been decided to break down the doors instead of fiddling with the locks.

Rather than catching the Doomers in bed, they were actually counting on them running out into the front room where the Guardians could hit all four at the same time with taser darts. After that, fangs and venom would finish the work.

"Go!"

Brundar kicked the door, expecting the lock to give and the wood to splinter. Instead, pain shot through his leg all the way to his spine, and he stumbled back.

The bloody door was reinforced?

"What the hell?" Raibert pulled out his gun, the regular one, and emptied a round into the wood, creating an opening inside the door.

As the culprit became visible, Brundar cursed under his breath. It was a simple iron bar that ran across the opening, and now that it was visible, Raibert kicked one side of it to loosen the screws holding it attached to the wall.

The other teams on their floor followed his example, and given the sounds of gunshots coming from upstairs, Anandur's teams were doing the same.

Fuck. It was going to get messy.

With the element of surprise gone, the Doomers were ready for them, aiming their guns and firing through the hole in the door before the Guardians made it through.

Brundar hadn't fared any better than his friends.

Even though he was ready, both his tasers armed and aimed, Brundar got hit before he could release a shot. The first bullet was stopped by the vest, but the other hit the SWAT issue armored suit that wasn't designed to stop bullets. With the searing heat ripping through his thigh, Brundar's aim faltered, but he still managed to hit his first target before the Doomer had a chance to fire another bullet.

Except, there were three more Doomers, and Raibert was down after being shot multiple times.

Somehow, Brundar managed to slip into the zone despite the burning pain, moving with a speed that was unnatural even for him and hitting the remaining three one after the next.

Except, before going down, the Doomers kept shooting and two more bullets had hit home in his body, and one grazed his helmet right next to where his earpiece was, rendering him momentarily deaf.

With a curse, he ripped the thing off and descended on the Doomers, clobbering each one over the head while they were still twitching on the floor.

He would have gladly sunk his fangs in the first one, but Raibert wasn't moving and Brundar rushed to his side.

The Guardian was breathing, thank the merciful Fates, but he was bleeding profusely from his thigh. The bullet must have hit an artery.

Whipping a tourniquet from one of his vest pockets,

Brundar tied it above the wound, then looked at the corridor. "Is anyone out there? I need someone to carry Raibert to the medic bus!"

When there was no response, Brundar cursed and lifted the wounded Guardian over his shoulder, his injured leg nearly collapsing under him. Gritting his teeth, he limped out into the corridor and looked around.

None of the Guardians were there, and he had to assume that they were assisting in the other apartments.

Fucking mess.

Hopefully, Anandur was doing better on the second floor.

Outside the building, the situation wasn't better, which was worrisome. If the Guardians securing the perimeter were gone, it meant that they were giving chase.

Without the earpiece, he had no idea what was going on.

In a flash of brilliance, he removed Raibert's and put it on. "What's going on?"

"A fucking mess," Onegus answered. "It's a bloodbath."

"Them or us?"

"Both."

"Can you send the bus? Raibert is out, and I'm injured."

"It's already moving. Should be there in a couple of seconds."

"Thanks."

Brundar let Raibert's body slide down but remained standing. If he sat down, he wasn't going to get up, and there were Doomers inside who needed to get either envenomed or clobbered over the head once again.

The medic bus turned the corner and then came into a screeching stop in front of him. Julian jumped out and hefted the injured Guardian over his shoulder.

As Brundar limped away, Julian called after him, "You are bleeding. Come back and let me take care of that leg."

"After I dispatch the Doomers." Brundar kept going.

34

YAMANU

"*T*hat must have been the worst executed mission in our history," Anandur grumbled.

Next to Yamanu in the back seat, Brundar nodded in agreement.

Both brothers were injured, and yet they had both gone back to help their fellow Guardians as soon as they'd gotten patched up by the doctors. All available fangs had been needed, and it had to be done while the aggression was still pumping through their veins.

After the Doomers were taken care of and loaded into the trucks, the injured Guardians had been sent home, and the uninjured ones stayed behind to clean up and transport the Doomers to the warehouse.

Hopefully, they'd gotten all of them, but since an exact count hadn't been available, it was possible that a Doomer or two had managed to escape. The likelihood of them getting by the Guardians securing the perimeter was low, but it wasn't entirely non-existent.

"Considering the clusterfuck this was, we were lucky," Anandur said. "Most injuries were minor, like Brundar's and mine, but some guys took a lot of heat. The medic bus was full to capacity." He shifted, trying to find a more comfortable position. "I'm glad to be going home in a private car."

They had left the fake SWAT vehicles in the parking lot of one of the clan's downtown buildings, where they were going to get a new paint job. Kian hadn't decided yet whether he was going to keep them for future missions or sell them.

"What I wonder," Yamanu said, "is whether the operation would have gone smoother if Turner had planned it."

A simple precaution, an iron bar across the door, had almost been their downfall. And wasn't that a humbling experience.

"I don't think so," Brundar said. "The human team Turner sent to snoop around didn't discover the bars on the doors either. It's almost as if the Doomers were ready for us."

Anandur turned around to look at his brother. "Bridget said that the bullets they used were designed to explode and cause as much damage as possible. That's why they hurt so fucking bad, and why it took her so long to take all the pieces out."

Brundar shifted, wincing as his bandaged leg moved. "Their boss must have suspected something after the last raid."

Anandur shook his head. "We were very thorough. There was no hint of a struggle left and we staged it perfectly. It looked like they stole the drugs and the money and defected."

"We've learned a few things since then," Brundar said. "Like the fact that it is not easy for Doomers to defect because they are compelled to be loyal to Navuh."

"Yeah, but we also know that the longer the Doomers are away from the island and Navuh's influence, the weaker the compulsion becomes. Those guys have been in the Bay Area for months."

Brundar shrugged. "Nevertheless, what happened tonight is proof that either they or their boss suspected that we were involved. They wouldn't have bothered to get those mother-fucking nasty bullets for humans."

"Yeah." Anandur rubbed his arm. "Next time we are going fully suited up. We can make our armor look like government issue. Just slap some acronym letters on it."

"I wonder what will happen to their boss," Yamanu said. "If I were him, I would pick up and run. Navuh is going to make shish kabob out of his carcass."

Anandur smirked. "Maybe we should do the guy a favor and snatch him too. He'd be better off in our dungeon."

"I like it," Brundar said. "Call Kian and tell him to do that."

"At four o'clock in the morning? You call him."

"He's not sleeping," Yamanu said. "Kian is waiting for everyone to return home."

Until the last of the Guardians was safely home, Kian wasn't going to call it a night.

Yamanu wondered whether Mey was sleeping or anxiously waiting for him at home. Should he call her? What was the protocol for that? He'd sent her a text, saying that the mission had been successful and that he was coming home. The second part was true, the first one not really. With half of the Guardians getting hit and the possibility of an escaped Doomer, he would not call it a success.

"Did you guys call your mates?"

Anandur winced. "I didn't want to call Wonder and tell her that I was injured. She would have made a big fuss about it."

"Is she waiting for you?" Yamanu asked.

"Probably."

"Then call her. She's probably worried." He turned to Brundar. "What about you?"

"I texted Callie that I'm fine and on my way home. But I didn't mention getting hit. By the time we get there, it will most likely be healed anyway."

Behind the wheel, Oidche chuckled. "Now I don't feel as bad about being the only bachelor here. All this reporting is a pain in the arse."

Yamanu wanted to correct him and point out that he was technically still a bachelor as well, but that would have garnered questions he didn't want to answer, so he kept his yap shut.

"I'm in the car on my way home," Anandur said into the phone. "I got hit, but it's nothing. Bridget already patched me up."

Out of respect for Anandur, Yamanu tried to tune out Wonder's response, but it was difficult since she was chewing him out for not calling before.

"I didn't want to worry you. It's really nothing. A bullet grazed my arm."

On the other end of the line, Wonder gasped and asked about Brundar and the rest of the Guardians.

"Some got hit way worse than I did, but there were no casualties, thank the merciful Fates. We also managed not to kill any of the Doomers, which was a miracle given what went down."

"What about Brundar?" Wonder asked.

"He's fine. Got hit a couple of times, but it's nothing serious."

Callie's background shriek was so loud that they all cringed in unison.

"No, he's fine. Tell her to relax. He's right here next to me, trying to kill me with his eyes."

"Give him the phone!" Callie commanded after taking over from Wonder.

"Sorry, bro," Anandur smiled sheepishly as he handed the device to Brundar.

"You are going to pay for this." Brundar's face looked far

from angelic as he took it.

"I have no doubt." Anandur crossed his arms over his chest and shrugged. "He should have told her."

Yamanu smirked. "Aren't you glad that you listened to my advice? Imagine what would have happened if you arrived home without first telling Wonder that you were injured."

35

MEY

"I can't believe he didn't tell me," Callie fumed. "I'm going home." She took the empty ice cream bucket to the trash and headed for the door. "Are you coming, Wonder?"

"Yeah. I want to be home when Anandur comes back." She smirked and turned to Mey. "Get ready for some happy time. After a mission, the guys usually come back pumped up." She winked and then blushed.

Callie opened the door. "Brundar is not going to be happy, I promise you that."

"Don't be so harsh," Wonder said. "He texted you to say that he was okay a whole hour before Anandur called me. And he didn't tell you about the injury because he didn't want to worry you."

"I know that. But I will not tolerate that macho crap. I'm not some delicate flower that will faint from a whisper of bad news. I'm his partner, and he should share everything with me. The good and the bad."

Searching for support, Wonder looked at Mey. "What do you think?"

"I think that Callie is right, but I don't think that punishing Brundar is the way to go. Just sit him down and talk to him. He meant well."

Callie let out a breath. "Yeah, you're right. I guess all that stress had to explode and it was just looking for a good reason. I'll cool down on the way home." She came back in and pulled Mey into a quick hug. "Thanks for having us."

"Thanks for coming. I would have gone nuts waiting here for Yamanu by myself."

Wonder returned for a hug as well. "You know that he wasn't in any danger, right? His job is to shroud. He rarely takes an active part in raids."

"But sometimes he does. It sounds like they encountered way more trouble than they'd expected, and I'm sure he jumped in to help the moment he could let go of that thing he does. The shrouding." She shook her head. "I'm still trying to figure out how it's possible. It sounds like magic."

Callie chuckled. "Yamanu, the voodoo shaman. He even looks like one."

"I see that your mood has improved." Mey patted her arm. "You'd better get going if you want to greet your guys when they come back."

"We're going." Callie kissed her cheek. "I know that you want to get rid of us and get ready for happy times."

Covering her mouth with her hand, Wonder giggled.

Mey smiled. "Goodnight, or rather good morning."

She stood in the doorway watching them go, waved goodbye one last time, and then closed the door.

Callie and Wonder weren't wrong about men returning all pumped up from the battlefield, their aggression morphing into sexual energy. Some of Mey's most memorable times with Shimon had been after his return from missions.

But if Yamanu hadn't taken an active part in the fight, he'd had no reason to get all pumped with energy. And besides, he wasn't going to act on it anyway.

Not tonight, right after he'd used his powers to shield his fellow Guardians. She hadn't known him for long, but it was enough to figure out what made him tick.

Yamanu was a defender. It wasn't what he did, it was who he was. That was why it was so difficult for him to risk giving it up.

If she could only convince him that it was all in his head and that there was no way that his sacrifice was what made him powerful.

He just believed in that.

What she couldn't understand, and it bugged the hell out of her, was how come the doctor hadn't told him that. A medical doctor should believe in scientific facts. Not superstitious mumbo jumbo. Merlin should have told Yamanu that his power emanated from him, and that it was probably fueled by his belief, but it didn't stem from it.

He would have believed the doctor, or at least some of his conviction would have faltered.

With a sigh, she padded to the kitchen and opened the fridge. After eating about half a gallon of ice cream she wasn't hungry, but perhaps Yamanu would be. That was another thing warriors returning from battle usually craved, although it certainly took second place after sex.

Except in Yamanu's case, offering him food would be a better choice.

There were a couple of steaks in the freezer, and she pulled them out. There was no time to defrost them, but she could heat them up in the pan. She also found a pack of frozen corn on the cob and dropped them into a pot of hot water.

Fifteen minutes later, the modest meal was ready, and five minutes after that, she heard the front door open.

KIAN

*T*he mission had been a mess, and Kian was responsible for it.

Or was he?

Turner had sent a team of humans to investigate, but they hadn't thought to check the doors for anything other than the material they were made of and whether they were fortified with alarm sensors.

Then again, Turner hadn't had the time to be as thorough as he usually was. Except, Kian doubted it would have crossed his mind to check for a basic safety measure like the installation of iron rods across the doors.

Other than that oversight, Kian had taken every precaution possible, given the limited number of Guardians he had.

But he'd been hasty. He should have waited for better intel. As it was, they had no idea if they'd gotten all of the Doomers. It wasn't likely that anyone managed to escape, but still, without an exact headcount, one or two might have slipped through the cracks.

When Bridget's ringtone sounded from his phone, he snatched it off the coffee table. "What's up?"

"There were no trackers. We ran all the Doomers through the equipment, and they had no foreign objects in them. Just in case, though, when Julian comes back, he is going to put them through another round."

"That's good news, and good job on patching up everyone and bringing them home. I'm glad you had Julian and the nurses to help you."

She chuckled. "Deep down, you must have known we were going to encounter problems. Otherwise, you wouldn't have invested in the medic bus, which was a lifesaver. Thank you for that."

"At least I did one good thing. Can't say that about the rest of the mission."

She sighed, sounding tired. "Don't beat yourself up about it. What's done is done. The injuries weren't too bad, and hopefully, we got all the Doomers. None of them are dead either, which should make your mother happy. I'm cleaning up their wounds and bandaging them so they don't get infected. With their bodies in stasis, they might not be as resilient."

"Perhaps it's a good opportunity for you to run some tests. Leave an injury untreated and see what happens."

There was a long moment of silence. "It's tempting, but I can't do that. I swore to do no harm. But if any of ours volunteers for an experiment, I'll gladly do that."

Kian's fingers tightened around the phone. "I don't get it. So, you are willing to put one of your own in harm's way but not a Doomer?"

She chuckled. "If the Doomer were conscious and volunteered for the test or agreed to it in exchange for some form of compensation, I would have preferred that. I'm just not willing to experiment on an unconscious guy without his consent."

"Semantics, Bridget. They didn't give their consent to getting shot or envenomized either."

"That's different, and you know it."

He raked his fingers through his hair. "Yeah, I do. I'm tired and irritated, and I'm talking nonsense. Forgive me."

"You're forgiven. Go get some sleep, but before you do, tell me what you want to do with the Doomers. Should we leave them here or bring them to the keep as we originally planned?"

"After Julian's checked them again, you can bring them to the keep."

"That's what I thought. Goodnight, Kian. Or rather good morning."

"Thanks. Wrap it up and get some sleep."

"As soon as I can."

When he hung up with Bridget, Kian called Julian. "How are you holding up?"

"No problems here. I'm heading back to the warehouse to help my mother."

"Are the Guardians back home? Or are some still in the clinic?"

"Everyone is home. None of the injuries required a hospital stay. By morning, ninety-five percent of them will be as good as new."

"That's music to my ears. What about the other five percent?"

"No later than this evening."

"Excellent. I understand that you want to run the Doomers through the machines again."

"Yeah. My motto is better safe than sorry. If we want to store them in the keep, we need to make sure they are clean." He chuckled. "Surprisingly, most of them are. I'm starting to think that the stinky Doomer is a myth."

"Nope, not a myth. I guess these men were selected because they were higher caliber than the average Doomer. They needed to appeal to American girls."

37

YAMANU

"Yamanu!" Mey ran up to him and wrapped her arms around his neck.

As she kissed him, Yamanu cupped her bottom and lifted her up. Getting with the program, she wrapped her legs around his waist and deepened the kiss.

Thirty more seconds of that, and he was going to carry her to bed, which was a bad idea. What was more troubling, though, was that he was aroused when he shouldn't be. Unlike the other men, he usually felt spent after a mission. Holding up a shroud for hours took everything he'd had, and that included every last bit of energy.

Except, holding Mey's round ass, having her core pressed against his groin and her breasts against his chest, was affecting him when it shouldn't.

Lowering her back to the floor, he inhaled. "I smell steak."

Mey was quick, wiping the look of disappointment from her face and putting on a broad smile. "I thought you'd be hungry. Come, they are still hot." She took him by the hand and led him to the table. "Would you like a beer?"

"You read my mind." He started pushing up from the chair, but she put a hand on his shoulder.

"I'll get it. You must be tired."

"Exhausted. Keeping a shroud over a large area like that takes a lot out of me."

"I can imagine."

Mey ducked into the kitchen and a moment later returned with a platter loaded with two steaks and four corn on the cob. "I know it's not much. But that's all I found in the freezer." She pulled the beer out from her back pocket and put it in front of him on the table. "We should go grocery shopping."

As she sat across from him, Yamanu lifted a brow. "Aren't you going to join me?"

"I had about a gallon of ice cream. Callie and Wonder came over to keep me company, and they brought the ice cream with them."

He cut into the first steak. "That was nice of them."

"It was. Although I almost had a heart attack when they knocked on the door."

Yamanu cocked a brow. "Why? You know that the village is safe."

She leaned back and crossed her arms over her chest. "I wasn't afraid of burglars knocking in the middle of the night. Where I come from, a knock at an ungodly hour means bad news. That is always delivered in person."

It took him a moment to understand what she'd been referring to. "Fallen soldiers?"

She nodded. "Everyone is afraid of that. And of the brown envelope."

"What comes in a brown envelope?"

"Summons for reserve duty. Up to a certain age, every citizen has to give a month a year, and no one likes it." She chuckled. "Except for those who want a vacation from the wife.

Some men actually look forward to seeing the brown envelope in the mailbox. Or so the joke goes. Personally, I think it's just male posturing."

Yamanu finished chewing and popped the lid on the beer. "Women don't get called for reserve duty?"

"We do, but we get released at an earlier age, and married women are exempt, except for highly trained professionals like doctors."

He cut another piece of steak. "I wonder if this mandatory military service for everyone fosters more equality between the sexes."

Mey nodded. "I think so. Especially in the workforce. Here, employers might be concerned with women taking long maternity leave. Over there, the men have to serve for one entire month of every year until they are in their fifties. Officers have to serve even longer, and at times of war, the duty goes for as long as they are needed. Maternity leave becomes inconsequential in comparison. Still, men are men, and they always think that they are better." She smiled. "Naturally, we ladies know the truth."

"I don't think like that. In my opinion, women are better than men at most things."

She waved a hand. "You're just trying to be politically correct."

"Not true. The clan is a matriarchal society. Our Clan Mother is the ultimate authority."

"Isn't she just a figurehead, though? I was under the impression that Kian runs things."

"He does here. His sister is in charge in Scotland. It's Annani's choice to let them run things as they please. But sometimes she puts her foot down and demands things be done the way she wants. Like not killing Doomers and putting them in stasis instead. It would make our lives much easier if we could just kill them."

Feeling his aggression surface, Yamanu redirected it toward the second steak, cutting a piece off together with the paper plate under it.

"Damn." He flicked the cardboard away. "And that's where I'm a bit of a chauvinist. I think men's aggressive natures make them much better suited for combat. I don't like the idea of women on the battlefield."

"It was tough tonight, eh?" Mey asked, ignoring his comment about female fighters.

"Yeah. I can't remember when we sustained so many injuries. We didn't have enough intel, and we weren't as well-prepared as we thought."

"What happened?"

He chuckled. "They used a simple safety measure. An iron rod across the door, secured on both sides to the walls. The Guardians didn't expect it. When they tried to break the doors down, it took a few extra seconds, and the noise was enough to wake the Doomers up. With the element of surprise gone, the Guardians were greeted with bullets instead of snores."

Mey winced. "Was there a way to find out about the rods?"

"Of course. With a couple more days of reconnaissance, using humans to check the apartments would have prevented this clusterfuck. But Kian was in a rush. He didn't want to give the Doomers the chance to snatch even one girl."

"I can understand that."

Yamanu shook his head. "That's why Turner is better at this. The guy is pure logic. Emotions don't factor into his plans."

"Why wasn't he consulted then?"

"Pride would be my guess. Since Turner joined the clan, he's taken over that part of Kian's job, and it must have rankled. Besides, Turner still runs his private operation, and he needs time for that. Still, Kian enlisted his help at the last moment, and Turner sent a human team to investigate, but it was done in a rush. They checked only the basics."

"What is Turner's private business?"

"High-risk rescues. If you have a loved one who's been kidnapped for ransom, Turner is the one to turn to for help."

38

MEY

*M*ey's interest was piqued. "Can he help me find Jin?"

"He's the one who told Kian about what's really going on in that Quiet Zone, but that's the kind of information anyone can find out with an internet search. I'm sure he can dig up more for us. And if she is there, and we need to get her out, I wouldn't trust anyone else to plan the mission."

Having the clan and a specialist like Turner helping her was great, but Mey had to wonder about the costs, and who was going to cover them. She certainly didn't have that kind of money, and neither did her parents. Her father was a retired history professor, and her mom was a pediatric nurse who was still working part-time. Perhaps she could borrow it?

Or, she could play the ostrich and not ask. No one had mentioned money, so maybe they were going to do it pro bono? After all, the clan was doing a lot of humanitarian work, battling traffickers and rehabilitating the girls they'd rescued.

Except, she knew that they were doing it for her because she was Yamanu's girlfriend, or rather future mate. If that was ever going to happen.

He'd said he'd make up his mind after the raid, and she'd been hoping that the battle rush and the ensuing sexual hunger would tip the scales in her favor. What she hadn't taken into account was that Yamanu's part in the mission didn't require him to fight, and that it had exhausted him.

Normally, she wouldn't have had a problem with that, but time was running out.

"You're talking as if we have all the time in the world to find Jin, and if she needs rescuing, plan for it and do it. But we have ten days."

A pained look flitted through Yamanu's eyes. "Jin's rescue has nothing to do with your transition, and it's not urgent. It's not like her life is in danger."

Mey shook her head. "Is the clan still going to do that once I'm gone? If I don't transition, you are going to erase my memories and send me back to New York. I will have to find Jin on my own."

Reaching across the table, he took her hand and clasped it between his. "Let's not succumb to pessimism. You are going to transition, and the clan is going to do everything to help your sister, provided she needs help. It's possible that she's where she wants to be."

Letting out an exasperated breath, Mey let her shoulders slump. "You might be right. The way she sounded in that echo I've heard, she knew what she was doing. But she is still a kid. She might have gotten in over her head."

Yamanu smiled. "She is less than two years younger than you."

"I know. Still, she's my kid sister, and I feel responsible for her."

"Naturally. But don't worry. We are going to find out where she is and whether she needs rescuing."

"Thank you. I still don't understand why you are doing this

for me. It seems that I'm more trouble than I'm worth."

He frowned. "How can you say that?"

She pulled her hand out of his clasp and crossed her arms over her chest. "Because of me, you are faced with a difficult decision. I know that Dormants are important to the clan and all that, but they are not as important as keeping everyone safe, which you believe is entirely dependent on you."

"Not entirely, but to a large extent." He sighed. "And tonight was a perfect example of that. If I hadn't been there to shroud the area, the multiple gunshots would have caused massive panic, the police would have shown up, and I have no doubt that a large number of Doomers would have escaped." He rubbed his jaw. "I hope none have, but it was such a mess that it's possible, and that would be disastrous."

"Why?"

"Because the whole idea was to make it look like the government arrested these Doomers on suspicion of either terrorism or selling drugs and human trafficking. That's the way we staged it to look. If there were any eyewitnesses, they would have reported that a SWAT team entered the building and took out suspects. Naturally, I would have added to that, planting memories to support the illusion. But if even one of them managed to escape, he will inform his superior that it was us. Their leader might retaliate by sending a much larger force to hunt us down."

"Then you shouldn't have done it. The risks outweighed the benefits."

He looked into her eyes. "Not everything is two plus two equals four. Sometimes it's five and sometimes it's three. Life is not a math equation or even a probability field. Sometimes you need to go with what you know is right. In hindsight, the consequences might not be worth it, but going in, you always think that you will prevail."

Mey wondered if Yamanu was aware of the irony. If he applied the same logic to himself, his decision should have been made days ago. Except, she wasn't sure that it would have been the one she hoped for.

"I can't argue with your life experience, so I'll take your word for it. But if you believe in what you've just said, why are you having such a hard time deciding?" Her voice wavering just a little, she continued. "What does your gut tell you?"

As he looked at her with those sad eyes of his, Mey didn't dare inhale.

What was he going to tell her? That he'd already decided and that the safety of his clan must come before his own happiness?

She should have waited until tomorrow to ask that, and not do it right after he'd come back from a mission that had required his shrouding abilities.

He sighed. "My gut tells me that I've done enough, and that after centuries of sacrifice, it's okay for me to be selfish and do what's right for me. But my conscience is slapping me around for daring to think like that. I know that I promised you an answer after the raid, but I need a little more time."

Mey wondered if another gallon of ice cream could erase the taste of disappointment smothered with a hefty topping of helplessness.

She couldn't even get mad at Yamanu because she understood all too well what he was going through. He was right, it wasn't as easy as two plus two.

She nodded. "Take as long you need. I won't pester you about it anymore. I'm putting my faith in fate."

The last comment had been tinged with sarcasm, but Yamanu hadn't picked up on that.

"Thank you." He pushed up to his feet. "I'm going for a walk to try to clear my head."

39

YAMANU

*A*s Yamanu stepped out the door, he vowed not to come back without making a decision.

The sun was rising, and people would be waking up in a couple of hours. Until then, though, the trails would be deserted, providing the peaceful atmosphere necessary for contemplation. Except, he'd had days to decide and couldn't, so how was he going to do that in a couple of hours?

Stringing Mey along and leaving her in a perpetual state of anxiety wasn't fair to her. None of this was her fault, and yet she blamed herself for putting him in this situation. And that wasn't fair either.

He couldn't keep straddling the fence and hope for some divine intervention to provide him with the wisdom to decide. Apparently, the Fates wanted him to do that on his own and take responsibility for his actions. They were not going to make it easy for him, and perhaps they were right.

To fully appreciate what he had, he needed to grab it by the horns and proclaim ownership. He either kept owning the martyr scepter, in which case he would need to come out and admit to Mey and everyone else why he was abstaining. Then he would need to apologize to Mey for leading her on and let her choose someone else. It was going to kill him, but that was what martyrs did.

They sacrificed, and they suffered.

Or he should grab the crown of a mated man, put it on his head, and pass the martyr scepter to someone else.

Hey, that was a thought.

If he could harness the sexual energy and channel it into his shrouding and thralling ability, another male should be able to do that as well.

Right. As if anyone else would be willing to give up sex and the chance of a fated mate to keep the clan safe.

Except, if it was possible for someone else to do it, Yamanu shouldn't feel bad about tossing that burden into the middle of the village square and announcing that a volunteer was needed to pick it up.

And if there were none, so be it.

But what if the one who picked it up was already sacrificing a lot? If Arwel volunteered, or Kian. Yamanu's conscience wouldn't be happy with that. Or Kian.

Damn. There should be more selfless males around, but he couldn't think of anyone who would step up and haul that burden onto his shoulders.

Thinking back to his conversation with Mey, he wondered whether any of the females could do that as well, but he discarded the idea. As lustful as immortal females were, their sexual energy wasn't as powerful as that of the males. Nature, or the scientist responsible for their genetic makeup, made the males much more predatory.

And if he needed proof of that, there was Ruth.

Others might have not noticed, but Yamanu had paid attention. Before she'd gotten the job managing Nathalie's café and later meeting Nick, Ruth had been a recluse. Yamanu couldn't be a hundred percent sure, but he suspected that after giving birth to her daughter, Ruth had been celibate until she and Nick had mated. And yet she hadn't gained any superpowers in exchange for her abstinence.

Not before meeting Nick, and not during their courtship.

Everyone had been waiting for them to seal the deal, but like a couple of virgins, they had taken their time. Three months was an awfully long time for immortals to dance around intimacy.

And that was exactly what he was doing now in regards to making up his damn mind. He was letting it wander aimlessly instead of deciding one way or the other.

So, here were his options.

The idea to take a break from celibacy and then go back to it was not going to work. Even with shitloads of potion, he wouldn't be able to abstain as long as Mey was around.

He wanted her too much.

Which meant that all of Mey's creative ideas of how to induce her transition without him breaking his vow were a waste of her brainpower. Well, maybe not. He should tell Merlin and Bridget about them in case they could help someone else in the future.

Not that he could see any of the males summoning aggression to fight a woman. They could barely do that to fight scrawny Roni. The kid had had to come up with the creative idea to spur Kian's anger by reciting slam poetry.

Damn, he was doing it again. Letting his mind wander in any direction just to avoid making a decision.

It was quite simple.

Mey or the clan.

He couldn't have both.

ANNANI

*a*s was her custom while residing in the village, Annani woke up when the sun came up. Her pale skin and sensitive eyes could not tolerate the midday light, but the soft glow of early morning hours, especially when the sky was overcast, was her favorite time of day. Dusk and dawn were when she ventured outside and sat on the lounger in the modestly sized garden of her temporary abode.

Soon she would be going home, and except for her short excursions to nearby towns, there would be no more natural sunlight for her.

She was going to miss it, and she was going to miss the Friday night dinners with the family and the afternoon teas with other invited guests.

Should she stay?

This time around, she and Kian had been careful not to step on each other's toes. He did not inquire about her whereabouts too often, and she tried to be as mindful and as careful about her safety as was reasonable when venturing outside the village.

Still, when Alena got back, they were going home. Perhaps she would come to visit more often, though. But before Annani visited the village again, she had to pay Sari a visit. Fates forbid Sari would think that her mother was showing favoritism to Kian and Amanda.

No matter how old her children were, as a mother, she had to be mindful of things like that.

"Here is your coffee, Clan Mother." Ogidu put the tray on the side table and bowed. "Would you care for anything else? Perhaps a shawl? It is a bit chilly outside."

"Thank you. That is very thoughtful of you."

"I shall be right back, Clan Mother." He bowed and turned on his heel.

Picking up the cup, she brought it to her lips and took a long sip. It was perfectly done. Not too hot and not too cold. Ogidu had perfected the art of making coffee.

Pulling her feet up under her gown, she leaned back on the lounger. The sweet sound of a bird chirping its mating song had Annani look up. Over the fence, she spotted the little guy among the tree branches swaying in the gentle breeze, but as she lowered her eyes, she saw the top of someone's head bobbing as he walked by.

Well, not just anyone. Given the height, it could be only Dalhu or Yamanu, but Dalhu's hair was coarse and wavy, while Yamanu's was sleek and straight.

What was he doing up so early?

Perhaps he had not gone to sleep yet?

The Guardians had returned from their mission not too long ago. Kian had told her that everything had gone well, but seeing Yamanu striding along the path instead of sleeping raised her suspicions. She had not seen him doing that any of the other mornings.

Perhaps Kian had not told her the entire story.

Swinging her legs over the side of the lounger, Annani slipped her feet into her shoes and got up.

"Here is your shawl, Clan Mother." Ogidu handed it to her.

"Thank you." She shrugged it over her shoulders. "I am going out for a walk."

"I shall walk with you." He bowed.

"There is no need. I have spotted a Guardian outside, and I want to join him."

Ogidu bowed again. "Then I shall accompany you until we catch up to him."

"Very well."

She could not fault her butler for his programming. After all, it was exactly what she had instructed him and his brothers to do.

Serve and protect, like the motto of the police department.

Annani smiled. She had invented it first.

"Master Yamanu!" Ogidu called out after the Guardian. "The Clan Mother wishes to join you on your morning stroll."

Yamanu stopped and turned around, then walked back and bowed to her. "Good morning, Clan Mother."

"Good morning to you too." She turned to Ogidu. "Thank you. You may leave now."

"Yes, Clan Mother." He bowed but waited until she threaded her arm through Yamanu's and started walking before pivoting on his heel and turning back.

Perhaps she should change this old programming. It was a remnant from times when it had been considered impolite for a servant to turn his back on his master or mistress.

Beside her, Yamanu felt tense, probably uncomfortable with her show of familiarity.

"Does it bother you that I have my arm through yours?" Annani asked.

"It doesn't bother me. I'm honored, Clan Mother."

"You seem tense. Did something go wrong tonight? Kian said that except for a few minor injuries, everyone came back in one piece and that none of the Doomers have been killed either. I have a feeling that he was sugarcoating it for my benefit."

She knew she was putting Yamanu in an awkward position, but she needed to know the truth. Not just the positive outcomes, but all of them.

"Everything Kian said was true. None of the injuries were severe, but there were more of them than he expected, and they were more painful. The Doomers used special bullets that explode after penetrating the flesh. It has taken Bridget and Julian a long time to dig out all of the pieces."

"Do you think they knew you were coming?"

He nodded. "They didn't know when it would happen, but they had taken precautions. Very basic ones, but nevertheless effective. Aside from the bullets, they had the doors reinforced with a simple iron rod bolted across the opening. This one simple trick cost us the surprise."

Annani frowned. "I hope Lokan did not warn his adopted brother. I would be very disappointed if he had."

"Do you think he is playing both sides?"

As unpleasant as the thought was, it had crossed her mind. "I hope not. I would rather assume that Losham was cautious. Lokan's questions about the move might have made him suspicious."

Yamanu groaned softly. "I hope that this mission hasn't cost us a valuable informant. It would be a shame to lose Lokan as a source."

Annani shivered, but not from the cold. "Do you think he is in danger?"

"I don't know. But maybe it would be wise to apprehend Losham just in case he suspects Lokan's involvement."

Annani nodded. "I will speak with Kian." She looked up at Yamanu's handsome face. "Is this why you are strolling out here instead of sleeping in your bed? Are you worried?"

41

YAMANU

For about a nanosecond, Yamanu thought of lying.

He could have said that yes, he was worried about Lokan, or that he was worried about the safety of the clan, which would have at least been true, but this was Annani, the Clan Mother, and lying to her felt as wrong as lying to the Fates.

Besides, she had the wisdom of ages. Perhaps she could tell him what to do.

Her slim shoulders didn't look like they could carry his burden, but he knew that to be an illusion. Annani wasn't powerful just because she was a goddess. The tiny lady threading her arm through his could move mountains with her sheer willpower and determination, and she had.

"I wish I could say that this was the reason I couldn't sleep, but the truth is that I have other matters on my mind. Personal ones."

She lifted one perfect red brow. "I heard that you found a mate? Is she not what you have hoped for?"

"Mey is perfect, but I wish that she wasn't. It would have made my decision much easier."

Annani stopped and turned to him. "I do not understand. Finding your fated mate should be the best thing that has ever happened to you, a source of joy, not of anguish."

"For anyone but me, that would be true. But in order for me to be with Mey, I have to let go of my power. And if I let go of it, I leave the clan exposed to danger because no one can do what I can. Or maybe someone can, but I doubt anyone would volunteer once they realize what they have to give up."

As Annani looked up at him for a long moment, her smart, ancient eyes boring down into his soul, Yamanu wondered whether she'd already guessed his secret.

"Let us take a seat." She threaded her arm through his again and led him toward the nearest bench. "I have a feeling that this story requires sitting down."

He couldn't argue with that.

The bench Annani found was a good spot, not directly on the pathway but inset into the greenery that had grown much higher since it had been planted, which hadn't been that long ago. The landscape architect who'd designed the village's outdoor areas had done a great job. What was his name, Ruben? He was one of the younger immortals in the Scottish keep who was born after Yamanu had moved with half of the clan to America.

Yamanu shook his head. He was doing it again, letting his mind wander off-topic to avoid thinking about the big things.

"Okay." Annani wrapped the shawl tighter around her bare arms. "You should start from the beginning and explain what this is all about."

He nodded. "Do you remember when you sentenced me to six months of banishment?"

"Of course, I do. You were so guilt-stricken that I figured you needed the time to reflect and forgive yourself. Was I too harsh?"

"Not at all. If anything, you were too lenient. I still felt guilty when I came back. But I digress. The side effect of the banishment was abstinence, which I thought befitted my sins perfectly. What I didn't expect was the ability to channel all that pent-up sexual energy into my shrouding. I was good at it before the exile, but I wasn't anywhere near as powerful as I am now. I discovered it by chance when the neighboring village was attacked, and I managed to shroud the entire place, including their fields and livestock. The marauders shook their heads in disbelief and kept going."

"Maybe the increase in power was the result of your six-month-long contemplation?"

He chuckled sadly. "I wish. The episode happened a day after my return. I volunteered to go shopping for supplies because I wanted to visit the village prostitutes and end my enforced celibacy. After the shrouding, I no longer had the urge. All that energy had been channeled into the shroud. The same thing happens every time I have to perform a massive thrall or shroud. It's like a climax, just not as pleasurable."

Annani looked at him with narrowed eyes. "What do you do in between? As far as I can remember, your services are not required on a daily or even monthly basis."

Smart goddess.

"I found a wise old human who knew a lot about herbs. She brewed a concoction for me that eased my need. I've been using her recipe ever since."

Annani's brows dipped. "I hope that you have not suffered permanent damage from using it for so long. Even our bodies cannot take that much abuse. If we overeat on a regular basis we get heavy, and if we drink to excess, we get headaches. We are not immune to everything. We just heal fast."

"I know. But trust me, everything still works fine, except for the potion, that is. With Mey around, it seems to be ineffective.

In fact, I got aroused even after all the energy I used up on the shroud I pulled last night."

"Do you still feel guilty?"

"About what I did to deserve my banishment?"

She nodded.

"Yes. I was stupid and vain, and I caused a terrible tragedy. I don't think I will ever get over the guilt."

"That explains it. That is why you remained celibate for so long. But I think that you have paid your dues and then some a long time ago. It is time for you to start living." She shook her head. "I cannot believe that you have been paying for your sins for so many centuries and keeping it to yourself. Why did you keep it a secret?"

Annani's response baffled Yamanu. She wasn't addressing the issue of the clan's safety at all, thinking that his continued abstinence had been fueled by his guilt.

"I didn't remain celibate to punish myself. I did that because I became the clan's shield, and I could not in good conscience stop being that. And as for why I didn't tell anyone, it was because I didn't want to be treated like a martyr. I've been sacrificing enough, and I didn't want to put my friendships on that altar as well. I would have made people uncomfortable."

"I understand. But your martyrdom ends today."

It was a command, not a suggestion.

"What about the clan?"

The goddess waved a dismissive hand. "A different solution will be found. You've paid your dues."

Yamanu rubbed a hand over his jaw. He hadn't shaved since yesterday, and he didn't like the stubble that had sprouted on his face.

His mind was doing it again. Taking him away from where he needed to be.

"I'm terrified, Clan Mother. If something happens to the clan because I cannot defend it, I would never forgive myself."

She put her hand on his arm and leaned in closer. "The Fates have rewarded you with a truelove mate. To refuse their gift is dangerous. If you anger them, they might take away your love as well as your powers."

Yamanu was a believer, and Annani had raised a valid point. "I hadn't thought of that. But that only scares me more. I'm damned if I do, and I'm damned if I don't."

Annani sighed and leaned away. "I think you still suffer from the affliction of vanity. There is always another solution, and no one is irreplaceable. We can try what Sari's people are doing and combine the power of several strong shrouders. Over there, the shroud does not need to be as strong because they are just keeping their castle hidden, not the sounds of explosions and the like, but I bet their method can be improved on. Also, technology is progressing, and our William might invent us a cloaking device."

He chuckled. "Have you been watching *Star Trek*, Clan Mother?"

"Yes, and it is a wonderful show. It shows us what is possible. The idea has to come first, and then someone finds a way to make it a reality. The science fiction of today is the technology of tomorrow, am I right?"

"Absolutely. I think all of Jules Verne's inventions became true."

Annani smiled and patted his arm. "Start living, Yamanu. The clan will survive without your shield. And who knows? Perhaps the Fates will smile upon you and allow you to keep both your love and your powers. Have you thought about that?"

"I didn't dare to hope."

42

LOSHAM

"It was the clan, sir. They were dressed in SWAT uniforms, but those were Guardians."

Losham eyed the lone warrior who had managed to escape the massacre.

Was he a hero or a traitor?

Sixty-five warriors were gone, and they had been the best the Brotherhood had to offer, handpicked to charm female students into accompanying them to the island.

What a loss.

It was a catastrophe Losham wasn't sure how he was going to recuperate from. The other time he'd managed to cover the mass defection with a fake plane crash, but he couldn't use the same cover twice.

Besides, there was the lone survivor. Shafen.

"How can you be sure of that? Did you see fangs? Did you see anyone getting bitten?"

The guy shook his head. "I didn't wait around to see what happened. I drove away."

"How far away were you?"

"They blocked the street, so it was pretty far, but I saw the building, and I saw them storming it. I backed away and got as far from there as I could."

"Why did you wait so long to call me?"

Shafen scratched his beard. "I was scared. Being the bearer of bad news is dangerous. I went back there a couple of hours later, and it was all over. They'd put yellow tape on the entrance."

"Perhaps they were the real police? It might have been a drug bust."

"The men would have thralled the policemen, not shot at them."

Losham narrowed his eyes at Shafen. "How did you know the men shot at the troopers? Didn't you just say that you drove away?"

Each warrior had a handgun and a silencer, but since it had been a surprise attack, they might have not stopped to assemble them. Shafen might have heard the shots.

"When I returned, I saw bullet holes in some of the windows. I can go back and talk to the neighbors, ask if they heard anything."

Why would the men fire at the windows?

The only reason would have been to create an escape path. If the policemen had gone through the door, that left the windows as the only option.

After the defection, Losham had investigated possibilities for attaching trackers to the warriors' spinal cords, but Navuh had objected. Mostly, because he didn't know that Losham's previous crew had not perished in a plane crash, but had absconded with the money and the drugs.

Still, if Shafen was right and the clan took his comrades, then the trackers would have been invaluable. At least they could find the bodies and verify the causes of death.

And if the police had taken the men, it would have enabled

Losham to find them and free them.

The question was what story he was going to tell Navuh.

If he went with the police scenario, Navuh would task him with finding the men, which would buy Losham time to investigate. But if he claimed that the men had been taken by the clan, Navuh might get angry and respond in one of two ways.

He would either recall Losham and punish him for his failure to safeguard the warriors, or he would send an army to find the clan's stronghold and finally take them out.

It was risky.

On the one hand, Losham might get further demoted, but on the other hand, he might be put in charge of a large force and given the okay to hunt the clan.

It wasn't a decision he could make on the spot.

He looked at Shafen. "Just so we are clear. Are you basing your opinion about the identity of the attackers on the bullet holes you saw in the windows?"

The guy nodded. "That's only one thing. I know these men. They weren't stupid or inept. If they'd been faced with human police, they would've gotten away."

"Not if they were neutralized before they had the chance."

Suddenly, Shafen didn't look as convinced. "I don't think that the police would have just shot them without trying to apprehend them first."

Losham put a hand on the guy's shoulder. "The men might have panicked and shot first. If even one bullet was fired, it would have given the police justification to open fire."

"That might be true. But if that's what happened, the majority of the men are not dead, and we need to find them and free them."

Losham nodded. "I hope that they will manage to do so on their own, but if not, we will need reinforcements to search for them."

43

MEY

For a long time, Mey lay awake in bed, waiting for Yamanu to return. But even as distraught and as anxious as she felt, her body eventually gave in to nature's demands, and she drifted off into a restless sleep.

In her dream, she and Jin were running away from a bunch of men in black suits, all wearing identical aviator sunglasses and polished shoes. They looked like the agents in *The Matrix* movies, except that their faces were all different. Nevertheless, even in sleep, she knew it wasn't real. What felt real, though, was Jin's hand in hers.

Mey stopped running and turned to her sister. "Are you trying to tell me something?"

Jin shook her head and tugged on Mey's hand. "We need to keep moving."

Mey's eyes popped open. Did the dream mean anything?

Probably not. Sharing dreams had never been something she and Jin had done. They were close, so naturally Jin appeared in some of Mey's dreams and the other way around, but there had been nothing special about them.

What was real, however, was Yamanu's big body spooning

behind her, and his heavy arm draped over her middle. She must have been deep asleep, not to feel him getting into bed.

"Good morning." He nuzzled her neck.

Mey debated whether to answer him or pretend that she was still asleep. The truth was that she didn't feel like talking to him. She'd promised not to pester him to make up his mind, but she was getting tired of his indecision, his irrational belief in superstition, and most of all, she was tired of feeling disappointed.

Heck, she should be used to that.

Every man she had dated had been disappointing in one way or another. Was she expecting too much?

Not really.

Mey's list of requirements was short and uncomplicated. She wanted her guy to find her attractive and interesting, and she wanted to feel the same about him. She wanted for the two of them to prefer each other's company to that of anyone else's, and she wanted fidelity.

Everything else was negotiable.

Yamanu fulfilled all of her criteria, but the problem was that he might choose what he believed was his duty over her. Should she add choosing her first to that short list of requirements?

The problem with that was that she didn't want her guy to be irresponsible. Someone who just threw everything away for love was not her type either.

She respected Yamanu for his devotion to the clan.

"I know that you are not sleeping." He moved her hair away from her shoulder and kissed it. "Are you mad at me?"

"I'm not mad at you. I'm mad at the situation. But I promised not to nag you about it, so I'm not going to. I'd rather keep on sleeping."

"I've done a lot of thinking this morning. We need to talk."

Mey's gut clenched. If his decision was to induce her, he would have just said it.

The dreaded 'we need to talk' statement could mean only one thing. Yamanu had decided that he couldn't do it and that he was going to keep his vow.

He would probably coat it with a lot of explanations and apologies, but in the end, he would tell her that she had to choose someone else for her induction.

Could she even do that?

Probably not. But maybe one of the scrawnier clan members would agree to fight her and test her hypothesis that female Dormants could be induced in the same way the males were.

Talk about equality.

For a clan that was headed by a female, they were very close-minded about the traditional induction process. How come it hadn't occurred to anyone that females could be good fighters? They could spur aggression in males that had nothing to do with sex, and it would make the entire process so much easier for them.

There would be no need to find a partner and commit to him from the get-go. Kian's two-week ultimatum was ridiculous.

"I'll make coffee." Yamanu planted one more kiss on the back of her neck and got out of bed.

"Okay."

As Yamanu left the room and shut the door behind him, Mey slid from under the comforter. For a moment, she just sat on the bed and tried to get her stomach under control.

She felt nauseous, but that was probably the ice cream's fault, not Yamanu's impending speech about why he couldn't be with her.

With a sigh, she pushed up to her feet and padded to the bathroom.

Perhaps a long hot shower would help calm her nerves. And if everything else failed, she could puke all that nasty ice cream into the toilet.

In any case, she was in no hurry to join Yamanu in the kitchen.

Prisoners on death row did not rush to their own execution.

44

YAMANU

*W*hile waiting for Mey to be done in the shower, Yamanu brewed coffee and made breakfast. He'd even gone on the internet to check out Israeli cuisine. The country's traditional morning meal included a chopped salad, eggs, and a slice of toasted bread with cottage cheese.

He'd made the salad and the eggs. But he didn't have the cheese, so he pulled out a jar of jam from the fridge and a pack of sausages from the freezer. It was going to be a hybrid affair, a meshing of Scottish and Israeli breakfasts.

Looking at the assortment, Yamanu was quite proud of himself. Mey, however, didn't seem to appreciate his efforts. Padding over to the table, she sat down and reached for the coffee mug without saying a thing.

With the pinched expression on her face and the way she was rhythmically tapping her foot on the floor, Yamanu didn't need an immortal's super senses to realize how anxious she was.

He'd better get on with it.

"Since you seem stressed, I'll start at the end of the speech I've prepared. I've decided that it is time to break my vow, and not as a temporary measure. I'm ready to close that chapter of my life."

Mey let out a relieved breath. "Thank God, the merciful Fates, and whatever higher power that guided your decision. And thank you." Her hands were trembling so badly that some of the coffee spilled on the table. She put the mug down. "I want to get up and kiss you, but my legs don't seem to work."

Poor girl. His indecision had put her through the wringer.

Pushing away from the table, he got up, walked over to Mey, and picked her up in his arms. "Now you can kiss me."

With the tears that had pooled in the corners of her eyes succumbing to gravity, twin rivulets started down her cheeks.

As he walked toward the couch, he kissed each tear away, her eyelids, her lips.

"I'm sorry," he said as he sat down, holding Mey close to his chest. "It was a difficult decision to make, and in the end, I needed help to reach it."

"From whom?" Mey wiped her wet cheeks with the back of her hands.

"I guess the Fates."

He chuckled at Mey's raised brow. His girl was not a believer.

"During my morning stroll, I somehow found myself next to Annani's house. She saw me and decided to join me on my walk. We talked, and I told her my dilemma. She told me that I've paid my dues and that I should start living my life."

Mey smiled. "Can I thank her in person? Will she agree to see me?"

"I don't know. The goddess decides who she wants to invite over and when. I don't think she accepts requests for audiences." He rubbed Mey's back. "Aren't you curious to hear what she had to say?"

"I'm guessing that it was something along the lines of telling you to stop believing in superstition and that your vow has nothing to do with your powers. That it is all in your head."

For a long moment, he just gaped at her. "That's what you thought it was? That I invoked the Fates to grant me super-powers in exchange for my vow of celibacy?"

Now Mey looked unsure. "What else could it have been? People usually make vows in exchange for something they desperately need, like protection for their loved ones or cure from disease. In times of great trouble, it's a way for them to feel a little less helpless and hopeless."

"That might be true for humans, but that wasn't what started me on this path. In my case, there is a direct correlation between my abstinence and the increase in power. I channel all of my pent-up sexual energy into my shrouds and thralls."

Mey put her hand on his shoulder. "Seriously? How did you find out that it worked like that? Did you join a monastery or something? Because you had to abstain first to discover that it increased your powers."

Evidently, she was still doubtful.

"It wasn't a voluntary thing. I was banished to an uninhab-ited island for six months. Annani wanted me to have a long time to reflect on my sins, and the punishment she came up with fitted my crime perfectly."

"What did you do? I can't believe that you've ever intention-ally committed a crime. Especially not against your own people."

He leaned and kissed her forehead. "Thank you for believing the best about me." He sighed. "You are right. There was no malice in what I did. I was young and vain, and I thought that pleasuring ladies, whether they were married or not, was my way of spreading the joy."

She smirked. "Typical male with an overinflated ego. But how was that a crime?"

"Those were different times, Mey. And I was supposed to limit myself to widows and paid service providers. Annani specifically warned us against seducing virgins and married women. They were off-limits."

Mey rolled her eyes. "Big deal. So, you had some fun with ladies you weren't supposed to. I bet that you weren't the only one and that the husbands of those ladies were playing around as well."

He shook his head. "Perhaps that was all true, but in my case, I should have been doubly careful and heeded Annani's warning. I didn't look like the average Scot, and when one of my lovers gave birth to my child, it was very obvious to her husband that it wasn't his. He murdered her and my child on the birthing bed, claiming later that they had both died in childbirth. Back then, it wasn't uncommon, but I suspected something."

"What did you do?"

"I entered his mind and saw what he did. Suffice it to say that he didn't wake up the next morning."

Mey's eyes blazed with anger, but it wasn't directed at him. "Good for you. You did the right thing."

"I don't regret that. The murderer had to die. But it was my vanity and rule-breaking that had caused the tragedy. I was stricken with grief and guilt, and I confessed my crimes to the goddess. In her infinite wisdom, she sent me to that uninhabited island, where I had to build a shelter for myself to keep warm in the bitter winter and to hunt for my food. It was a harsh and inhospitable place, and it was perfect for my penance. When it was done, and I came back, I discovered what the long abstinence had done for me. I accepted it as a sign from the Fates that my mission from that point on was to defend the clan. It gave meaning to my suffering."

"Did you ever try to take a break from it? You should have

checked whether releasing your sexual energy naturally diminished your powers."

He shook his head. "I didn't dare. Besides, the way I felt after an intense shroud or thrall was almost like after a climax. I was spent, exhausted, and felt no urge to have sex." He smiled. "Until you came along. Even after the massive shroud that I pulled yesterday, when I came home to you, my libido sprang to life as soon as you jumped on me."

"I'm sorry."

45

MEY

"*W*hy are you sorry?"

As the full impact of Yamanu's confession hit Mey, the tears started flowing again.

The clan depended on him for its safety, and it wasn't about a belief. This wasn't something that existed only in Yamanu's head, it was real, and it had been tested.

More or less.

What he'd said about feeling spent after shrouding or thralling made sense. He used up the reserves of energy he'd built by abstaining.

Frankly, she couldn't understand the goddess. It was true that Yamanu had paid his dues, and it was also true that it wasn't fair to demand further sacrifice from him. But the needs of the many outweighed the needs of the individual, especially when their survival depended on it.

How could she have told him to break his vow?

The goddess probably felt bad for him. Hell, Mey felt devastating sorrow for both of them. She was already mourning the relationship they could have had. But she was also pragmatic.

In fact, Mey was sure that Kian would have never given

Yamanu the okay. As the de facto leader of his people and as someone with a military and strategic background, he would have never given up on an asset like Yamanu only because he felt sorry for him.

"Mey? Why are you crying? I thought you'd be happy."

Resting her forehead against his chest, she whispered, "I can't."

"You can't what?" He hooked a finger under her chin and lifted her head, so she had to look into his eyes. "Talk to me."

"The goddess told you that you've paid your dues and that you've sacrificed enough. That's all true. But if your clan depends on you for its safety, how can you turn your back on that?" Through the mist of tears, she tried to read his expression. "I can't be that selfish, and neither can you." She wrapped her arms around his neck and pressed herself to his solid chest. "As much as it hurts, you need to let me go."

Those had been the hardest words that Mey had ever had to say, and now that they were out, she started sobbing in earnest.

His arms tightened around her. "I can't do that. I won't."

"People depend on you, Yamanu. You have to either erase my memories and send me back to New York or pass me to someone else."

Stroking her hair, he rocked her like a baby. "I'm not going to do either of those things. You are mine, Mey, and I'm going to keep you. The only way I'm letting you go is if you tell me that you don't want me."

"You know that I do." She'd almost blurted that she loved him, but that would have just heaped up more hurt on top of the pain that was already too excruciating to bear.

"The clan will manage without me. As the goddess pointed out, no one is irreplaceable. The Scottish arm of the clan maintains a permanent shroud around their castle by combining the power of several shrouders working in shifts. We can try to do the same here. Also, technology is progressing, and our tech people could come up with some interesting devices. Besides, if abstaining from sex powered my abilities, someone else might be able to do the same. I think it is time I passed my martyr scepter to another male." He kissed the top of her head. "I'm ready for the crown of a mated man. After all, my mate is a queen, so that makes me a king."

Mey chuckled through the tears. "I'm just an ex-beauty queen, not a real one."

"You are my queen."

Lifting the bottom of her long T-shirt, she wiped the tears of her eyes and cheeks. "I bet Kian would not be as merciful and gracious as the goddess. Losing your protection is not something he can afford to do."

"I talked to Kian before I talked to Annani, and you are right, he was hesitant about giving me the green light. But he left the decision up to me."

Mey shook her head. "Your people are really special. Humans are not like that. If the government has my sister, and they know what she can do, they are never going to let her go. They are going to use her without giving a damn about what it does to her or whether she wants to do it or not."

"In my case, never is a very long time. Annani and Kian accept that I've done enough. The Fates rewarded me for the many centuries of sacrifice by bringing you into my life, and to refuse their gift is to court their wrath. They might retaliate by taking you as well as my ability away." He leaned and kissed her lips. "I'm willing to risk my ability, but not you. Besides, who knows? If I'm super nice and express my gratitude in every way I can, they might let me keep both you and my powers."

He was just saying that to ease her conscience. If that was a possibility, he wouldn't have obsessed so much about his decision.

Still, there was nothing wrong with hoping, even if it was illogical.

Not that any of it made sense. If sexual drive was such a powerful force, then monks and nuns would have been performing miracles throughout history.

Except, what if they had? Maybe not all of the stories had been fabrications and exaggerations?

"You are still frowning," Yamanu said. "Not convinced yet?"

She sighed. "I was thinking about all the monks and nuns and how abstinence hasn't made them miracle workers. But then I thought that maybe some of those stories were actually true."

Yamanu rubbed a hand over his jaw. "There might be something to it. But comparing human sex drive to that of immortals is like comparing the engine of a motorcycle to that of a jet fighter. The harnessed energy is limited, and therefore can power much less."

She narrowed her eyes at him. "Sex wasn't among the superpowers you mentioned before."

"Given the circumstances, there was no point in bringing it up." He scratched at his stubble. "But now that I think of it, maybe it's not a good idea for me to stop drinking the potion cold turkey. Maybe I should just lower the dosage. I don't want to unleash the beast while you are still human. He's way too hungry and dangerous."

Yamanu was probably exaggerating. Nevertheless, the idea of him turning into a ravenous beast wasn't frightening. It was arousing.

46

YAMANU

*A*s the scent of Mey's arousal flared, causing a parallel stirring in Yamanu, he realized that she couldn't possibly grasp the difference between human and immortal sex drive, probably because he hadn't explained it.

Instead of dumping the information on her all at once, Yamanu had expected to elaborate when she asked questions. He would have clarified his beast comment, revealing one thing at a time and easing her into it.

Mey wasn't the type who scared easily, but she was still human. He wasn't sure how she would react to the news flash that not only was he thrice as strong as a human male, but he also didn't need time to recuperate between one climax to the next.

Before, when Yamanu had occasionally fantasized about breaking his vow, he'd envisioned booking the entire staff of an escort service for a couple of weeks and going through them one or two at a time.

That way, he could have his fill without exhausting or harming anyone.

Mey shifted in his arms and smiled coyly. "Breaking your

vow is even more monumental than a virgin's wedding night. It should be one hell of a celebration, and it shouldn't be watered down by drugs." Her eyes widened. "I have an idea..."

He put a finger on her lips. "Hold that thought." Scenting the surge in Mey's desire for him, Yamanu loathed tamping down her excitement, but she needed to understand that he hadn't been exaggerating or boasting like a human might. "Before you get all excited, you should know what you're dealing with, and why I can never let go with you while you are still a human."

Her smirk confirmed his suspicion that she wasn't taking his warning seriously. "I'm not afraid of you, Yamanu. You might be big and strong and really starved for sex, but I'm big and strong as well." She kissed the underside of his jaw. "You've chosen your mate wisely."

Hearing Mey refer to herself as his mate warmed Yamanu's heart. It meant that she believed it and accepted the reality of their bond. But referring to herself as big and strong was laughable.

Not that he was going to comment on that. Mey might take offense.

He kissed her forehead. "If anyone should get credit for the wise choice, it's the Fates. They put us in each other's paths. All we deserve credit for is not ignoring their gentle nudge."

Mey snorted. "Gentle? Meeting you was like getting hit by a bolt of lightning. When I gave Alena my business card, I had an ulterior motive. I knew that I had to see you again." She frowned. "I was so disappointed when you didn't come out to meet me. I thought that you were not interested."

"The reason I stayed in my room was that I was way too interested. My reaction to you was just as potent as yours was to me, and if not for the potion tamping down my primal urges, I might have thrown you over my shoulder and run off with you."

Mey laughed. "I would have put up token resistance, just so you wouldn't think me easy, but I would have been smiling all the way to your lair."

He was flattered, but she still wasn't taking his warning seriously.

"Before we get sidetracked again, I need to tell you a few things about immortal sex, and why I think a gradual weaning off the potion is necessary. It's not just my strength that I'm worried about, although this is a major consideration as well. I'm at least three times stronger than a human male my size. Immortal males need practically no recuperating time before they can go again, and they are usually not satisfied with one or two rounds."

He stopped there, letting the information sink in.

Given how long he had abstained and how much he wanted Mey, he could probably go for an entire week until he had his fill. Even an immortal female could not withstand that. A human, well, it was a no.

Mey nodded. "I get what you're trying to say. But I trust you, Yamanu. You will never do anything to harm me, and I know you will stop the moment you realize that I've had enough. The thing is, the potion numbs you, and I don't want you to be numb for our first time together."

"I don't know about that." Yamanu went back to rubbing slow circles on Mey's back. "I've never hurt a woman, during sex or otherwise, but after all this time, I'm not sure how much self-control I have. The potion will give me peace of mind."

She shook her head. "No way. I'd rather chain you to the bed than have you drugged." She smirked. "A kinky wedding night."

So far, Mey had mentioned a wedding night twice. Was that a hint?

The goddess was in the village, so he could probably arrange for a quick, private ceremony. But the problem was that there was still a small chance that Mey wasn't a Dormant, and he couldn't pledge himself to her before that was determined, or better yet, she transitioned.

Still, they could make it special without a formal ceremony.

Maybe an engagement?

The gods used to have those, humans still did, so why not introduce a new tradition to the clan?

Since finding mates was a recent phenomenon, the clan was still in the process of developing the traditions surrounding the mated bond. So far, every wedding had been different, and some couples had opted not to have one at all.

None had bothered with an engagement, though.

Should he and Mey be the first?

Except, he was pretty sure a ring was required, and he didn't have one. What else did he need?

Mey cupped his cheek. "Are you still thinking about my proposal? Because I was joking. I don't want you tied up any more than I want you drugged. I'm an old-fashioned kind of girl, and I like my man to take the lead in bed." She smiled sheepishly. "But if you need reassurances that you are not going to kill me with too much sex, you can give me one of those taser guns you guys used on the Doomers. Wonder told me how effective they are. I can put it under the pillow in case the beast refuses to be tamed by words alone."

Yamanu was sure that Mey had been joking again, but that was actually not a bad idea.

MEY

G iddy with excitement, Mey had come up with one absurd idea after another, but even though her suggestions hadn't been serious, she really didn't want Yamanu to be drugged anymore.

Not only because she wanted to experience the real him, but because she had a feeling that more than his sex drive had been numbed for centuries. It was time he started enjoying life to its fullest, and not through hazy sunglasses.

"That's actually not a bad idea." He scratched at his day-old stubble. "It will give me peace of mind knowing that you can stop me if I go nuts."

Mey laughed. "I don't need a taser. A rolling pin could be just as effective. A baseball bat would be even better, but it's not going to be comfortable under the pillow. Maybe a frying pan? You know, one of those old-fashioned cast iron ones." She pretended to swing one at his head. "Boom, out goes the light."

He tweaked her nose. "You think that you are being funny, but it's not a laughing matter. I'm serious."

With a sigh, she rested her cheek on his chest, listening to his big heart beat slow and steady. "Don't worry. If all else fails, I'll perform the Vulcan nerve pinch."

"You're still joking."

Yamanu was starting to sound exasperated, and Mey debated whether to pull out her secret weapon now or save it for later. If she used it now, it would lose the shock effect, which she was certain would stop him no matter how far gone he was.

Then again, if she kept it for later, Yamanu might sneak in a dose or two of his damned potion because he was afraid of hurting her.

Then there was her own fear of rejection, but that was highly unlikely. Mey knew how Yamanu felt about her, even if he hadn't told her. After all, he was breaking a centuries-long vow and was willing to leave his clan unprotected for her. She didn't need any more proof of how deep his feelings ran.

Still, there were two things that were fueling her insecurity.

One was her being a potential Dormant, which made her highly desirable to Yamanu as well as to all the other single clan males. That alone would have guaranteed a long line of suitors regardless of who she was as a person, and whether she was even attractive or not.

The other one was Yamanu himself, and the fact that he hadn't verbalized his feelings for her yet.

It would have been nice to hear him say it first.

Then again, if he was breaking a freaking super important vow for her, she could at least thank him with the best she had to offer.

"I know what will stop you, and this time it's not a joke."

"That I would like to hear."

She chuckled. "I bet. So here it goes. I love you, Yamanu, and I'm pretty sure that you love me too. Your love for me won't let you hurt me, and if in the height of passion you forget, I will remind you."

The only response she got was Yamanu's arms tightening around her.

Was he too stunned to say anything?

Or had she been mistaken about his feelings, and it was all about finding a suitable mate who could one day have his children, and not about love?

"Aren't you going to say anything?"

He swallowed. "I love you. I was trying to come up with something that sounded better than that, but all I could think of was asking you to marry me. Not right now, but maybe after we find your sister. I know that you would like to have her at our wedding. And your parents too, although that means that I'll have to ask the goddess to compel them to silence, and I don't know if she's still going to be here in two weeks."

Tears prickled the backs of Mey's eyes.

Sweet, sweet Yamanu was babbling like a schoolboy, and it was the most endearing thing ever to see the big, powerful man lose it because he was overwhelmed with emotion.

Lifting her hands, she cupped his cheeks and kissed him lightly on the lips. "Yes, I'll marry you, but only after I transition. There is still a chance that I won't."

He kissed her back, just a soft brush of his lips. "I'll pray to the Fates every morning, noon, and night until you are safely on the other side." He shook his head. "This was probably the most underwhelming proposal ever, and I'm so sorry about that. I don't even have a ring to give you. But I'm going to get one. Today." He looked into her eyes. "Do you want to choose it? How is it usually done?"

Her heart overflowing with happiness, Mey laughed. "You don't have to rush to get me a ring. We can wait with that for the wedding. And just to ease your mind, I'm not big on proto-col, I am big on feelings. Let's make tonight special."

"How?"

If she could run out to a store, she could have come up with a few creative ideas. But since she was stuck in the village until her transition, she would either have to make do with what she could find in the house, which probably wasn't much, or solicit the help of her new friends.

The problem with that was that they would ask what was the special occasion. Could she claim that she wanted to cele-brate their ten-day anniversary?

Heck, why not?

It was crazy, but it was also romantic, and from the stories they had told her, the insanity was not unusual for immortal couples, or rather immortals and Dormants.

Talk about hit by lightning.

The girls were going to love it.

The other problem was how to plan anything with Yamanu in the house. Seeing her preparing things for tonight would take away from the experience.

"Leave it to me." She kissed his cheek, then frowned. "Did you take your potion today already?"

He shook his head. "Last night was the last time."

"Good. The question is whether one day is long enough for your body to get rid of it all."

He chuckled. "Trust me, it is. I don't know how I'm going to last until the evening." He eyed her speculatively. "Unless you are willing to forgo the preparations and get in bed right now."

"No way!" She slapped his chest. "This night needs to be special, and I'm going to do my damnedest to make it so. But in order for that to work, I need you out of the house." She scrunched her nose. "That's the part I feel bad about. I don't want to kick you out of your own home, but I can't prepare anything with you watching. It would ruin the fun."

"Don't feel bad. If I want to last until the night, I need to get away from you and spend the entire time in the gym. Hopefully, the physical exhaustion will tame the beast." He tilted his head. "Or is that not okay with you either?"

"No, that's fine. I just don't want you to be drugged. I want you to be fully into the experience."

48

LOKAN

"What should I wear?" Carol asked.

Looking at her standing in front of the closet, wearing only a skimpy bra and an even skimpier pair of panties, Lokan could only think about her taking them off and not about what she should put over them.

"Something elegantly casual."

Pursing her lips, she put her hands on her hips. "You're not helping. You are taking me to an important business meeting, and I don't know whether I should put on a dress or a suit."

He leaned back on his forearms to get a better viewing angle. "A dress. You are supposed to be the distraction, so I can enter Malcolm's mind while he is drooling over you."

Carol looked at him over her shoulder. "That might be risky. What if you get jealous and your eyes start glowing, or worse, your fangs make an appearance?"

"Not going to happen. I know you have a thing for powerful men, but I'm not worried. Malcolm is in his late seventies."

She arched a brow. "And he still runs the business? Good for him."

"He is still one of the sharpest guys I know, and he's a workaholic. He's going to die clutching his keyboard."

Malcolm Roderick was the founder and CEO of a cybersecurity firm that provided services for the US government when discretion was key. Which was why he was one of the few people who knew about the existence of the secret paranormal division. Naturally, the guy hadn't volunteered the information, and Lokan had stumbled upon it accidentally while searching Malcolm's brain for something else.

At the time, he hadn't dug too deeply, but later on, he'd regretted not going for more details.

Today, he was going to remedy that oversight, not for his own purposes, but per Kian's request.

Carol smiled like a she-devil. "I'll wear this." She pulled a form-fitting dark blue dress out of the closet. "It's elegant, but not overly so, and it displays my assets to perfection."

Unable to help himself, he reached for her hand and pulled her down to him. "I think we have time for a quickie."

Carol put a finger on his lips, preventing him from kissing her. "Save it for later, tiger. You're going to mess up my makeup, and I won't have time to reapply it." She pushed back by bracing on his chest.

With a sigh, he let her go.

They had dinner reservations for five, and given the unpredictability of traffic, it was best if they left the hotel in ten minutes or so.

Luckily, Carol didn't take long to finish getting dressed.

"How do I look?" she asked.

He smiled. She did it every time they went out, and his answer was always the same. "Ravishing."

"I'm going to get you a thesaurus app for your phone."

He lifted his hands. "What is wrong with ravishing? There is no better word to describe you. It encompasses beautiful, alluring, elegant, delightful, sexy… should I go on?"

"Not if we want to make it on time." Carol stifled a smirk as she lifted her purse off the dresser. "Let's go."

Even with the rush hour traffic, they arrived at the restaurant a few minutes before Malcolm, which was how Lokan liked it. Small things like that mattered. People appreciated not having to wait and viewed tardiness as disrespectful.

As Lokan had expected, the moment Malcolm walked in, his eyes zeroed in on Carol and a wide grin spread over his face.

Getting up, Lokan offered the guy his hand. "Hello, Malcolm. Let me introduce my fiancée, Carol."

Carol followed his example and got up as well. "Hi." She smiled as she offered him her hand.

"Enchanted." He lifted it to his lips for a kiss. "Congratulations. When is the wedding, and do I have time to steal you away from this handsome devil?"

Carol laughed. "I'm afraid it's too late for that. I'm hooked."

"What a shame." Malcolm pulled out a chair and sat down. "Let's order a bottle of wine to celebrate your engagement."

For the next half an hour or so, Lokan pretended to be interested in soliciting Malcolm's services for an imaginary client, hinting that he was referring to the island. Regrettably, Malcolm had visited only once and hadn't shown any desire to come back. Which meant that any information they wanted to pick up from his brain had to be done on his turf.

After coffee and dessert were served, Malcolm turned his attention back to Carol. "So, what do you do, young lady?"

"I write a foodie blog. Next time you are in Washington, check it out before choosing where to eat."

As the two chatted about the various eateries and Carol's unique rating system, Lokan reached into Malcolm's brain.

Disarmed by Carol's easy charm, the guy had his defenses all the way down, and probing him was like flipping through an open picture album.

There was a lot of technical stuff in there, most of which Lokan couldn't begin to understand, some meetings and phone conversations with government officials, and interactions with friends and family.

Regrettably, the memory of hearing someone talking about the government's paranormal division was the same one Lokan had already seen, and there were no new ones.

It seemed that Malcolm was a dead end as far as that went. Still, it was a good opportunity to probe him for other things that might prove useful to the Brotherhood.

"What about you, Malcolm?" Carol asked. "I'm sure you've done work for some interesting people. I know that you can't drop names, but I'm sure you have some fascinating stories." She leaned closer to him. "You can tell me. I'm good at keeping secrets." She added a wink.

Damn, he should take her with him to all his meetings. If she could have Roderick wrapped around her little finger like that, she could be an incredibly useful tool.

"Well, there was this one guy," Malcolm said. "A couple of years ago, a reclusive billionaire, whose name I won't mention, bought a huge house in one of the most affluent cities in the Bay Area. The odd thing about this job was that next to the existing house, he built an even bigger underground structure that went three stories deep. It was like freaking NORAD, including the latest and best in computer equipment and communications."

"What's NORAD?" Carol asked.

"It's the North American Aerospace Defense Command. It's a secure bunker built inside the Cheyenne Mountain, protected against EMP pulses. During an emergency, its stored supplies can last one thousand people for a month. I'm only telling you that because that's public knowledge. There are other doomsday scenario facilities that I can't talk about." He shook his head. "I have no idea how he got permits for that. My guess is that he either bribed someone or donated a shitload of money to the mayor's re-election campaign."

Or if the billionaire was a powerful immortal, he could've either thralled or compelled the city officials to grant him the permits for his compound.

Lokan's interest was piqued. "How many people could live in that underground structure?"

Malcolm shrugged. "Comfortably, about a hundred. A little more, packed, probably three to four times as many. Perhaps he wants to run his business from home, so to speak, and provide his staff with living quarters. He would have never been allowed to build such a monster above ground, so that might have been the motivation for it."

"Did you meet the guy in person?" Lokan probed further in case he'd missed seeing it in Malcolm's brain.

Malcolm shook his head. "Everything was done online, and no one was living in the place while we worked there. I won't mention how much he paid for our services, but I can say that it was the biggest private job we've ever done."

Carol and Lokan exchanged glances.

What Malcolm had described resembled the keep's infrastructure, which made it a perfect setup for a bunch of immortals seeking a secure hideout. Since it didn't belong to the clan or to the Brotherhood, could it belong to a group of unidentified immortals?

It was a long shot, but it was worth investigating.

It sounded like the ideal environment for Kalugal and his men.

"Anyone know where his money comes from?" Lokan asked.

Malcolm shrugged. "No. I'm pretty sure that he uses an alias too. He could be a Russian oligarch or a Wall Street maverick."

Lokan chuckled. "Why only those two options?"

"A hunch. You can tell a lot about people by the vocabulary they use. His English was perfect, but here and there I caught a phrase that didn't fit as precisely. Those are the kind of mistakes that well-educated foreigners make, which made me think either a Russian oligarch or an oil prince. I discarded the oil prince because he would have no need for an underground facility."

"What about Wall Street? What made you think in that direction?"

"Again, his vocabulary. He used many trade-specific terms." Malcolm shrugged again. "But I'm playing Sherlock here. I might be totally off. He could an international drug lord for all I know."

"But you don't think so."

"No, not really."

49

MEY

*A*fter looking through the kitchen cabinets, the pantry, the laundry room, and Yamanu's closet, Mey hadn't found a single thing she could use to create a romantic atmosphere.

There were no candles to light, no incense to provide a pleasant aroma, and no roses were growing in Yamanu's back or front yard to collect petals from.

He didn't even have wine.

Whiskey and that awful beer he liked to drink were not exactly romantic drinks.

She had no choice. If she wanted to make tonight special, she had to call one of her new friends.

Wonder was the first one that came to mind because she had the best rapport with her, but she didn't seem like the type to go for romantic gestures. Callie was second, but her idea of a romantic evening was probably a pair of handcuffs and a flogger.

Mey chuckled.

She would've never suspected sweet, unassuming Callie to be into the kinky stuff. Her mate, however, that was a different story. Mey could certainly imagine Brundar in a pair of leather pants.

Bad girl. She admonished herself. This wasn't the time to think about other couples' sex lives.

Kian's wife seemed like the romantic type, but Mey wouldn't dare call her even if she happened to have her number. Carol would have been a perfect choice, but she wasn't around.

It was either Wonder or Callie.

She chose Callie. Maybe kinky couples did romantic stuff too.

"Hi, Callie. I'm calling to find out if Brundar is still alive, or did you kill him and hide the body in your backyard?"

"Ha, ha. Very funny. He's alive. How about Yamanu? I bet he is exhausted after the shrouding he did last night."

"Actually, he's in the gym. We slept until late, though. Listen, I need a favor."

"Anything."

"I'm planning a romantic evening for Yamanu to celebrate our engagement."

Damn, she hadn't planned on using this as an excuse. It just came out of her mouth without thinking.

The shriek Callie released was deafening. "Congratulations! Who proposed to whom and when?"

"Yamanu proposed to me this morning, but don't get too excited. It's a tentative proposal that is conditional on my transition. So please don't tell anyone."

"Oh, girl, this is going to be so hard, but I'll keep my mouth shut. I promise. What do you need me to do?"

"I didn't find anything in the house that I could use to create a romantic atmosphere. No candles or candlesticks, no wine, and the fridge is practically empty, so I can't make anything good for dinner. If I could, I would run to the nearest store and buy whatever I need, but until I transition, I'm grounded here."

"Say no more. The food is no problem. My house is always fully stocked. Anything in particular you have in mind?"

"Frankly, I have no clue. I just know that it's not frozen pizza."

"Let me think. We don't want anything too heavy or too garlicky." Callie chuckled. "You don't want to chase away the vampire. You want to get him in the right mood. Pasta is messy, and steak is too everyday. How about fish? I can make an awesome salmon dish."

"Sounds good to me. Do you know if Yamanu likes fish?"

It was embarrassing how little she knew about the guy she'd just agreed to marry.

"No clue. But I haven't met anyone yet who didn't like this dish. I think it's a safe bet. So that's settled. I also have a nice selection of wines. I don't have candles, but that's not a problem. I can go on a quick scavenging run and get everything you need. How about sexy lingerie? I know Amanda always has new designer stuff that she'd be overjoyed to contribute."

"I'm good in that department."

"What else? I can hook you up with several silk scarves, those are multipurpose. You can use one as a blindfold and the others to tie Yamanu to the bed."

Mey laughed. "You are making me blush."

"That was the intention. But seriously. There is a lot you can do with silk scarves, and it doesn't need to be kinky. Go on YouTube to get some ideas."

"Thanks for the suggestion. I will. And thank you so much for doing this for me. I owe you."

"Nonsense. You can pay me back by making me one of your bridesmaids."

"The spot is yours regardless. But once I'm a fully accepted member of the clan and can go shopping, I'm going to invite you and Brundar for dinner. I'm not nearly as good a cook as you are, but I'm decent."

"Offer accepted. See you in an hour." Callie ended the call.

Mey glanced at her watch. How did Callie plan on cooking dinner and collecting romantic paraphernalia in such a short time?

The better question was, what was Mey going to do in the meantime?

Perhaps she could go on YouTube and find out what silk scarves could be used for.

50

KIAN

*K*ian glanced at his watch. It was after six and time to call it a day. Syssi expected him home by seven, and he was looking forward to eating dinner with her and hearing all about her day. The question was whether he should relax first with a cigarillo on the roof or go home and smoke it in the backyard.

His phone ringing solved the dilemma.

Kian had been expecting a call from Lokan after his meeting with the government contact, and hopefully, the guy had some good news about the paranormal division's location.

If there was one.

He accepted the call while heading for the stairs. "Hello, Lokan. Got anything for me?"

"I do, but it's not what you've been expecting. The guy I met had no new information about the paranormal talent collection effort, but he told Carol and me a very interesting story about a civilian job he did a couple of years ago. A reclusive billionaire, whose name he obviously couldn't reveal, bought a mansion in the Bay Area and added a three-story deep underground bunker that could house a hundred people comfortably, and installed a state-of-the-art computer and communications system. He hired my guy to handle the cyber-security for the house and for the basement complex."

Kian pulled out the cigarillo box and sat down on the rocker chair. "It's an interesting story, but I don't see how it has anything to do with our search for the paranormals the government is supposedly collecting." He lit up and took a puff.

Lokan chuckled. "Your head is still geared toward the para-normals. This is about something completely unrelated."

"Like what?"

"Doesn't the setup make you curious? A big underground facility? A reclusive billionaire who my contact suspects made his money on Wall Street?"

As soon as Lokan mentioned Wall Street, the cogs in Kian's mind shifted gears. "You think that it might be Kalugal?"

"It's a possibility that is worth checking out."

"It's probably a long shot, but I can have my hackers gather more information about the guy. Do you have the address?"

"I do. After Malcolm told us the story, I peeked into his brain and got the name of the city as well as a visual of the location. That was enough for me to find it on Google Maps."

"Good work. Text it to me."

A long moment passed before Lokan spoke again. "I need your word that you are not going to take out Kalugal and his men. I will not aid you in doing that."

That was to be expected, but Kian couldn't give his word without knowing what he was dealing with first. He also didn't need Lokan to tell him the address.

As long as he knew the mansion was in the Bay Area, he could find out the rest by checking out real estate transactions that were about two years old, and then cross-referencing the information with city records of building permits granted in the same timeframe. Even in an affluent area, probably not many mega mansions had exchanged owners about two years ago, and even fewer had undergone extensive renovations and expansions.

Still, Lokan had called him with the information, and he needed assurances that he hadn't betrayed his brother by doing so.

"Look. My mother asked me to look for Kalugal as a favor to yours, so it's not like I have malicious intentions toward the guy. But if I discover that he poses a threat to my clan or that he is involved in something really bad, I can't promise you that I will do nothing about it. I can promise you, however, that I will not take any steps against him or concerning him without consulting with you first."

"Fair enough. Let me know the moment you learn anything."

"I will. You have my word."

A few moments later Kian got a message with the address, forwarded it to William, and then called the guy.

"Where did you get it?" William asked.

"From Lokan." Kian relayed the rest of the information. "I want you to check it out. See if you can hack into the security system."

"From what you've told me, that system is not going to be hackable. What I can do, however, is hack into the security feed of nearby restaurants and cafés. If he ventures outside his home, which he must if he wants to meet any ladies to seduce, then we can probably catch his face on one of those."

"Sounds like a plan."

"Do you want me to stop the other searches? We are maxed out."

"Yeah, I think this is worth checking out first. How long will it take you?"

"How far back do you want me to go? A week? A month?"

"Let's make it a month. I want to either confirm that it's him or discard the information and move on. What do you think, should I send someone with a drone to snoop around? Or maybe install a camera across the street from his gate?"

"If the guy hired the best cybersecurity firm in the country to protect his data, I'm sure he has done no less with his other security measures. We don't want to spook him prematurely. After we confirm that it's him, we can decide what to do next."

"Right. Except, even if you don't find his puss in the feeds, it doesn't mean that he's not there."

"I'm aware of that. But again, let's exhaust this first. After investing so many millions in this location, the guy is not going anywhere unless he feels threatened, and I doubt he stays home and never goes out."

"True."

After hanging up with William, Kian lit up another cigarillo and pushed back on the rocker. Holding the phone with one hand, he scrolled through his saved photos until he found Kalugal's. It was a scan of the portrait Tim had drawn, but even on the device's small screen, Kalugal's personality shone through.

He was a good-looking fellow, with striking blue eyes and brown hair, but his best feature was his smile.

The guy was a charmer.

His coloring was lighter than Lokan's, but they shared the same cunning expression in their eyes. Except, where Lokan looked serious and intense, Kalugal looked amused.

If he was the reclusive billionaire, though, then he was obviously not as light-hearted as he appeared in the portrait, and he was very serious about security. Which meant that finding out what he was doing in that bunker of his was going to be extremely difficult. Even more so than infiltrating a secret government facility holding paranormals.

Yamanu's shrouding and thralling wasn't going to be helpful because it only worked on humans, and conventional means of spying weren't going to work either because the recluse was at the top of his game in that regard.

Which brought to Kian's mind Mey and Jin's extraordinary spying talents. Could Jin's ability work on immortals?

What she could do was quite incredible. With one touch, she formed a connection to a person and could then spy on him or her whenever needed.

The question was whether she could do the same with immortals.

Mey's talent worked on both, but then she listened to information stored in the walls, and it wasn't about mental connection. Jin's talent required hands-on, literally, so it might be ineffective on immortals.

Still, there was a chance that it was.

If they managed to find her, Jin could help them spy on Kalugal. Provided that he was indeed the reclusive billionaire, she could walk into a restaurant or a café he was visiting, touch him, and that was it. From that point on, it would be as if they had a hidden camera attached to his forehead.

51

ANNANI

"Hello, my darling son." Annani motioned for Kian to bend down so she could kiss him. "I hope you came because you missed me and not because you have bad news."

"In fact, I might have a bit of good news, although it could be premature."

Kian had given her a thorough update about the mission without smoothing the edges for a change. He had not tried to minimize the consequences of what might happen if some of the Doomers had managed to escape and report that it had been the clan and not the police who had seized their comrades.

Annani appreciated that. Shielding her from the clan's problems was absurd, and she was glad Kian had finally realized it.

"I am always eager for good news." She motioned to the couch.

He waited until she was seated before sitting down himself. "I asked Lokan to arrange meetings with the contacts from whom he'd learned about the paranormal program. Earlier today, he had such a meeting in the Bay Area, and although he didn't learn anything new about the government's paranormal division, he discovered other interesting information."

Annani listened to his report without interrupting, but her eyebrows hiked up a few times. It was not like Kian to make assumptions on so little information.

"The reclusive billionaire could be anyone, Kian. And his reason for building an emergency bunker might be simple paranoia and not a cadre of immortal warriors he needs to hide. Many people are concerned with nuclear power in the hands of unstable dictatorial regimes. Without proper safeguards, a crazy despot could cause the end of the world. Sometimes I get afflicted by such fears as well, and then I think that we should build proper shelters for our people."

"That's actually not a bad idea. Except, those are insanely expensive to build, and we can't afford them at this time." He sighed. "Sometimes, I wish we didn't have such high standards for ourselves. We could have all the money we needed by doing what we suspect Kalugal does. You can get very rich very fast by trading stocks when you have inside information."

"That is true." She patted his knee. "But that would be cheating, and innocent people would be affected negatively. Our mission is to make life better for everyone on the planet, and we do that by promoting new and better technologies and democracy."

"I know, Mother. It's just that sometimes I get frustrated with how long it takes."

"There are no shortcuts, my son." She chuckled. "I read all those ridiculous claims of people achieving great things by working only a few hours a day or even a week, and I feel sorry for all the fools who believe in that, spending their lives searching for those shortcuts, or hacks as they call them now, instead of working hard. I am all for working smart, mind you, but nothing significant can be achieved without putting in the time and effort first."

Kian nodded. "Then I'll rephrase. I wish I were smarter and could achieve more in less time."

"Another way to approach this problem is to surround yourself with smart people who can aid you. But I know that you have tried and have not seen much success."

"I've had some. Turner is a great asset, and if not for my damn pride, I could have relegated all security matters to him. Bridget is awesome at leading the war against traffickers and rescuing their victims, Vanessa is managing the rehabilitation center without any input from me, and Julian is doing a great job with the halfway house."

"Indeed. It is only in business that you have a hard time finding competent people."

"Right, but we got sidetracked. I came to tell you about the new clue and to ask you about the various powers the gods used to have. Do you remember anyone having Mey's ability?"

"Listening to the echoes of past conversations embedded in walls?"

He nodded.

"I am not sure. There were many rumors, some of which were spread by the gods with the intention of making them look even more powerful than they were. I heard about a lot of bizarre abilities, but I cannot tell you whether they were real."

"What about what Mey's sister can do? Touching a person and creating a permanent link to him or her?"

Annani shook her head. "I have never heard of a thing like that. I can remote view on occasion, and the viewing takes place in real time as well, but it is an unpredictable ability, and I cannot use it at will. So, in a way, Jin is more powerful than I am. On the other hand, I do not need to touch the person or even to know him or her to see what they are doing. I regard it as something the Fates wish for me to see, and not a power that I possess."

Kian leaned forward and braced his elbow on his knees. "I wonder about Mey and Jin's peculiar abilities and how they came to be. What if they are the next step in human evolution and have nothing to do with us? If they exhibit powers that even the gods did not have, they might not be carriers of the godly genes."

"Fates forbid." Annani put her hand over her heart. "Poor Yamanu would be devastated. I saw him walking outside early this morning and went out to see what was troubling him. He told me about his dilemma."

Kian narrowed his eyes. "What exactly did he tell you?"

"I am not at liberty to reveal his secrets, but he is worried about losing his powers if he takes Mey as his mate."

Letting out a breath, Kian relaxed his shoulders. "I assume that he told you about his celibacy and the reasons for it."

"He did. Did he tell you as well?"

"Yes, and I didn't know what advice to give him. On the one hand, I can't expect Yamanu to keep it up because it is grossly unfair to him, but on the other hand, I'm afraid of losing his ability to protect the clan and to shroud missions. I can't begin to imagine how much worse last night's fiasco would have been without Yamanu's shroud. And that's another matter I wanted to discuss with you. If Yamanu is not willing to pass Mey to another male, we might consider inducing her the way we did with Turner. Although I can't think of a way that we could explain how she transitioned without revealing your part in it."

Annani nodded. "That won't be necessary. I told Yamanu to go ahead and claim his mate. If he loses his powers, which I hope he will not, we will find another solution."

"I think it is safe to assume that he will lose it. From the way he explained it, I understand that his repressed sexual energy is channeled into his shrouds and thralls. Without it, there would be no fuel."

Annani put a hand on Kian's arm. "I am not sure about that at all. Yamanu is an old immortal, and he has been doing this for a very long time. I think there is a good chance he will still be able to harness the necessary energy when needed. He can do that with meditation, or maybe even with short-term abstinence. Several days without sex might be all he needs. In any case, he cannot refuse a gift from the Fates. To do so is to court their wrath."

52

YAMANU

"You've had enough, my man." Anandur caught the bar, lifted it off Yamanu's chest, and put it back on the rack. "If you want, I can put on lower weights. But I think you should call it a day."

"You're right."

The truth was that Yamanu was so done that he probably couldn't lift a chair, but fear was driving him to push harder. The more exhausted he was, the less chance there was of him hurting Mey.

"What time is it?"

Anandur glanced at his watch. "It's six-thirty."

Yamanu was supposed to get back home in an hour, and he still needed to shower, shave, and get dressed.

"Can I ask what this is all about?" Anandur threw a bunch of paper towels on his chest. "You usually train hard, but not this hard."

Pushing up to a sitting position, Yamanu grabbed a couple of the towels and wiped the sweat off the back of his neck. "Killing time. I didn't do shit in New York, and I was starting to feel flabby."

Not a lie, just not the complete truth.

Anandur let out a breath. "Good. I was starting to worry that there was trouble in paradise. Everything okay at home?"

"Perfect." Yamanu pushed up to his feet. "Thanks for spotting me. I'm going to hit the showers."

Anandur shook his head. "I don't know why you guys use the gym's when we all live only minutes away. It's gross."

"I want to come home clean and smelling of cologne. Not sweat."

"You have a valid point. Except, my Wonder likes me ragged, and since I start my workout with a clean body, I don't stink at the end of it."

Lifting his arm, Yamanu sniffed at his armpit. "It's not too bad, but I'd rather come home looking and smelling fresh. You and Wonder are an old couple by now. I'm still in the courtship stage."

Anandur grinned. "If you are still courting, you should get flowers for your lady. And a box of chocolates is always appreciated."

Damn, he should have thought of that.

"Thanks for the advice. I need to get going."

As he rushed toward the showers, Yamanu heard Anandur chuckle softly. Hopefully, it wasn't because the advice he'd given was misleading.

Yamanu was rusty as hell, and he had no idea what constituted courtship these days. Six centuries ago, flowers and sweets were customary tools of seduction. Jewelry had been even better. But now? People were hooking up, not courting, and chivalry was dead.

Or just about.

Except, perhaps it was better this way. More honest. There was a clear demarcation between seeking a partner for a relationship or for sex, and the two were no longer considered one and the same. There were fewer mixed signals, and everyone knew what they were signing up for.

More or less.

Still, it was safer to show up with flowers and candy than without.

The problem was that he couldn't buy anything in the time he had. The drive back and forth would take him at least an hour, and he had about fifty minutes left.

He needed to improvise.

As he smeared conditioner over his long hair, Yamanu went through his list of friends, trying to remember who grew flowers in their front or back yards. None of the Guardians did. Gertrude only grew herbs. Then he remembered Roni mentioning that Ruth liked to grow things in her garden. The question was whether those things were flowers.

He could stop by her place on his way home.

As for chocolates, he knew that Ella had a weakness for Godiva, so maybe she had a hidden stash she was willing to part with for a good cause.

An excellent cause.

Even after the exhausting workout, thinking about what was waiting for him at home had him sprout a flagpole. Luckily, Anandur went home to shower, and there was no one else there to make fun of him.

Not that he would have cared.

For the first time in forever, Yamanu felt truly alive. If not for the fear of hurting Mey churning in his gut, he would have shouted his happiness to the world, singing and dancing in the village square like a fool.

One day without the bloody potion and he already felt like a new man. He hadn't realized how much that thing had been stifling his senses. Suddenly, Yamanu felt everything more acutely, from the water cascading down his back, to the soap on his skin, the smells, the sounds, everything was sharper, more alive.

It was like he'd been living on mute for all those centuries and watching the world through mud-covered lenses.

Apparently, he'd been sacrificing much more than sex for his people.

53

MEY

The table was set, the bedding was laundered and put back, and Mey was soaking in the bathroom trying to relax.

Callie had delivered everything she'd promised and then some.

Two aromatic candles were burning in the bedroom, a delicious meal was keeping warm in the oven, and a bottle of fine white wine was chilling in the fridge.

She'd even brought an elegant tablecloth, which was smart of her because all Mey had found in Yamanu and Arwel's cabinets was a pack of paper ones.

Still, even though everything was ready and the bath was supposed to soothe her frayed nerves, the urge to chew on her nails was almost uncontrollable.

She wasn't a virgin for goodness sake, so why was she so nervous? And it wasn't as if she and Yamanu had dated for a long time, and she was desperate to get him in bed either.

It was about how monumental it was going to be for Yamanu. After such a long abstinence, Mey had nothing to fear as far as performance went. There was no way he would find her unsatisfactory. Heck, as long as she got excited for him, which wasn't going to be a problem, he was going to be happy.

Or so she hoped.

With the way her stress level was climbing by the minute, when the time came to be a sex goddess, she might freeze up. Anxiety was the kryptonite of arousal.

To relax, Mey needed to meditate, but doing so in Yamanu's home felt like an intrusion, an invasion of privacy. She might hear the echoes of private conversations between him and Arwel that were about Guardian business and hadn't been meant for civilian ears. Especially for those of someone who wasn't a fully-fledged citizen of the village yet.

She'd already chosen what she was going to wear. The red wrap dress had been an easy choice because Yamanu seemed to like it, and it was easy to take off. He'd already seen her in it a couple of times, but that was okay.

He wasn't going to mind.

Besides, she hadn't packed much, and her selection was limited. Unless she wanted to use the scarves that Callie had brought. She could fashion an outfit out of them, and then remove them one at a time while belly dancing. That was what she'd found on YouTube as far as sexy times with scarves went.

The problem was that she didn't know how to belly dance, and what she'd tried in front of the mirror had looked pathetic. She had never been a good dancer, probably because she was too self-conscious about her height and trying to slouch so she wouldn't tower over her partners.

Regrettably, there would be no scarf dance tonight, and it was time to get out of the bathtub and get ready.

Stepping out of the water, Mey wrapped herself in a fluffy bath sheet and walked over to the vanity. Her hair wasn't overly long, but it was thick, and it took a long time to blow-dry. The good thing was that no styling was needed unless she decided to pin it up in some interesting way.

Nah, that was only going to interfere.

Without the potion stifling his desire, Yamanu might not even have the patience to eat dinner first.

He was probably going to attack her like a hungry beast.

Mey smiled. It would actually be best if Yamanu walked in, lifted her up, and took her to bed. There would be no time for an awkward conversation or for the anxiety to build up.

Perhaps she should wait for him with nothing on but the towel wrapped around her body. That would send a clear message. But then all her efforts to make this evening special would be wasted.

What would it be?

A romantic dinner and hopefully a conversation that would be about love and commitment and future plans, or a full-frontal assault and wild sex?

Frankly, she wasn't sure which one she preferred.

Leave it up to Yamanu and see what happens. That was the best and least stressful approach. If the decision was out of her hands, she had nothing to get anxious about.

Just like she used to do before an important test in school, Mey thought about everything she had done to prepare. If she had done everything she could and there was nothing further she could have done, then there was no reason to keep on stressing. From that point on, it was up to luck or fate or the teacher's whims.

As her mother always said, "You do the best you possibly can, and then give yourself a reward for a job well done. The rest doesn't matter. The only one you need to please is you."

Yeah, but what if she did the best she could, and it wasn't enough?

To accept failure after putting up the best effort wasn't easy. Especially when so much was riding on it.

Don't be silly, she said to the mirror. *It's only sex, and as long as you don't freeze up, it's going to be okay.*

Satisfying a man who had gone without for centuries was going to be easy. The big question was whether she was going to live up to six hundred years' worth of expectations.

No pressure.

54

YAMANU

*A*rmed with a lovely bouquet of flowers and a box of chocolates, Yamanu ambled toward his home.

The village was an amazing community, and he was thankful to be part of it. Ruth had cut down some of her prize roses without batting an eyelash, tied a red ribbon around the stems, and wished him good luck. Ella had given him her last unopened box and told him that she was going to keep her fingers crossed for Mey's successful transition.

Everyone assumed that this was the special occasion he was preparing for, and since it was part of it, Yamanu had no problem with letting them think that.

Other than Annani, Kian, and Merlin, no one knew about his long abstinence, and hopefully, no one was ever going to find out. Once it was known that his powers were gone, there might be some questions, but he wasn't going to worry about it now.

Who knew? Maybe the Fates would indeed be merciful and let him keep them?

On some level, he didn't want that. How stupid would he

feel if he discovered that he had been sacrificing his joy in life for nothing?

Not for nothing.

He'd been rewarded in the best possible way. Giving up six and a half centuries of meaningless sex for a truelove mate was a no-brainer. If the Fates had appeared to him back then and offered him this bargain, he would have taken it even without the added bonus of getting superpowers.

Love with a lifelong companion was worth every sacrifice.

That was it, that was the missing piece in the tapestry of his destiny.

He realized that it had all been worth it and that even if he didn't lose his powers once he no longer abstained, he hadn't been an idiot for not testing it sooner.

What a difference a change in perspective made. One small shift in the way he thought about things had changed his entire outlook on life.

No longer dreading a future as an ordinary Guardian, one who'd left his clan unprotected for his own selfish reasons, Yamanu suddenly felt lighter. With a spring in his step and a grin on his face, he strode toward his home with renewed confidence.

Everything was going to work out fine.

Just as Mey had told him, all he needed to do was to think about how much he loved her, and there was no chance he was going to hurt her. He was going to treat this evening as proper courtship, and not make it just about sex.

He'd waited six and a half centuries, he could wait a few more hours, and if the beast bared his fangs, Yamanu was going to beat it into submission.

Mey wanted to make it a memorable event, and he was going to make sure it was. He was going to be patient, not assume anything, and once they got intimate, he was going to be careful and treat her like his precious queen.

Not only tonight but for the rest of their very long lives.

Upon reaching his front door, Yamanu stopped, and instead of just walking in, he knocked.

A man holding a bouquet of flowers and a box of chocolates shouldn't just walk in on his lady love. He should be invited first.

Silly?

Maybe.

But after doubting himself for way too long, Yamanu was back to trusting his instincts, and they told him to knock and wait for Mey to open the door.

He didn't have to wait long. By the fast-paced clicking sound, he knew that Mey had put on her high heels, and it made him happy that she'd dressed up for him.

He wondered what else she had done in preparation.

As she threw the door open, he dipped his head. "Good evening, my lady Mey. You look resplendent."

A nervous giggle escaped her throat, but she responded in kind, executing a beautiful curtsy. "Good evening, my lord Yamanu. You look more handsome than ever. And I see that you came bearing gifts."

"Flowers and chocolates for my beautiful lady." He handed her both and then leaned to kiss her cheek. "Careful with the roses. There might be still a few thorns left."

Mey looked surprised by the gentle peck, but pleasantly so. "They are beautiful. Where did you get them?"

Yamanu felt very proud of himself for acting like a gentleman and not letting his animal urges take over. Not bad for a guy who'd waited for this moment for centuries.

You are a vain bastard. He shook his head. Annani was right about that.

As he followed Mey inside, he could hardly recognize his own house. Where had she gotten all of the decorations, and a white tablecloth that wasn't made from paper?

"I got the roses from a friend with a garden," he said. "How about you? Where did all this come from?" He waved a hand at the beautifully set table, and the silk-covered cushions.

The welcoming committee had brought a few simple ones, a throw blanket, and Dalhu had donated a couple of his landscapes, but Mey had somehow embellished on that.

She smiled. "From a very resourceful friend who enlisted the help of other friends."

MEY

*Y*amanu looked amazing. His long hair was gathered in the back with a tie, he was freshly shaved and smelled as good as he looked.

He was also on his best behavior. A perfect gentleman with impeccable manners who was as far from the hungry beast she'd expected as could be.

It was a relief.

As much as the idea of facing the beast had excited her, deep down Mey knew that it wasn't what she wanted. Not for their first time, anyway. Perhaps that was the reason she'd been so anxious.

This evening was about love and companionship as much as it was about sex.

Nowadays, sex was a cheap commodity that was readily available. Love and commitment were the rare finds that should be nurtured and cherished above all.

Given the circumstances, perhaps it wasn't true for Yamanu, but it was for her. Well, that wasn't a hundred percent true either, since in her case she needed the sex to transition, and without transitioning, there would be no love and commitment. So, the two were intertwined.

"I hope you are hungry." She put the flowers in a tall beer glass, which was the only container she could find for them.

"I am, and the salmon smells delicious."

She smiled. "I keep forgetting how good your sense of smell is. I might have guessed it was fish, but not which kind."

"Can I help bring things to the table?" He followed her into the kitchen.

"In fact, you can. Callie brought this enormous tray with everything already arranged on it, and it's heavy." She handed him the oven mittens. "By the way, I was surprised to find these. I thought you guys were impervious to hot ovens."

He put the mittens on. "We can heal fast, but that doesn't mean that injuries and burns don't hurt. I'd rather avoid pain if I can."

He lifted the platter and brought it to the table, setting it carefully on the marble cutting board she'd put in the middle.

"Thank you for making this evening special," Yamanu said as he pulled out a chair for her.

"I couldn't have done any of it without Callie's help."

Yamanu glanced at the couch. "Did she also bring those beautiful cushion covers?"

Mey chuckled. "Those are silk scarves that I wrapped around them and tied in the back. Callie had different ideas in mind when she brought them."

He cocked a brow. "Oh, yeah? Like what?"

To hide her embarrassment, Mey got busy loading Yamanu's plate. Did he know about the games Callie and Brundar played? But even if he did, talking about their friends' sex life seemed inappropriate.

"She said I can get creative with those and suggested that I look for ideas on YouTube." Perhaps he would let it go at that.

"Did you find anything interesting? I mean other than decorating ideas."

She loaded her own plate. "There was something about a scarf dance, but it was too elaborate for me."

He poured them both wine and lifted his glass. "To us."

"To us," Mey repeated as they clinked glasses.

It was such a loaded salute, and it encompassed everything, starting with her transition, which their future depended on.

Suddenly, her anxiety came back full force. What if she wasn't a Dormant?

None of the immortals she'd met so far had ever heard about abilities like hers and Jin's. And if none of the descendants of the gods exhibited anything like it, then chances were that she and Jin were not dormant carriers of their genes.

"What's wrong?" Yamanu put his fork down and reached for her hand.

Mey shook her head. She'd always wanted to have a man who got her, who was attuned to her, but perhaps it wasn't such a good thing. There was no hiding from Yamanu. He either smelled or sensed every change in her mood.

"Talk to me, Mey. Are you nervous because of what I've told you about the uncontrollable beast? If you are, don't be. I have him under control." He smiled. "You were right. My love for you will never let me harm you." He lifted her hand to his lips and kissed the back of it. "You will always be my queen."

"That's not it at all. I meant it when I said that I trust you. I was just thinking that Jin's and my abilities are not shared by any of your people. Which might mean that we are not carriers of the godly genes. We are something different."

"Like what?" He smiled. "As far as we know, we are the only divergent humanoid species on the planet." He shook his head. "Or the other way around. We are probably the original, and humans are the divergence, but that's beside the point. You and Jin are either human or dormant. There is no third option. And since I've never heard of any humans who can do what you two can, I believe that you are Dormants."

Mey wasn't convinced that he was right. "What if there are others like you but different who are hiding among the human population? Your people and the Doomers are proof that it's possible."

"Possible, yes. Likely, no." He put his other hand on top of hers. "On the way home, I had a sort of epiphany. When I left here this morning, I was full of fears. I was afraid that without the potion, I was going to hurt you. I was afraid of losing my powers and leaving my people unprotected. I was afraid of becoming just a regular, nothing-special Guardian. Those were all logical fears, but I was also afraid of not losing my powers. Because if I didn't, then all those centuries of abstinence were for naught, and I would have felt like a moron for not testing it sooner."

She hadn't thought that Yamanu might fear not losing his powers, but what he'd said made sense.

"So, what was your epiphany?"

"That you were worth the wait. Because even if my sacrifice hasn't been needed to fuel my powers, it has earned me the Fates' favor. Meaning you. And if back then, they had offered me a bargain, six and a half centuries of abstinence in exchange for a truelove mate, I would have taken it with or without the added bonus of gaining godlike powers."

Wow, and wow again. Yamanu would have been willing to do that for her? For love?

Mey was speechless.

Except, his epiphany had nothing to do with her fears.

He smiled. "I see that you are confused. What I was trying

to explain was that the Fates brought you to me for a reason, and it wasn't to crush me. I'm a believer, Mey, and I believe that you are my reward, and therefore, there is no way that you are not a descendant of the gods."

56

YAMANU

*M*ey still looked unsure, and it seemed like nothing he could say to her would ease her fears.

"I'm touched by your conviction." She put her other hand on top of his, completing the stack. "But in my experience, not all good deeds are rewarded. In fact, they rarely are."

Apparently, despite her words of love, Mey hadn't internalized yet that she was his, and that they were meant to be. The sooner he induced her transition, the better, and Yamanu was of a mind to start right away.

Suddenly, it didn't matter that his plate was still mostly full and that dinner wasn't nearly done. The urge that he'd been forcing down for the past hour had slipped from its anchor and shot to the surface, unceremoniously ending the polite courtship stage.

They'd drunk wine, they'd eaten a few bites, it would have to do.

"You are not going to shake my belief." He pulled his hands back. "So, don't even try. You are mine."

Given the acceleration in Mey's heartbeat, she must have sensed the change in his mood.

Reaching for a napkin, Yamanu wiped his mouth and then took another long sip from the wine, mainly to clean his palate in anticipation of the ambrosia he was about to taste.

"Where are you going?" Mey asked when he pushed to his feet.

"To worship my queen." He walked over to her chair and turned it around, so its back was to the table, and then he knelt in front of her.

Her red wrap dress was perfect for what he had in mind, and the moment he put his hands on her knees, Mey knew precisely what it was and parted her thighs, letting the dress fall to the sides and expose her legs.

"Beautiful." He applied a little pressure, urging her to part a little wider.

She did, but then glanced at the light fixture hanging over the table, and then back at him, letting him know that she was uncomfortable with getting intimate in the full light.

"You realize that it doesn't matter to me whether the light is on or off. I will still see all your treasures just as clearly." His palm traveled up her inner thigh. "This is all mine."

Mey blushed. "I keep forgetting your super senses."

He inhaled deeply, the scent of her arousal making him dizzy with want.

She chuckled. "And that too. It's so embarrassing that you can smell me."

"Why? It's the best scent in the world to me. I've just gotten lightheaded because all the blood in my body rushed into my groin."

He was teasing to help her relax, but he was exaggerating only a little.

She tried to bring her knees back together. "Then maybe we should go to the bedroom. I don't want you to wait any longer."

He put his hands back on her knees, parting them, and then tugged at the same time, bringing her bottom to the edge of the chair. "I want this, and not only because I need to prepare you."

Mey nodded. "This is your night, Yamanu. We will do things exactly how you want them."

It was Mey's night too, but he knew that she was going to enjoy submitting to his will, and if believing that she was doing it for him helped her make peace with that, so be it.

Eventually, she would grow confident enough in his love to admit that she enjoyed letting go. It was a game as ancient as time, and even though he hadn't partaken in centuries, it seemed that not much had changed in that regard.

Lowering his head, he kissed the soft skin of her inner thigh, working his way up with small nips and kisses until his mouth hovered over her panty-covered treasures.

The panties were red like her dress and soaked through.

"So lovely." He tugged on the two strings holding them up and lowered them down Mey's shapely legs, kissing and sucking her skin on the way down and then once again on the way up.

By the time he reached her wet folds, Mey was panting and shivering with need, and he was very aware that his fangs were at their full length, and he needed to be careful not to nick her.

Using just the tip of his tongue, he parted her lips with soft strokes, his eyes rolling back in his head from the taste of her.

Her hands gripping the seat, Mey arched against him, silently begging for more.

Soon, he was going to give in, but not yet. The longer he managed to prolong the foreplay, the stronger her climax would be.

57

MEY

This night was supposed to be Yamanu's, but instead of the ravishing Mey had expected, she was the one getting pleasured again.

And teased mercilessly.

She needed that talented tongue of his not on her folds, but on the throbbing center of her desire that Yamanu was making sure to avoid while licking and kissing everywhere else.

If not for her promise to let him do as he pleased, she would have screamed in frustration or pulled on his long hair. Instead, she was gripping the chair and biting her lower lip while writhing under his ministrations.

"Yes!" When he finally flattened his tongue on that most sensitive spot, Mey nearly shot up from the chair.

His grip on her thighs never wavered, holding her down as he went for more. She was going to have bruises in the shape of his fingers, but right now she couldn't feel anything other than the pulsating of blood in her feminine center.

Her cry must have snapped his restraint, and suddenly she was under attack. With his tongue flicking over her clit harder and faster, the simmering heat turned into an inferno, bringing her to the crest. She was already hovering over the edge, ready to tip over and start her free fall, when he pushed two fingers inside her and closed his lips over that pulsating little bud.

Instead of falling, Mey shot up, the climax exploding from her with a loud cry.

Kissing her gently, Yamanu waited for the shivers to subside before lifting her off the chair and carrying her to the bedroom.

Finally.

With her panties already gone, removing the dress and bra took Yamanu no more than a split second, and then she was lying on the bed, her body quaking in anticipation as she watched him whip his shirt over his head.

She'd seen his bare torso before, but she would never get tired of looking at it. Yamanu was magnificent, so beautifully made that he didn't look real. A talented sculptor could not have done a better job.

When he didn't continue the reveal and climbed in bed with his pants on, Mey stifled a protest, the words remaining lodged in her throat.

He caressed her, his palm sliding gently over her trembling stomach. "If I take my pants off, it's going to be over in a minute. I want to savor this."

Hadn't he said that he needed zero recuperating time?

Then again, there was only one first time, and she couldn't fault Yamanu for wanting to make it special.

"You are so beautiful, my lady Mey." His hand traveled up her ribcage, finding her breast and palming it for a moment before moving to pinch her aching nipple.

His other hand joined the first, teasing her, his pinching and plucking just shy of being painful. He took her right up to the edge again with just that, the orgasm building up inside her so fast that she was sure to erupt if he only kissed her.

He hadn't kissed her yet. Not tonight. Well, not on her mouth, anyway. Was there a significance in that, or had it been just an oversight?

Lifting his head, Yamanu looked at her with his glowing eyes. "I'm losing you. What were you thinking just now that has upset you?"

"You didn't kiss me yet."

"My bad." He kissed her nipple, adding a slow lazy lick for good measure.

"Not there. Well, there too."

He kissed her other nipple. "Here?"

If he was teasing her, then the lack of a kiss had indeed been an oversight, and she could play along.

"Yes, but not just there."

He pushed up and kissed her neck, sucking the skin hard enough to leave a mark. "This is good?"

Mey moaned. "Yes, but keep going."

He did, kissing and nipping the side of her neck until he reached her earlobe. He nipped a little harder, then licked the little hurt away.

How Yamanu was managing to be so gentle with those huge fangs of his was a mystery. He was very careful with her.

Perhaps that was why the pants stayed on. So he could have better control.

When he finally reached her lips, it was the closest Mey had ever gotten to climaxing from a kiss, and when his hand found her wet center, and he slipped two fingers inside her, fireworks exploded behind her closed eyelids, and she screamed his name into his mouth.

He kept kissing her as she trembled in his arms, saying

words of endearment she couldn't hear because the blood was still roaring in her ears. She heard, however, when he said those precious five words.

"I love you, my Mey."

YAMANU

P recious.

Yamanu was never going to forget how Mey looked right now. Her face blissed out, her hair messed up, and her magnificent nude body vibrating softly against his.

By some miracle, he hadn't erupted in his pants, but he'd gotten pretty damn close. Sheer determination had prevented him from giving up.

When he orgasmed for the first time in centuries, he was going to do it inside his woman, not his pants, and he was going to bite her. The potency of both his seed and his venom should be off the charts, and he wouldn't be surprised if he induced her transition and got her pregnant at the same time.

That thought managed to chill his fervor.

Hopefully, that wasn't going to happen because no one knew whether transitioning was dangerous for the embryo.

Damn, he was succumbing to his old sin of vanity again.

There was practically no chance he could get Mey pregnant on the first go. It would take a miracle for an immortal male to be able to do so. Besides, like most young women these days, Mey was probably using some sort of contraceptive.

Letting out a relieved breath, he dipped his head and kissed her lips softly.

Her eyelids fluttered open. "Yamanu," she whispered and wrapped her arms around his neck, bringing him down for another kiss.

As he let Mey pull him over her, he pushed his pants down, but his boxer shorts snagged on his hard as a rock shaft, eliciting a pained hiss.

Mey let go of his mouth. "What happened?"

Smooth.

Yamanu had forgotten that pants and undershorts hadn't been a thing when he'd been a randy lad, and he had no practice in removing modern articles of clothing while kissing a lady.

"Nothing." He shifted to his side, using both hands this time.

There was no direct light in the bedroom, but the door was slightly ajar, and the light from the living room was enough for Mey to get a good look at the flagpole sticking out of his hips.

"Oh, wow, Yamanu. You are really big all over." Fortunately, she sounded awed, not scared or repulsed. "And obviously, the potion didn't do any lasting damage."

It hadn't even occurred to him that she might have been worried about that. Unlike Mey, he had been acutely aware of how well everything still functioned despite the potion.

As she reached for his shaft, he caught her wrist. "Don't." Then added in a softer tone, "Not this time."

When he wasn't on the verge of eruption, she could touch him as much as she wanted.

"Okay." She took his hand instead, pulling him back over her. "I'd rather feel you in me anyway." She parted her legs, cradling him between them.

He groaned as the tip of his shaft touched her soft center,

twitching to get inside. Yamanu didn't dare to put his own hand on it to guide it. It would have to find its own way.

Pressing his chest to Mey, he looked into her soft, brown eyes. "I love you."

She smiled. "I love you too. Now make us one." Cupping his buttocks, she arched up, and the tip of his shaft slid inside her.

That was the point of no return.

As he surged all the way in, Yamanu's vision blurred, and he felt as if he was going to pass out. For a long moment, he didn't move, savoring the feeling.

Awed by it.

They were one, the connection so powerful, so all-encompassing, that he didn't know where he ended and Mey began. It was about much more than sex, even much more than love, it was about their unbreakable bond.

"You are mine." He pulled back and surged in again, amazed that he hadn't orgasmed yet and thankful to the Fates for it.

Every moment of this night was going to be etched forever in his memory, and he wanted as many of those moments as he could possibly collect.

Taking Mey's hands, he guided them over her head and threaded his fingers through hers. "I've waited nearly my entire life for you. And now you are here."

He pulled out and pushed back, trying to keep it slow and steady but soon losing the fight and going fast and hard.

The climax was building up momentum rapidly, and Yamanu knew that he had mere moments before their first time was going to be over.

As he dipped down and latched his lips to the spot he was going to bite, Mey tilted her head to the side, elongating the smooth column of her neck in the most graceful gesture of surrender.

He had just enough presence of mind to lick that sweet spot

before his vision tunneled, and all he could focus on was the seed rushing up his shaft and the venom dripping down his fangs.

With a hiss, he bit down, releasing the venom into Mey's neck at the same time as his seed geysered into her sheath.

59

MEY

*R*apture.

It was coming.

Even through the intense pounding Yamanu was treating her to, Mey could feel his shaft swelling even thicker inside her.

When she'd seen his size, she'd been taken aback, but she shouldn't have worried. The freaking Fates had known exactly what they had been doing when they'd matched her and Yamanu.

They were made for each other. This was a perfect harmony of body and spirit and much more powerful than anything Mey had ever experienced.

Even the prospect of getting bitten by Yamanu's monstrous fangs wasn't scary. Heck, it was hot, and she couldn't wait for him to do that.

A split second of pain, and then there would be bliss. That was what Wonder and Callie had told her. According to them, nothing could compare to the post-coital bliss of a venom bite. Protecting Yamanu's secret, she'd pretended to know what they'd been talking about, and had just smiled shyly and nodded.

Bring it on! She was beyond ready.

As Yamanu dipped his head and put his lips on the spot where her neck met her shoulder, Mey knew it was about to happen in the next couple of seconds.

Relax, don't fight it, just surrender to it. It's worth it. She turned her head to the side and held her breath.

Damn. It hurt, and instinctively she tried to jerk away. But Yamanu's hands clamped on her head, immobilizing it just long enough for the cool venom to slither in and deliver everything he had promised and more.

The pain evaporated as if it had never been, and a heatwave of intense arousal washed over her, triggering the mother of all orgasms, and after that at least five of its aunts. As one climax after the other rocked her body, Yamanu kept filling her with his essence through both points of entry. At the rate he was going, there would be nothing left of him once he was done.

This was the last coherent thought Mey had before the heatwave abated, and a euphoric calm spread through her, lifting her into another realm.

Floating, she soared up and up, watching with awe the impossible landscapes she was passing by.

Surreal.

Wondrous.

When she next opened her eyes, it was to gaze into Yamanu's worried face.

He breathed out. "Thank the merciful Fates. You've been out for hours."

"I was? It felt like minutes." She smiled and tried lifting her arms to put them around Yamanu's neck, but they refused to cooperate. "I need help."

"What's wrong?"

"Nothing. I'm still boneless, and I can't lift my arms. Help me bring them around your neck?"

The creases in his forehead smoothed out, and he did as she asked. "How are you feeling? Was I too rough?"

"Pfft. Not at all. If that was the beast, I have to say that he's pretty tame." She managed to pull up a bit and kissed the underside of Yamanu's jaw. "Thank you. That was out of this world, literally. I soared on a cloud and watched alien landscapes. And if I sound drunk, that's because I feel like I am."

He smiled. "I'm the one who should be thanking you. You brought me back to life. I didn't realize that I was living on mute for all those years."

Leaning down, he cupped her cheek and planted a soft kiss on her lips. "I was so worried that I called Kian in the middle of the night. He told me that it was normal."

Even as drunk as she felt, Mey blushed. That was so damn embarrassing. After that, how was she ever going to look Kian in the eyes?

"It wasn't your first time with a human. It must have happened to the others you've been with too."

He shook his head. "Half an hour or an hour. That was the maximum time I remember. You were out for over six."

"Really?" Mey glanced at the window.

The automatic shutters were up, which meant that the night was over and that the sun had risen. It was still dark outside, but the sky was starting to lighten.

"Yeah, really. That's why I was so worried. I was afraid that I overdosed you, but Kian assured me that the same happened to Syssi their first time together."

Well, if Kian had shared such private intel with Yamanu, then she had no reason to be embarrassed about Yamanu calling him up and reporting that they had started her induction process.

"Interesting. And what did they do after Syssi woke up?"

"Kian didn't say."

Mey smiled coyly. "I bet that they went for another round."

Yamanu's eyes started glowing. "Are you up for it? A moment ago, you couldn't lift your arms."

"I still can't. But I'm fine with you doing all the work." She smirked. "You told me that you didn't need any time to recuperate, and it has been six hours."

60

YAMANU

*B*y the position of the sun, it was late morning, but Yamanu didn't want to move even to pick up his phone from the nightstand and check the time.

Lying on his side, he watched Mey sleeping. Her cheeks flushed, and her hair mussed, she was the most beautiful female to ever walk the earth. He wondered if the ghost of a smile on her lips meant that she was dreaming about him.

His heart overflowing with love, he couldn't tear his eyes away from her.

Mey was his entire world.

They had made love three times, and he'd bitten her twice. After the second bite, Mey drifted away and hadn't woken up even when he'd used a bunch of warm washcloths to wipe her from top to bottom. They had both worked up quite a sweat.

This time, however, he didn't worry. Kian had assured him that it was normal. And besides, Mey had every right to be exhausted. As much as he'd tried to be gentle, it must have been brutal for her.

Thank the merciful Fates for the venom's healing properties. Even as careful as he'd been, without the venom Mey would have woken up covered in bruises.

Fates, he adored this woman. So strong and so brave, she'd given him everything she had and then some. Fearlessly, self-lessly, she'd made last night as special and as memorable as she could for him, achieving her goal and then some.

He'd been worried that the first time wouldn't last long and that he wouldn't have enough memories of it. Except, his mind had merged the entire night and morning into one first, and he was going to commit it to memory as such.

Epic.

That was the best word he had for it.

Life-altering was fitting as well. Mey had literally brought him back to life.

One thing Yamanu was sure of—no matter what happened, he was never going back to celibacy. Let someone else carry that load. He was never giving up Mey or the life they were going to have together.

She wanted a house full of children, and he was going to give it to her. And if she wanted to run a fashion business with her sister, he was going to quit the force and become a stay-at-home dad.

How was that for a career change?

Yamanu chuckled. It might not be considered manly, but he didn't give a fuck. His vanity had always gotten him in trouble, it was time he shoved it aside and concentrated on what made him happy and not what others thought of him.

Was he strong enough to actually do that, though?

It took guts to go against social norms and expectations. Even for someone who had proved his worth as a Guardian.

But those musings were premature. First, Mey had to tran-sition, then they would get married in whatever tradition she preferred, and then they would try for a child.

He'd almost forgotten about Jin. Finding her needed to happen after Mey's transition and before the marriage. Mey would want her to be at the wedding.

As his stomach rumbled, reminding him that they hadn't finished dinner last night, Yamanu gently kissed Mey's forehead. When she didn't react, he pushed a strand of hair away from her cheek and kissed it too. She didn't react to that either.

He should let her sleep and go get breakfast.

Mey would love to wake up to the smell of fresh pastries and cappuccinos from the café.

Just in case she woke up before he returned, he scribbled a note and left it on the nightstand next to her phone. She would see it when she checked the time.

First, though, he needed to shower. He loved smelling Mey on himself, but he had no intention of advertising what they had shared last night by walking into the café with her scent all over him.

Thankfully, when he got there, the place wasn't packed, with only two of the tables occupied and just Wonder behind the counter.

"Good morning." He smiled at her. "Any pastries left after the breakfast rush?"

"Take a look." She pointed at the display.

There wasn't much, but it would do. "Can I get all of it? And two cappuccinos, please."

She tried to hide the smirk. "Someone woke up hungry this morning."

Damn. Mey must have told Callie about her plans for last night, and the rumor had probably spread all over the village. The question was, what exactly had she told them?

"Ravenous." He winked, hoping she would volunteer what she knew.

Wonder blushed and turned toward the pastries display. "Would you like me to heat them up for you?"

"Yes, please."

While the pastries were in the oven, Wonder made the cappuccinos and handed Yamanu a tray with the two tall paper cups. When the oven beeped, she took out the pastries, put them in a paper bag, and handed it to him as well.

"Say hi to Mey for me and tell her that I wish her luck."

He cocked a brow. "Luck with what?"

Wonder frowned. "Transitioning, of course. What did you think I was referring to?"

So that was what Mey had told Callie? That they were about to start working on her transition?

That was good.

"There are many things you can wish Mey luck for. Like finding her sister or winning the lottery. Except, she already won the jackpot. She got me." He winked.

Wonder laughed. "No, it was actually I who won, but I guess it's a matter of personal opinion."

"I guess so. But I'm still the best."

As he headed back, Yamanu started singing softly, a happy tune from his childhood that matched his joyous mood.

"I know that song." Merlin appeared from behind the bend. "But it has been a long time since I've heard it." He walked over to Yamanu and offered his hand. "I hear that congratulations are in order. You and Mey started the induction process."

Yamanu put the paper bag on the tray to free his hand and shook Merlin's. "Thank you. But it's really annoying how there is no privacy in this village. How did everyone already hear about it?"

Merlin shrugged. "As long as it's good news, why not? Your mate is lovely, and we all wish for her to transition easily and join our community." The doctor glanced around, making sure no one could overhear them.

"Did you test your powers?"

Yamanu shook his head. "Not yet. I'm still celebrating, and I don't want to spoil the mood."

"Understandable. Later on, when you are done celebrating, you might want to come over to the clinic and freeze some seed for the future."

"Thanks for the offer, but I'm done with celibacy for good. If I come to the clinic, it will be to ask for your fertility potion. Mey wants a house full of children, and I intend to give her everything she wants."

Merlin laughed and clapped Yamanu on the back. "Slow down, Yamanu. The lady needs to transition first, and then she will probably want a mating ceremony. After that, you might want to ask her when she wants to start working on having children."

61

KIAN

*K*ian was about to wrap up his meeting with Onegus and Bridget when his desk phone rang.

He really needed to get a receptionist to screen his calls. How was he supposed to get any work done with his cellphone or desk phone always ringing?

He snatched it off the receiver without glancing at the display. "I'm busy."

"You want to make time for this," William said. "I found him."

There was only one *him* he could be referring to, but it was such unexpected news that Kian had to verify. "Kalugal?"

Bridget and Onegus leaned closer.

"The one and only. I got him on the security feed from a bar not far from his house."

"Are you sure it's him?"

"It's a crappy black and white recording, but he looked straight into the camera. I fed the still through the program, and it's a ninety-two percent match with the sketch, which is stellar. I also watched about twenty minutes of it as he made his rounds. The way he carried himself and the way he moved was indicative of an immortal with military training. An excellent posture and fluid, economical moves. You can come down here and watch for yourself. I'm afraid the recording is too grainy for me to send to you. The details are blurry even after manipulating the picture quality with my equipment."

"I'm coming down."

Bridget grinned. "You can call Alena and her crew back home."

"Not yet. We need to verify that it's really him first."

"How are you going to do that?" Onegus asked.

"I'll worry about that later. Right now, I want to see what William has. Either of you want to join me?"

Bridget shook her head. "I wish I could, but I still have work to do before I can close shop for the weekend."

"I'll walk you over there," Onegus said.

On the way to the underground structure, Onegus pulled Kalugal's picture up on his phone. "Tim is a real asset. It's hard to believe how accurately he draws those sketches just from listening to other people's descriptions."

"Maybe he has supernatural talent?" Kian said it as a joke, but then he frowned. "I'll be damned. Tim might be a Dormant. Just like Nick's talent with electronics borders on magic, so does Tim's with his sketches."

Onegus snorted. "Do you really want that guy to join our community? He is an annoying prick."

The pavilion's sliding doors parted, and they walked through, heading for the elevators. "That's an interesting moral question." Kian called the cab up. "Do we pick and choose who we want to induce? We haven't faced that problem yet, but we might."

"I say that we do." Onegus followed him inside the elevator. "This is our community, our village, and we don't have to invite anyone we don't want. We've been lucky so far, with all the

Dormants being great people and finding mates. But we need to have a system in place in case an undesirable Dormant shows up on our steps."

It was a good suggestion. Kian didn't want to have to decide on whether someone deserved immortality or not. Because if a person was rejected by the village, he or she could not be induced.

Perhaps the big assembly should decide on such matters. Someone would need to represent the Dormant and present his or her case to the village.

As they reached the lab, Kian was surprised to find Ella there, sitting next to Roni at his station. Not that he minded. After all, she had been instrumental in finding and catching Lokan, and without Lokan, they wouldn't be looking for Kalugal. He just found it odd that she was spending time with Roni. As far as he knew, they weren't pals. Then again, they were about the same age, so there was that.

"Hello, everyone," Onegus said. "I was told that a special screening was happening here today." He made quotation marks with his fingers. "The immortal reclusive billionaire."

Ella smiled. "The title needs work." She tapped the tip of her nose with her finger. "The reclusive billionaire's secret."

William shook his head. "Are you all done?"

"They are," Kian said. "Please proceed."

As the recording played in slow motion on one of William's huge computer screens, Kian pulled out his phone and glanced at Kalugal's portrait, then back at the screen. "Can you zoom in on the face and freeze it?"

William did as he asked, enlarging the picture as much as he could without making it too blurry.

Kian looked between the two pictures. The hair cut was different, and unlike Tim's sketch, the guy on the big screen wasn't smiling, the different expression making it difficult to compare. Also, the black and white didn't show eye color.

"Can you bring up Tim's portrait right next to this?" Onegus asked.

With a couple of clicks, the two pictures were one next to the other, appearing on two adjoining screens.

"We need to catch him smiling," Kian said. "I'm not sure it's the same guy."

"I'm sure," William said. "As good as your eyesight is, you can't compete with a computer. Ninety-two percent is as good as a hundred in this case. Don't forget that we are working with a drawing, not an actual photograph."

Onegus nodded. "I think it's safe to call off the New York operation. Our guy is right here in California."

"Perhaps." Kian leaned to take a closer look. "But I see no harm in Alena completing her modeling gig. The other plan can serve as backup in case this is not our guy."

"That's true," Onegus agreed.

"By the way," Roni started and then glanced at Ella. "Is it okay if I tell Kian about your aunt?"

"Sure. I was going to do it anyway." She grinned. "We might have another potential Dormant on the loose."

Kian frowned. "I thought that your mother was an only child?"

"She is, but my father had a sister." Ella rolled her eyes. "Talk about a recluse. I don't even remember what she looks like because we hardly ever got to see her. But my mom says that Eleanor was always an odd bird."

"That doesn't make her a Dormant," Onegus said.

"True, but there is more." Ella pointed to her head. "My telepathy is much stronger than my mom's, and my brother's compulsion ability is extremely rare. As far as we know, only Navuh and his two sons have it. That got me thinking that maybe my father was a Dormant as well. According to Amanda's theory, immortals and Dormants feel a special affinity for each other, so I think it's safe to extrapolate that Dormants feel it for each other as well. Which can explain why my mother and father clicked right from the start. And if my father was a Dormant, then Aunt Eleanor is a Dormant too."

"And that's where things start getting really interesting," Roni said. "Ella asked me to find out what her aunt was up to recently, and I did a little snooping around. What I found reminded me of Eva's story. Eleanor no longer works as a pharmaceutical rep, she is a ghost. I found a bank account in her name, with lots of money in it, but it hasn't been touched in over two years. The address on it is the apartment she used to live in before she ghosted, and the bank statements are delivered to her old email address. It looks like she reads her emails, but she doesn't send any out. Next, I checked her tax returns. She didn't file for the last two years, and it says that she's exempt from filing, which is also odd. The IRS is one of the hardest networks to hack into and change anything, so her exempt status had to be government approved."

The more Roni talked, the more Kian's interest was piqued. Could it be that Eleanor had been accidentally turned like Eva had?

"Did you check her driver's license?"

Roni cast him an offended look. "Of course. I was getting to it." He shifted in his enormous chair. "I ran her old driver's license picture through the facial recognition program, and guess what?"

The kid loved drama.

"What?"

"Her doppelgänger popped up with a West Virginia driver license under a different name."

The gears in Kian's head started spinning. Two years wasn't

long enough for Eleanor to show signs of aging, so that couldn't have been the reason behind a new license.

"How old is your aunt?" he asked Ella.

"She is thirty-eight," Roni said. "Thirty-nine in December."

"That's not old enough to be overly concerned with signs of aging."

Ella lifted a brow. "What are you talking about?"

Kian leaned against the desk and crossed his arms over his chest. "When Roni said that Eleanor's story reminded him of Eva's, it got me thinking that maybe she was accidentally turned immortal and fled because of that. But she is obviously too young to worry about not showing age. So that's not the reason she's ghosted, as Roni put it. Besides, she was a pharmaceutical rep, not an undercover agent like Eva. The simple explanation could be that she got in some kind of trouble, either personal or professional, and needed to disappear. But the West Virginia license makes me think of another possibility."

William nodded. "The mythical paranormal division that might not be mythical after all."

MEY

*P*leasant dreams had kept Mey asleep for longer than she'd expected, and when she finally opened her eyes and looked out the window, the position of the sun told her that it was about noon.

Yamanu wasn't in bed with her, which was a little disappointing, but then she couldn't expect him to stay with her all day. He had Guardian work to do.

Yeah, and she was the reason he might be out of a job, or at least out of the position he'd held as the clan's shield.

Crap, that thought was enough to ruin a perfect morning that had followed a perfect night.

Spectacular wasn't a strong enough word to describe it. Yamanu had exceeded her expectation by a margin as wide as the distance from the moon to the sun. After six and a half centuries of abstinence, he had not only held on long enough to ensure that she was ready, but he had also made a tremendous effort to be gentle with her.

Still, it had been one hell of a ride, and Yamanu had been on top of his game as if he had never taken a break.

Surprisingly, nothing hurt. Mey lifted the comforter to see

whether she had bruises left over from his powerful grip, but there were none. In fact, she felt amazing, invigorated, healthy, rested, and happy.

Selfishly happy.

She'd gotten what she'd wanted, but at what price?

Would her new friends still like her once they'd learned what she'd cost them?

Probably not.

She'd made this entire community of immortals vulnerable. These wonderful people who had accepted her so warmly were going to regret welcoming her in.

Could they kick her out even if she turned? Or would becoming an immortal grant her a permanent resident status in the village?

It was strange that there had been no evaluation process. Even the most mundane housing communities screened their residents, and yet the clan seemed to accept anyone with the right genes.

Even Israel, which officially accepted anyone born Jewish, screened undesirables. Criminals were not welcome, not even the super-rich.

As Mey slung her legs over the side of the bed, she noticed a piece of paper next to her phone. Lifting it, she smiled, then feeling silly, she kissed it.

Yamanu's penmanship was like the rest of him. Beautiful and stylish and with a bit of flair. She decided to keep it as a souvenir of the night they'd shared and put it in her purse.

It was so sweet of him to get her breakfast from the café, and even sweeter to add a lopsided heart to his note with the word forever written under it.

Expecting Yamanu to be back at any moment, Mey hurried, finishing her shower in record time and returning to the bedroom with a thick towel wrapped around her. She had just enough time to duck back in bed when the door opened, and Yamanu walked in.

"Good morning, my lady Mey."

She grinned, happiness radiating from her center as if it was a force field and not just a feeling. "Good afternoon, my lord Yamanu."

He sat on the bed and put the tray on the nightstand. "Coffee?"

"Please."

He handed her a tall paper cup. "Pastry?"

She shook her head. "I don't want crumbs on the bed."

"There will be no crumbs if I feed you."

It was an offer she couldn't refuse, especially since her stomach had reacted to the delicious smell with a pang of hunger.

"Okay. Just be careful."

"I will." He pulled a Danish out and tore off a little piece. "Open wide." He popped it into her mouth, then followed with a soft kiss. "I love you."

She swallowed the small bite and smiled. "I love you too. And I loved the note you left me with the heart and the forever written under it. I'm going to put it in a special album dedicated to memories of our special moments."

His lips curved in a smile. "I will make sure to provide you with enough to fill an entire library of albums."

She spread her arms, careful not to spill coffee on the pristine white bedding. "It will have to be huge. Can you imagine how many cherished memories ten kids will produce?"

"You still want that?'

"Of course. But I know that's a pipe dream because of the immortal low fertility rate." She smirked. "Although after last night, I feel like I should get a pregnancy test."

Yamanu's expression was a picture of male satisfaction. "About that. How are you feeling? Anything hurt?"

"Nope. I feel fabulous."

"I met Merlin on the way back. He asked me if I wanted to freeze some sperm for the future."

Mey's good mood evaporated. "What was your answer?"

"I told him no. Because I'm never going back to celibacy again. I'm done with that."

"Did you test your powers?"

He smiled. "It's funny. He asked me the same thing. I didn't. First of all, because I need to be among humans to test it, and second because I want to keep this joy in my heart for as long as I can." He leaned and kissed the crease in her forehead. "Don't worry. Everything is going to turn out fine. And I also told Merlin that once you transition and we get married, we are going to come to him for his fertility potion. As soon as we find your sister, I want us to start working on filling this house with kids. If you are up to it, that is. You are still young, and I know that you want to open a business with your sister…"

She didn't let him finish. Putting the coffee cup on the nightstand, Mey jumped on him and kissed him until she ran out of air. "Yes and yes and yes."

He wrapped his arms around her. "Naturally, we need to find Jin first."

"Yeah. Preferably before the wedding. I want my sister to be there, and my parents and my grandparents."

"I will do my best to make it happen."

"I know you will. But how about your people? I robbed them of their shield. The moment they make the connection, I will become the least popular person in the village, and I doubt anyone would want to help me."

He tightened his arms around her. "I guarantee you that's not going to happen."

"How can you be sure of that?"

"Because Annani won't have it. She practically commanded me to obey the Fates' wishes. No one will dare to challenge her decree."

That was a relief.

Mey let out a breath. "I hope you are right. I really like the people I've met so far, and I would hate it if they turned their backs on me. As it is, I feel like I'm imposing on everyone's goodwill by asking their help to find Jin."

"You are not imposing. Kian wants Jin because of her special abilities. So, he would have authorized a search even if she wasn't your sister."

She tilted her head. "What's more valuable about Jin, her spying ability or her being a possible Dormant?"

"Her being a Dormant. That trumps everything. The future of our clan depends on finding as many as we can."

"Good. It made me uncomfortable to think that Kian wants Jin just because he wants a one of a kind spy."

As Yamanu's phone buzzed with an incoming message, he pulled it out of his pocket and grinned. "Speak of the devil. Kian wants to see us whenever we are ready to leave the house."

That wasn't good.

"Why?"

Yamanu kissed her forehead again. "He didn't say. But you have nothing to worry about. I promise."

"I hope you are right."

YAMANU

"Come in," Kian growled when Yamanu knocked on the door.

It was the guy's usual voice, but next to him, Mey tensed.

Wrapping his arm around her, Yamanu gave her shoulder a reassuring squeeze and whispered. "Ignore his gruffness. He's a good guy."

"I know." She took in a deep breath.

As they walked in together, Kian greeted them with a smile, and Mey's shoulders lost some of the tension.

"Please sit down." He waved at the two chairs in front of his desk. "You are probably wondering why I called you in here. I have some possible good news and also some questions."

Mey crossed her legs. "Is it about Jin?"

"Possibly. There are two new developments, seemingly unconnected, but knowing how the Fates work, I'm sure we will soon find out that they are not coincidental."

"I never thought that there would come a day when you would turn into a believer." Yamanu shook his head. "You're the most adamant skeptic I've ever known."

Kian shrugged. "After getting hit over the head with a brick enough times, I finally had to admit that there was a brick."

"That's a colorful way to put it."

Kian ignored the remark and turned to Mey. "I want to ask you a few questions about your sister's talent."

She nodded.

"Does it work on everyone, or are some people immune to it?"

"Jin tried not to do it too often, but the few times she did, it worked."

"Interesting, so it doesn't happen with everyone she touches? She has to do something to create the connection?"

"Yes, but even she doesn't know how it happens. I was the first one she did it to. We were still pretty young, I think I was nine, and Jin was seven. She was upset because I left the neighborhood playground without telling her, and she got scared. I only went home to use the bathroom, and I was gone for no more than ten minutes, but I should have told her I was leaving, and I didn't." Mey smiled shyly. "I had to go pretty bad, and she was on the jungle gym. Anyway, when I came back, Jin was crying. She put her hand on my arm and said that she never wanted to lose me again or something like that. I don't remember the exact words. And that was how she discovered her ability. At first, we thought it was a sister thing, but then she did it with one of her friends, and it worked too."

"Did it work with random strangers as well, or just people she knew?"

Mey frowned. "I don't think that she ever tried it on strangers. That would have been too weird. Who wants to see what strangers are doing? What she does happens in real time, so she can catch someone sitting on the toilet, or scratching his behind, or worse. It can be really awkward and gross."

Kian leaned back and crossed his arms over his chest. "If

she was hired because of her talent, I'm sure she's expected to use it on strangers. What I wonder is whether it will work on immortals. If it does, she could be an incredible asset to the clan."

Yamanu shifted in his chair. "I hope you are not planning on using her on Doomers."

"No, not on Doomers. Just one. Kalugal."

"You found him?"

"We might have. I'm not sure yet. Lokan had a meeting with one of his contacts, and during the conversation the guy told him about a cybersecurity installation he had done for a reclusive billionaire in Silicon Valley. When the contact described the subterranean complex the client had built on the property, Lokan started suspecting that it might have been Kalugal. I had William and Roni divert their attention from scanning airports to concentrate on cafés and bars in the area around that mansion. They found a surveillance recording from a bar with someone who looks a lot like him. But that's not enough proof. We still need to verify his identity."

"Why do you need Jin for that?" Mey asked.

"The mansion and the grounds it sits on are protected by state of the art security. It's an impenetrable fortress. We don't know how many immortal warriors he has with him or what he is doing in that subterranean complex. Before we initiate contact, I want to know who we are dealing with. The problem is that none of my people can get past the security if the guards are indeed immortal. Jin, however, can go into a coffee shop or a bar while he is there, touch him, make the connection, and we are in. She can tell us what's going on. The intel would be invaluable to us."

Mey nodded. "I hope she can do it with a stranger. But even if she can, we need to find her first."

Kian smiled. "That's where the other thing I've learned

today comes in. Ella suspected that her aunt might be a Dormant and asked Roni to find out what she was up to. When he started to investigate, he discovered that she has disappeared. Then he ran her picture through the facial recognition program, and he found a match on a West Virginia driver license. The name was different, but it was the same face."

Mey gasped. "You think Ella's aunt is in the same program as Jin?"

"It's a long shot, but as I said, it might not be a coincidence. The good news about this is that if Eleanor is indeed in the same program, she isn't a prisoner. Since she has been issued a fake driver's license, and a very good one at that, she is free to drive around. Jin might still be a trainee, and that's why she is restricted to base. But if we find Eleanor, she might lead us to Jin."

Her eyes full of hope, Mey looked at Yamanu. "Maybe we can wait with the induction? This seems like the first real breakthrough, a solid lead, and I want to follow it as soon as I can."

Yamanu took her hand. "I'm afraid it's too late for that. We've already started. You might enter transition right away."

Kian cleared his throat. "First of all, congratulations. I wish you both the best of luck. Secondly, with all due respect, we don't need you to come along. In fact, I'd prefer that you don't. Third, you can't leave the village until you transition. Not with your memories intact."

Mey's shoulders slumped. "How long does it take to transition?"

Kian cleared his throat again. "Once you've started the process and kept at it, it shouldn't take long. A few days, a week maybe. And since you are young and healthy, you shouldn't be out for more than a day or two. But as I said before. There is no rush because we don't need you to get Jin."

Mey shook her head. "And how are you going to make her trust you enough to go with you? I need to be there."

"Mey might be right," Yamanu said. "If Jin were alone, we could probably thrall her into coming with us. But it's possible that she has made new friends in that program with abilities that we can't begin to guess at." He rubbed his jaw. "My gut tells me that we need Mey with us."

Mey cast him a grateful look.

Kian nodded. "Perhaps. Still, there is no rush because we don't have a plan yet. I need to brainstorm it with Turner, and then we need to gather intel. We are not going to make a move until all the pieces of the puzzle are in place." He grimaced. "One botched mission is enough for me. I don't intend to ever repeat the mistake of going in unprepared."

COMING UP NEXT
THE CHILDREN OF THE GODS BOOK 34
DARK QUEEN'S ARMY

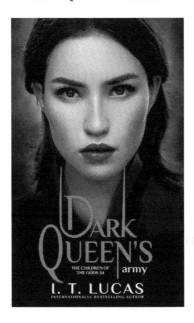

Dear reader,

Thank you for reading the ***Children of the Gods***.

As an independent author, I rely on your support to spread the word. So if you enjoyed the story, please share your experience with others, and if it isn't too much trouble, I would greatly appreciate a brief review on Amazon.

Kind words will get good Karma sent your way -:)

Click here to leave a review

Love & happy reading,
Isabell

FIND OUT MORE ABOUT ANNANI & AREANA'S PAST
THE CHILDREN OF THE GOOS ORIGINS
1: ANNANI & KHIANN'S STORY
GODDESS'S CHOICE
2: AREANA & NAVUH'S STORY
GODDESS'S HOPE

DON'T MISS OUT ON
THE PERFECT MATCH SERIES
PERFECT MATCH 1: VAMPIRE'S CONSORT
PERFECT MATCH 2: KING'S CHOSEN
PERFECT MATCH 3: CAPTAIN'S CONQUEST

dormant carrier of their genes. Ever the realist, Kian is skeptical and refuses Amanda's plea to attempt Syssi's activation. But when his enemies learn of the Dormant's existence, he's forced to rush her to the safety of his keep. Inexorably drawn to Syssi, Kian wrestles with his conscience as he is tempted to explore her budding interest in the darker shades of sensuality.

2: DARK STRANGER REVEALED

While sheltered in the clan's stronghold, Syssi is unaware that Kian and Amanda are not human, and neither are the supposedly religious fanatics that are after her. She feels a powerful connection to Kian, and as he introduces her to a world of pleasure she never dared imagine, his dominant sexuality is a revelation. Considering that she's completely out of her element, Syssi feels comfortable and safe letting go with him. That is, until she begins to suspect that all is not as it seems. Piecing the puzzle together, she draws a scary, yet wrong conclusion...

3: DARK STRANGER IMMORTAL

When Kian confesses his true nature, Syssi is not as much shocked by the revelation as she is wounded by what she perceives as his callous plans for her.

If she doesn't turn, he'll be forced to erase her memories and let her go. His family's safety demands secrecy – no one in the mortal world is allowed to know that immortals exist.

Resigned to the cruel reality that even if she stays on to never again leave the keep, she'll get old while Kian won't, Syssi is determined to enjoy what little time she has with him, one day at a time.

Can Kian let go of the mortal woman he loves? Will Syssi turn? And if she does, will she survive the dangerous transition?

4: DARK ENEMY TAKEN

Dalhu can't believe his luck when he stumbles upon the beautiful immortal professor. Presented with a once in a lifetime opportunity to grab an immortal female for himself, he kidnaps her and runs. If he ever gets caught, either by her people or his, his life is forfeit. But for a chance of a loving mate and a family of his own, Dalhu is prepared to do everything in his power to win Amanda's heart, and that includes leaving the Doom brotherhood and his old life behind.

Amanda soon discovers that there is more to the handsome Doomer than his dark past and a hulking, sexy body. But succumbing to her enemy's seduction, or worse, developing feelings for a ruthless killer is out of the question. No man is worth life on the run, not even the one and only immortal male she could claim as her own...

Her clan and her research must come first...

5: DARK ENEMY CAPTIVE

When the rescue team returns with Amanda and the chained Dalhu to the keep, Amanda is not as thrilled to be back as she thought she'd be. Between Kian's contempt for her and Dalhu's imprisonment, Amanda's budding relationship with Dalhu seems doomed. Things start to look up when Annani offers her help, and together with Syssi they resolve to find a way for Amanda to be with Dalhu. But will she still want him when she realizes that he is responsible for her nephew's murder? Could she? Will she take the easy way out and choose Andrew instead?

6: DARK ENEMY REDEEMED

Amanda suspects that something fishy is going on onboard the Anna. But when her investigation of the peculiar all-female Russian crew fails to uncover anything other than more speculation, she decides it's time to stop playing detective and face her real problem—a man she shouldn't want but can't live without.

6.5: MY DARK AMAZON

When Michael and Kri fight off a gang of humans, Michael gets stabbed. The injury to his immortal body recovers fast, but the one to his ego takes longer, putting a strain on his relationship with Kri.

7: DARK WARRIOR MINE

When Andrew is forced to retire from active duty, he believes that all he has to look forward to is a boring desk job. His glory days in special ops are over. But as it turns out, his thrill ride has just begun. Andrew discovers not only that immortals exist and have been manipulating global affairs since antiquity, but that he and his sister are rare possessors of the immortal genes.

Problem is, Andrew might be too old to attempt the activation process. His sister, who is fourteen years his junior, barely made it through the transition, so the odds of him coming out of it alive, let alone immortal, are slim.

But fate may force his hand.

Helping a friend find his long-lost daughter, Andrew finds a woman who's worth taking the risk for. Nathalie might be a Dormant, but the only way to find out for sure requires fangs and venom.

8: DARK WARRIOR'S PROMISE

Andrew and Nathalie's love flourishes, but the secrets they keep from each other taint their relationship with doubts and suspicions. In the meantime, Sebastian and his men are getting bolder, and the storm that's brewing will shift the balance of power in the millennia-old conflict between Annani's clan and its enemies.

9: DARK WARRIOR'S DESTINY

The new ghost in Nathalie's head remembers who he was in life, providing Andrew and her with indisputable proof that he is real and not a figment of her imagination.

Convinced that she is a Dormant, Andrew decides to go forward with his transition immediately after the rescue mission at the Doomers' HQ.

Fearing for his life, Nathalie pleads with him to reconsider. She'd rather spend the rest of her mortal days with Andrew than risk what they have for the fickle promise of immortality.

While the clan gets ready for battle, Carol gets help from an unlikely ally. Sebastian's second-in-command can no longer ignore the torment she suffers at the hands of his commander and offers to help her, but only if she agrees to his terms.

10: DARK WARRIOR'S LEGACY

Andrew's acclimation to his post-transition body isn't easy. His senses are sharper, he's bigger, stronger, and hungrier. Nathalie fears that the changes in the man she loves are more than physical. Measuring up to this new version of him is going to be a challenge.

Carol and Robert are disillusioned with each other. They are not destined mates, and love is not on the horizon. When Robert's three months are up, he might be left with nothing to show for his sacrifice.

Lana contacts Anandur with disturbing news; the yacht and its human cargo are in Mexico. Kian must find a way to apprehend Alex and rescue the women on board without causing an international incident.

11: Dark Guardian Found

What would you do if you stopped aging?

Eva runs. The ex-DEA agent doesn't know what caused her strange mutation, only that if discovered, she'll be dissected like a lab rat. What Eva doesn't know, though, is that she's a descendant of the gods, and that she is not alone. The man who rocked her world in one life-changing encounter over thirty years ago is an immortal as well.

To keep his people's existence secret, Bhathian was forced to turn his back on the only woman who ever captured his heart, but he's never forgotten and never stopped looking for her.

12: Dark Guardian Craved

Cautious after a lifetime of disappointments, Eva is mistrustful of Bhathian's professed feelings of love. She accepts him as a lover and a confidant but not as a life partner.

Jackson suspects that Tessa is his true love mate, but unless she overcomes her fears, he might never find out.

Carol gets an offer she can't refuse—a chance to prove that there is more to her than meets the eye. Robert believes she's about to commit a deadly mistake, but when he tries to dissuade her, she tells him to leave.

13: Dark Guardian's Mate

Prepare for the heart-warming culmination of Eva and Bhathian's story!

14: Dark Angel's Obsession

The cold and stoic warrior is an enigma even to those closest to him. His secrets are about to unravel...

15: Dark Angel's Seduction

Brundar is fighting a losing battle. Calypso is slowly chipping away his icy armor from the outside, while his need for her is melting it from the inside.

He can't allow it to happen. Calypso is a human with none of the Dormant indicators. There is no way he can keep her for more than a few weeks.

16: Dark Angel's Surrender

Get ready for the heart pounding conclusion to Brundar and Calypso's story.

Callie still couldn't wrap her head around it, nor could she summon even a smidgen of sorrow or regret. After all, she had some memories with him that weren't horrible. She should've felt something. But there was nothing, not even shock. Not even horror at what had transpired over the last couple of hours.

Maybe it was a typical response for survivors--feeling euphoric for the simple reason that they were alive. Especially when that survival was nothing short of miraculous.

Brundar's cold hand closed around hers, reminding her that they weren't out of the woods yet. Her injuries were superficial, and the most she had to worry about was some scarring. But, despite his and Anandur's reassurances, Brundar might never walk again.

If he ended up crippled because of her, she would never forgive herself for getting him involved in her crap.

"Are you okay, sweetling? Are you in pain?" Brundar asked.

Her injuries were nothing compared to his, and yet he was concerned about her. God, she loved this man. The thing was, if she told him that, he would run off, or crawl away as was the case.

Hey, maybe this was the perfect opportunity to spring it on him.

17: Dark Operative: A Shadow of Death

As a brilliant strategist and the only human entrusted with the secret of immortals' existence, Turner is both an asset and a liability to the clan. His request to attempt transition into immortality as an alternative to cancer treatments cannot be denied without risking the clan's exposure. On the other hand, approving it means risking his premature death. In both scenarios, the clan will lose a valuable ally.

When the decision is left to the clan's physician, Turner makes plans to manipulate her by taking advantage of her interest in him.

Will Bridget fall for the cold, calculated operative? Or will Turner fall into his own trap?

18: DARK OPERATIVE: A GLIMMER OF HOPE

As Turner and Bridget's relationship deepens, living together seems like the right move, but to make it work both need to make concessions.

Bridget is realistic and keeps her expectations low. Turner could never be the truelove mate she yearns for, but he is as good as she's going to get. Other than his emotional limitations, he's perfect in every way.

Turner's hard shell is starting to show cracks. He wants immortality, he wants to be part of the clan, and he wants Bridget, but he doesn't want to cause her pain.

His options are either abandon his quest for immortality and give Bridget his few remaining decades, or abandon Bridget by going for the transition and most likely dying. His rational mind dictates that he chooses the former, but his gut pulls him toward the latter. Which one is he going to trust?

19: DARK OPERATIVE: THE DAWN OF LOVE

Get ready for the exciting finale of Bridget and Turner's story!

20: DARK SURVIVOR AWAKENED

This was a strange new world she had awakened to.

Her memory loss must have been catastrophic because almost nothing was familiar. The language was foreign to her, with only a few words bearing some similarity to the language she thought in. Still, a full moon cycle had passed since her awakening, and little by little she was gaining basic understanding of it--only a few words and phrases, but she was learning more each day.

A week or so ago, a little girl on the street had tugged on her mother's sleeve and pointed at her. "Look, Mama, Wonder Woman!"

The mother smiled apologetically, saying something in the language these people spoke, then scurried away with the child looking behind her shoulder and grinning.

When it happened again with another child on the same day, it was settled.

Wonder Woman must have been the name of someone important in this strange world she had awoken to, and since both times it had been said with a smile it must have been a good one.

Wonder had a nice ring to it.

She just wished she knew what it meant.

21: Dark Survivor Echoes of Love

Wonder's journey continues in *Dark Survivor Echoes of Love*.

22: Dark Survivor Reunited

The exciting finale of Wonder and Anandur's story.

23: Dark Widow's Secret

Vivian and her daughter share a powerful telepathic connection, so when Ella can't be reached by conventional or psychic means, her mother fears the worst.

Help arrives from an unexpected source when Vivian gets a call from the young doctor she met at a psychic convention. Turns out Julian belongs to a private organization specializing in retrieving missing girls.

As Julian's clan mobilizes its considerable resources to rescue the daughter, Magnus is charged with keeping the gorgeous young mother safe.

Worry for Ella and the secrets Vivian and Magnus keep from each other should be enough to prevent the sparks of attraction from kindling a blaze of desire. Except, these pesky sparks have a mind of their own.

24: DARK WIDOW'S CURSE

A simple rescue operation turns into mission impossible when the Russian mafia gets involved. Bad things are supposed to come in threes, but in Vivian's case, it seems like there is no limit to bad luck. Her family and everyone who gets close to her is affected by her curse.

Will Magnus and his people prove her wrong?

25: DARK WIDOW'S BLESSING

The thrilling finale of the Dark Widow trilogy!

26: DARK DREAM'S TEMPTATION

Julian has known Ella is the one for him from the moment he saw her picture, but when he finally frees her from captivity, she seems indifferent to him. Could he have been mistaken?

Ella's rescue should've ended that chapter in her life, but it seems like the road back to normalcy has just begun and it's full of obstacles. Between the pitying looks she gets and her mother's attempts to get her into therapy, Ella feels like she's typecast as a victim, when nothing could be further from the truth. She's a tough survivor, and she's going to prove it.

Strangely, the only one who seems to understand is Logan, who keeps popping up in her dreams. But then, he's a figment of her imagination —or is he?

27: DARK DREAM'S UNRAVELING

While trying to figure out a way around Logan's silencing compulsion, Ella concocts an ambitious plan. What if instead of trying to keep him out of her dreams, she could pretend to like him and lure him into a trap?

Catching Navuh's son would be a major boon for the clan, as well as for Ella. She will have her revenge, turning the tables on another scumbag out to get her.

28: DARK DREAM'S TRAP

The trap is set, but who is the hunter and who is the prey? Find out in this heart-pounding conclusion to the *Dark Dream* trilogy.

29: Dark Prince's Enigma

As the son of the most dangerous male on the planet, Lokan lives by three rules:

Don't trust a soul.

Don't show emotions.

And don't get attached.

Will one extraordinary woman make him break all three?

30: Dark Prince's Dilemma

Will Kian decide that the benefits of trusting Lokan outweigh the risks?

Will Lokan betray his father and brothers for the greater good of his people?

Are Carol and Lokan true-love mates, or is one of them playing the other?

So many questions, the path ahead is anything but clear.

31: Dark Prince's Agenda

While Turner and Kian work out the details of Areana's rescue plan, Carol and Lokan's tumultuous relationship hits another snag. Is it a sign of things to come?

32 : Dark Queen's Quest

A former beauty queen, a retired undercover agent, and a successful model, Mey is not the typical damsel in distress. But when her sister drops off the radar and then someone starts following her around, she panics.

Following a vague clue that Kalugal might be in New York, Kian sends a team headed by Yamanu to search for him.

As Mey and Yamanu's paths cross, he offers her his help and protection, but will that be all?

33: Dark Queen's Knight

As the only member of his clan with a godlike power over human minds, Yamanu has been shielding his people for centuries, but that power comes at a steep price. When Mey enters his life, he's faced with the most difficult choice.

The safety of his clan or a future with his fated mate.

34: Dark Queen's Army

As Mey anxiously waits for her transition to begin and for Yamanu to test whether his godlike powers are gone, the clan sets out to solve two mysteries:

Where is Jin, and is she there voluntarily?

Where is Kalugal, and what is he up to?

35: Dark Spy Conscripted

Jin possesses a unique paranormal ability. Just by touching someone, she can insert a mental hook into their psyche and tie a string of her consciousness to it, creating a tether. That doesn't make her a spy, though, not unless her talent is discovered by those seeking to exploit it.

36: Dark Spy's Mission

Jin's first spying mission is supposed to be easy. Walk into the club, touch Kalugal to tether her consciousness to him, and walk out.

Except, they should have known better.

37: Dark Spy's Resolution

The best-laid plans often go awry...

38: Dark Overlord New Horizon

Jacki has two talents that set her apart from the rest of the human race.

She has unpredictable glimpses of other people's futures, and she is immune to mind manipulation.

Unfortunately, both talents are pretty useless for finding a job other than the one she had in the government's paranormal division.

It seemed like a sweet deal, until she found out that the director planned on producing super babies by compelling the recruits into pairing up. When an opportunity to escape the program presented itself, she took it, only to find out that humans are not at the top of the food chain.

Immortals are real, and at the very top of the hierarchy is Kalugal, the most powerful, arrogant, and sexiest male she has ever met.

With one look, he sets her blood on fire, but Jacki is not a fool. A man like him will never think of her as anything more than a tasty snack, while she will never settle for anything less than his heart.

39: Dark Overlord's Wife

Jacki is still clinging to her all-or-nothing policy, but Kalugal is chipping away at her resistance. Perhaps it's time to ease up on her convictions. A little less than all is still much better than nothing, and a couple of decades with a demigod is probably worth more than a lifetime with a mere mortal.

40: Dark Overlord's Clan

As Jacki and Kalugal prepare to celebrate their union, Kian takes every precaution to safeguard his people. Except, Kalugal and his men are not his only potential adversaries, and compulsion is not the only power he should fear.

41: Dark Choices The Quandary

When Rufsur and Edna meet, the attraction is as unexpected as it is undeniable. Except, she's the clan's judge and councilwoman, and he's Kalugal's second-in-command. Will loyalty and duty to their people keep them apart?

42: Dark Choices Paradigm Shift

Edna and Rufsur are miserable without each other, and their two-week separation seems like an eternity. Long-distance relationships are difficult, but for immortal couples they are impossible. Unless one of them is willing to leave everything behind for the other, things are just going to get worse. Except, the cost of compromise is far greater than giving up their comfortable lives and hard-earned positions. The future of their people is on the line.

43: Dark Choices The Accord

The winds of change blowing over the village demand hard choices. For better or worse, Kian's decisions will alter the trajectory of the clan's future, and he is not ready to take the plunge. But as Edna and Rufsur's plight gains widespread support, his resistance slowly begins to erode.

44: Dark Secrets Resurgence

On a sabbatical from his Stanford teaching position, Professor David Levinson finally has time to write the sci-fi novel he's been thinking about for years.

The phenomena of past life memories and near-death experiences are too controversial to include in his formal psychiatric research, while fiction is the perfect outlet for his esoteric ideas.

Hoping that a change of pace will provide the inspiration he needs, David accepts a friend's invitation to an old Scottish castle.

45: Dark Secrets Unveiled

When Professor David Levinson accepts a friend's invitation to an old Scottish castle, what he finds there is more fantastical than his most outlandish theories. The castle is home to a clan of immortals, their leader is a stunning demigoddess, and even more shockingly, it might be precisely where he belongs.

Except, the clan founder is hiding a secret that might cast a dark shadow on David's relationship with her daughter.

Nevertheless, when offered a chance at immortality, he agrees to undergo the dangerous induction process.

Will David survive his transition into immortality? And if he does, will his relationship with Sari survive the unveiling of her mother's secret?

46: Dark Secrets Absolved

Absolution.

David had given and received it.

The few short hours since he'd emerged from the coma had felt incredible. He'd finally been free of the guilt and pain, and for the first time since Jonah's death, he had felt truly happy and optimistic about the future.

He'd survived the transition into immortality, had been accepted into the clan, and was about to marry the best woman on the face of the planet, his true love mate, his salvation, his everything.

What could have possibly gone wrong?

Just about everything.

47: Dark haven Illusion

Welcome to Safe Haven, where not everything is what it seems.

On a quest to process personal pain, Anastasia joins the Safe Haven Spiritual Retreat.

Through meditation, self-reflection, and hard work, she hopes to make peace with the voices in her head.

This is where she belongs.

Except, membership comes with a hefty price, doubts are sacrilege, and leaving is not as easy as walking out the front gate.

Is living in utopia worth the sacrifice?

Anastasia believes so until the arrival of a new acolyte changes everything.

Apparently, the gods of old were not a myth, their immortal descendants share the planet with humans, and she might be a carrier of their genes.

48: Dark Haven Unmasked

As Anastasia leaves Safe Haven for a week-long romantic vacation with Leon, she hopes to explore her newly discovered passionate side, their budding relationship, and perhaps also solve the mystery of the voices in her head. What she discovers exceeds her wildest expectations.

In the meantime, Eleanor and Peter hope to solve another mystery. Who is Emmett Haderech, and what is he up to?

THE PERFECT MATCH SERIES

PERFECT MATCH 1: VAMPIRE'S CONSORT

When Gabriel's company is ready to start beta testing, he invites his old crush to inspect its medical safety protocol.

Curious about the revolutionary technology of the *Perfect Match Virtual Fantasy-Fulfillment studios*, Brenna agrees.

Neither expects to end up partnering for its first fully immersive test run.

PERFECT MATCH 2: KING'S CHOSEN

When Lisa's nutty friends get her a gift certificate to *Perfect Match Virtual Fantasy Studios*, she has no intentions of using it. But since the only way to get a refund is if no partner can be found for her, she makes sure to request a fantasy so girly and over the top that no sane guy will pick it up.

Except, someone does.

Warning: This fantasy contains a hot, domineering crown prince, sweet insta-love, steamy love scenes painted with light shades of gray, a wedding, and a HEA in both the virtual and real worlds.

Intended for mature audience.

PERFECT MATCH 3: CAPTAIN'S CONQUEST

Working as a Starbucks barista, Alicia fends off flirting all day long, but none of the guys are as charming and sexy as Gregg. His frequent visits are the highlight of her day, but since he's never asked her out, she assumes he's taken. Besides, between a day job and a budding music career, she has no time to start a new relationship.

That is until Gregg makes her an offer she can't refuse—a gift certificate to the virtual fantasy fulfillment service everyone is talking about. As a huge Star Trek fan, Alicia has a perfect match in mind—the captain of the Starship Enterprise.

Also by I. T. Lucas

Dark Secrets
44: Dark Secrets Resurgence
45: Dark Secrets Unveiled
46: Dark Secrets Absolved
Dark Haven
47: Dark haven Illusion
48: Dark Haven Unmasked

PERFECT MATCH
Perfect Match 1: Vampire's Consort
Perfect Match 2: King's Chosen
Perfect Match 3: Captain's Conquest

The Children of the Gods Series Sets

Books 1-3: Dark Stranger trilogy—Includes a bonus short story: The Fates take a Vacation

Books 4-6: Dark Enemy Trilogy —Includes a bonus short story—The Fates' Post-Wedding Celebration

Books 7-10: Dark Warrior Tetralogy
Books 11-13: Dark Guardian Trilogy
Books 14-16: Dark Angel Trilogy
Books 17-19: Dark Operative Trilogy
Books 20-22: Dark Survivor Trilogy
Books 23-25: Dark Widow Trilogy
Books 26-28: Dark Dream Trilogy
Books 29-31: Dark Prince Trilogy
Books 32-34: Dark Queen Trilogy

BOOKS 35-37: DARK SPY TRILOGY
BOOKS 38-40: DARK OVERLORD TRILOGY
BOOKS 41-43: DARK CHOICES TRILOGY
BOOKS 44-46: DARK SECRETS TRILOGY

MEGA SETS

THE CHILDREN OF THE GODS: BOOKS 1-6—INCLUDES CHARACTER LISTS

THE CHILDREN OF THE GODS: BOOKS 6.5-10—INCLUDES CHARACTER LISTS

TRY THE CHILDREN OF THE GODS SERIES ON AUDIBLE

2 FREE audiobooks with your new Audible subscription!

FOR EXCLUSIVE PEEKS AT UPCOMING RELEASES & A FREE COMPANION BOOK

Printed in Great Britain
by Amazon